Murder On the Rocks

A Stone and Steele Novel

Melissa Saulnier

PUBLICATION
CONSULTANTS
We Believe In The Power Of Authors

8370 Eleusis Drive, Anchorage, Alaska 99502-4630
books@publicationconsultants.com—www.publicationconsultants.com

ISBN Number: 978-1-59433-999-8
eBook ISBN Number: 978-1-63747-006-0

Library of Congress Number: 2025942142

Manufactured in the United States of America

Dedication

To all the tourists who visit our lovely state and those who live in Talkeetna, Alaska. May you enjoy this book!

Contents

TALKEETNA GOLD HISTORY

Gold was discovered in the Yentna-Cache Creek Mining District in Alaska's upper Susitna River Valley in 1898, soon followed by claim staking. Placer mining was reported in the Cache Creek drainage of the Dutch Hills by 1906. Quaternary glaciofluvial deposits, alluvial deposits, and Cenozoic conglomeratic white quartz-breccia units have been mined in the Dutch Hills. About 200,000 ounces of gold has been produced from these placer deposits.

By 1927, a road from Talkeetna was constructed into the mining area, known today as The Petersville Road. The mining camp of Petersville, Alaska served as the area Post Office for several years in the late 1920s and early 1930s. Two areas have been set aside for recreational gold mining: the North and South units of the Petersville State Recreation Mining Areas. Many smaller one-man and family placer mining operations continue today.

In addition to placer gold mining, this district in the Matanuska-Susitna borough has had some mining of tungsten from scheelite deposits, and small-scale lode mining for gold.

The district is well known due to the influence of artist Sydney Laurence and the still-unsolved murders of four miners in 1939 which gained nationwide attention (see The Mystery of the Cache Creek Murders by Roberta Sheldon).

A steam-powered dragline was used to mine the placer deposits of Peters Creek, below the canyon that cuts through the Peters Hills. The tailings of that operation can be seen today, and the area is part of the Petersville State Recreation Mining Area.

A cluster of deposits is in the main part of the Yentna district, near the Dutch Hills. The productive deposits here have been placer gold deposits with byproduct platinum and locally abundant cassiterite. Gold-bearing lodes in the Yentna district, which have not been as well described, include small and locally very rich deposits associated with felsic dikes and apparently low-grade deposits in major shear and altered zones. Assays exceeding 1 ounce of gold per ton have been obtained from three of these areas, and selected quartz-arsenopyrite vein material from one prospect assayed about 200 ounces of gold per ton.

The 1939 Cache Creek Murders

In the remote gold fields of Cache Creek near Talkeetna, Alaska, 1939 would mark the region with an enduring tragedy. Four brutal murders occurred on a single day, sending shockwaves through the tight-knit mining community and launching a mystery that would remain partially unsolved for more than sixty years.

At the center of the tragedy stood a bitter feud between two veteran miners, Dick Francis and Frank Jenkins, who had worked the same rugged terrain for nearly three decades. Their relationship had deteriorated into legal warfare during the 1930s as disputes over mining claims escalated into protracted court battles. The conflict reached a breaking point in 1938 when Francis's claims were auctioned to satisfy court-ordered damages awarded to Jenkins, a public humiliation that intensified the animosity between them.

As the 1939 mining season drew to a close, violence erupted across three separate locations. Frank Jenkins and his young employee were discovered bludgeoned to death at their operation in Wonder Gulch. Three miles away, Helen Jenkins was found murdered near the family cabin along Little Willow Creek. Meanwhile, at his Ruby Creek cabin, Dick Francis lay dead from gunshot wounds to the head, a revolver beside him suggesting suicide after a vengeful killing spree.

Initial assumptions about Francis's guilt were shattered when an autopsy revealed he had been shot twice in the head, an impossible feat for a suicide. This shocking revelation transformed the community's understanding of the crimes, with suspicions turning to the possibility that someone had exploited the notorious feud as cover to search for caches of gold rumored to be hidden on the Jenkins property.

The case captivated Alaskans, who demanded justice despite the challenges of law enforcement in such a remote region. Their calls for FBI intervention reflected the community's deep sense of violation. Now, previously unreleased evidence suggests the possibility that justice may have been denied, a whisper from the past that continues to haunt Cache Creek country more than six decades later.

PROLOGUE

The Talkeetna wilderness stretched endlessly in all directions, a vast expanse of untamed Alaska where secrets could be buried as deep as the permafrost. For those who knew where to look, the area offered countless places where a person could disappear forever without a trace.

Miles up the treacherous Petersville Road, where pavement surrendered to gravel and gravel eventually gave way to rutted dirt, abandoned gold mining operations lay hidden like forgotten graveyards in the dense forest. Rusted draglines stood frozen mid-excavation, their massive buckets still clawing at empty air after decades of silence. Partially collapsed tunnels burrowed into hillsides like wounded mouths, their timber supports rotting and sagging under the weight of time and earth. Equipment worth fortunes in their heyday now served as monuments to shattered dreams, creating eerie time capsules from Alaska's boom-and-bust cycles that few living souls remembered.

Beyond the reach of cell towers and emergency services, remote hunting cabins dotted the wilderness like scattered chess pieces on a board only the locals understood. Some appeared on no official maps, built by men who valued privacy above permits, known only to those who'd traversed these unforgiving lands for generations. These cabins changed hands through handshake agreements and word-of-mouth directions that sounded more like riddles: "Follow the creek past the bent birch until you reach the beaver dam, then head north toward the peak that looks like a sleeping lady."

The braided river systems created an ever-shifting maze of temporary islands and gravel bars that appeared and vanished with the seasons like nature's own magic trick. Spring snowmelt could wash away a sandbar overnight, while autumn's low water might reveal new hideaways that wouldn't exist come winter. A body weighted down on one of these ephemeral islands might surface miles downstream months later, or simply vanish into the glacial silt forever.

Perhaps most intriguing to those who understood the country's dark history was the network of unofficial trails leading to forgotten homesteads from failed settlement attempts. These paths, carved by desperate families seeking new lives in the Last Frontier, wound through stands of birch and spruce, over moss-covered ridges to clearings where nature had nearly reclaimed man-made structures. Collapsed cabins surrendered to alder thickets, their rooflines broken like the backs of the dreams that built them. Rusty stoves sat in meadows where kitchens once warmed families, and fragments of children's toys emerged from the underbrush like archaeological artifacts from lives abruptly abandoned when reality proved harsher than hope.

In such a place, where the wilderness swallowed human ambition as easily as it swallowed footprints in fresh snow, one more disappearance would barely register as unusual.

The fading light of an Alaskan summer evening painted long shadows across the rocky stream bed, turning the water into liquid copper. A man crouched behind a stand of spruce trees, his weathered hands trembling not from cold but from the white-hot rage building inside his chest like a pressure cooker about to blow. The young hiker, twenty-something, lean, with expensive hiking gear that screamed "outsider", was exactly where he shouldn't be, exactly where no one was supposed to be, crouching at the water's edge with his fingers sifting through the sediment like a prospector from the old days.

The old man had been watching him for the better part of an hour, his heart hammering against his ribs as the young man worked his way upstream, stopping every few yards to examine the streambed with growing excitement. The expensive camera hanging from his neck caught the dying light, and he could see the kid's face clearly now, the kind of soft, eager expression that belonged to someone who'd never learned that some discoveries came with a price paid in blood.

He watched the young man's face transform as he held something up to the golden light filtering through the canopy. A small nugget, no bigger than a pea, but gleaming with the unmistakable lustre that had driven men to madness for centuries. The hiker's expression of pure wonder, mouth slightly open, eyes wide with disbelief, confirmed his worst fear. The kid had found it. After thirty years of careful searching, of protecting this secret like a mother protects her child, some college boy with GPS and a camera had stumbled onto their future.

His jaw clenched so hard his teeth ached. This wasn't just about one nugget. He knew what lay beneath the surface of this stream, especially where it bent around the granite outcropping upstream. He'd found the source three months ago, a vein of gold so rich it had made his hands shake when he'd first seen it. More gold than he'd encountered in thirty years of prospecting across Alaska, enough gold to fund their community's final preparations for the collapse that was coming whether the outside world wanted to admit it or not.

Gold that rightfully belonged to him and his people after years of searching, suffering, and sacrifice. Gold that would secure their independence forever.

The hiker pocketed the nugget with reverent care, then began taking photographs of everything, the stream, the unusual rock formation, the play of light on water, the distinctive bend in the creek. The old man's stomach dropped as he watched the young man pull out a GPS device, punching buttons and recording coordinates with the methodical precision of someone who understood the value of what he'd found.

"No, no, no," he whispered, his breath fogging in the cooling air. The kid was marking the location. GPS coordinates meant satellite accuracy within three feet. Tomorrow, others would come. Government surveyors, mining companies, federal agents with their badges and warrants and legal papers that would strip away everything his community had built in the wilderness.

He forced himself to breathe slowly, to think clearly despite the adrenaline coursing through his veins. He'd been a mining engineer before the world had gone to hell, before he'd lost everything to government regulations and environmental lawsuits. He understood the process that would follow once word got out. Claims would be filed, surveys would be conducted, and their sanctuary would be overrun with strangers who had no respect for what they'd created here.

Silently, moving with the practiced stealth of a man who'd spent decades hunting these woods, he began to follow as the hiker continued upstream. He maintained a careful distance, using the dense undergrowth and the sound of running water to mask his approach. The sun dipped lower behind the mountains, painting the sky in shades of orange and purple while the forest floor grew dimmer with each passing minute. Perfect. He knew these woods like the lines on his own weathered face, had walked every game trail and creek bed within a twenty-mile radius. The hiker, meanwhile, was already showing signs of concern about the fading light, checking his map more frequently and glancing at his watch with increasing anxiety.

"What we've built is too important," he whispered to himself, his mind shifting into the cool, methodical mode that had served him well during his engineering days. They had created something pure out here, something that hadn't existed since the frontier days, a community free from government oversight, self-sufficient and prepared for the societal collapse that every thinking person could see coming. They grew their own food, generated their own power, and lived by principles that had sustained humanity for thousands of years before the modern world had gone soft and dependent.

The gold would fund their final preparations. Solar panels, medical supplies, ammunition, communications equipment, everything they needed to weather the storm that was coming. One person, one naive young man with a camera and a GPS device, couldn't be allowed to jeopardize everything they'd worked for.

The hiker paused at a fork in the trail, confusion evident in his body language as he consulted his map and compass. The old man held his breath, watching from behind a massive spruce whose trunk could have hidden a small car. The young man looked tired now, his shoulders sagging with the weight of his pack and the realization that he was deeper in the wilderness than he'd planned to be. After a moment of deliberation, he chose the left fork, the wrong path, the one that led deeper into the wilderness, away from the campgrounds and the relative safety of the established trails.

Away from witnesses.

He patted the smooth river rock in his jacket pocket, feeling its weight and thinking about the physics of blunt force trauma. Sometimes sacrifice was necessary to protect what mattered most. The stream's secret had to be kept, no matter the cost. They had searched too long, planned too carefully, invested too much of their lives in this vision to let an outsider take what belonged to them.

The hiker's pace quickened as full darkness descended like a curtain, panic setting in as he realized he was truly lost. The old man watched him fumble with his headlamp, the beam cutting through the darkness in frantic arcs as the young man tried to orient himself. Soon, very soon, he would make his move. The kid was maybe a mile from the nearest established trail now, in country where people routinely went missing and were never found. Bears, cliffs, hypothermia, getting turned around in the maze of game trails, the wilderness offered a dozen explanations for why a hiker might never make it home.

One life against the future of his entire community. When he looked at it that way, it wasn't really a choice at all.

The hiker had stopped now, his breathing rapid and shallow as he tried to decide which way to go. The old man could smell his fear, that sharp scent of adrenaline and sweat that prey animals gave off when they realized they were being hunted. The young man's hands shook as he tried to check his GPS again, but the device showed no signal this deep in the wilderness.

He emerged from the trees like a ghost, his gray hair catching the last glimmer of twilight. The hiker spun around, relief flooding his face at the sight of another human being.

"Oh, thank God," the young man gasped. "I thought I was alone out here. I'm completely lost. Do you know the way back to…"

"I'm sorry, son," he whispered, his voice carrying the weight of genuine regret. "But you found something that wasn't yours to find."

The hiker's expression shifted from relief to confusion to dawning terror in the space of a heartbeat. He started to back away, but the old man was already moving, his hand closing around the river rock with the certainty of a man who'd made his choice and would live with the consequences.

In the morning, they would find the young man's campsite abandoned, his car parked at the trailhead like so many others before it. The wilderness would keep its secrets, as it always had. And his community would continue to thrive, protected by the gold beneath the stream and the lengths one man was willing to go to preserve what he believed was right.

The stream gurgled softly in the darkness, washing away the evidence as it had washed away so many secrets before.

CHAPTER 1:
The Detective

Detective Emma Stone leaned against the worn brick exterior of the Anchorage Police Department, the late spring chill seeping through her leather jacket with the persistence of a winter that doesn't want to give up. She took a final long deep breath, savoring these last moments of solitude like the last cookie in the break room. The mountains loomed in the distance, spotted with last remnants of snow, a reminder that winter was hanging on with its usual indifference to human comfort, much like Emma's attitude toward mandatory department meetings.

"Stone! Meeting in five." Officer Davis stuck his head out the door, his breath visible in the cold air like a cartoon speech bubble missing its text.

Emma nodded without speaking, her version of a scintillating morning conversation. Davis hesitated, clearly expecting some verbal acknowledgment, maybe even a "good morning" if miracles happened, then disappeared back inside with a barely concealed eye roll that could have qualified him for the Olympics. She knew what they said about her when they thought she couldn't hear, Ice Queen, lone wolf, that uptight woman from Homicide who probably alphabetized her breakfast cereal. None of it bothered her much. The distance was deliberate, a carefully constructed barrier between herself and the forced camaraderie of precinct life, as essential to her as coffee and silence before 9 a.m.

Inside, the fluorescent lights buzzed overhead like caffeinated bees as she made her way to the conference room. Eyes followed her, some curious, others dismissive. At thirty-six, Emma was neither young enough to be considered a prodigy nor experienced enough to command automatic respect. Her slim build and striking features often led people to underestimate her, a mistake they rarely made twice and frequently regretted making once.

Emma slid into a seat at the back of the room just as Captain Harrison began the morning briefing. She listened with half an ear as he ran through the usual updates, ongoing cases, administrative reminders, the standard chorus of complaints about budget cuts that had become the department's unofficial fight song. Her attention sharpened only when he mentioned the string of home burglaries in the South Addition neighborhood.

"Nothing taken except jewelry and cash," Harrison was saying. "No forced entry. Three houses hit in the past two weeks."

Emma frowned, a detail nagging at the edges of her memory like an out-of-tune piano note. She hadn't been assigned to the burglary cases, she worked homicide, where the victims had the decency to stay put, but something about them triggered a connection.

"The homeowners weren't home during any of the break-ins," Detective Ellis added, directing his comments toward everyone except her, as if she might be contagious. "Professional job. Clean."

"What about the security systems?" Emma found herself asking, breaking her usual silence with all the unexpectedness of a vegetarian at a barbecue.

Ellis turned, surprise, evident on his face that she'd spoken at all, as if a department store mannequin had suddenly offered fashion advice. "Disabled. Guy knows what he's doing."

Emma closed her eyes briefly, summoning the image that had been flickering at the edge of her consciousness. Three weeks ago, she'd been called to a suspicious death that turned out to be natural causes. The deceased, an elderly man named Harold Morgan, had lived in South Anchorage. While waiting for the coroner, she'd noticed something odd in his home office, besides the concerning number of cat figurines for a man who lived alone.

"Check if any of the victims used Blue Harbor Security," she said. "Morgan had their sticker on his window, but I remember seeing their installation guide open on his desk with notes in the margins. Looked like someone was studying how to bypass it, unless he was planning a very ambitious career change at eighty-seven."

Ellis narrowed his eyes. "Morgan wasn't robbed."

"No, but he had a live-in caretaker," Emma continued, the details clarifying in her mind like a photograph coming into focus. "Asian woman, early thirties. She was upset, but something felt off about it, like watching someone cry during a cellphone commercial. Said she'd been with him for six months. Check if she has any connection to the other victims."

Captain Harrison looked at her with renewed interest, the way one might regard a vending machine that unexpectedly dispensed two snacks instead of one. "Ellis, follow up on that. Stone, I want you in on this too."

Emma suppressed a sigh with the practiced skill of someone who'd sat through countless family holiday dinners where politics were discussed. This was exactly why she kept to herself. One observation and suddenly she'd be pulled into team meetings, expected to collaborate with Ellis, who clearly resented her input the way cats resent baths.

The briefing continued, but Emma's mind had already moved on. She'd write up her observations in an email to Ellis and leave it at that. Getting entangled in another detective's case rarely ended well, especially when that detective already viewed her as an intruder in his professional tree fort.

As the meeting wound down, Captain Harrison cleared his throat. "One more announcement. As most of you know, I'll be retiring at the end of the month."

A murmur ran through the room like ripples from a stone tossed in a pond. Everyone knew it was coming, but the official announcement still sent a ripple of reaction through the assembled officers. Emma remained still, her face betraying nothing despite the sudden tightness in her chest. Harrison had been the one constant in her five years at APD, the only supervisor who seemed to understand her methods and respect her need for space, a rare quality in a profession where personal questions were wielded like battering rams.

"Deputy Chief Rogers will be handling the transition until my replacement is named," Harrison continued. "I expect everyone to make this as smooth as possible."

His eyes lingered briefly on Emma, and she understood the unspoken message with crystal clarity. Rogers had made it clear on multiple occasions that he found her working style problematic, in the same way penguins might find the Sahara "a bit warm." Without Harrison's buffer, her carefully constructed isolation could quickly become a liability.

As the room emptied, Harrison gestured to her to stay behind. Emma remained seated, watching as the last of her colleagues filed out, several casting curious glances back at her with all the subtlety of toddlers staring at a museum exhibit.

"You should try getting along with them," Harrison said once they were alone. "They're not all idiots."

Emma allowed herself a small smile. "High praise, coming from you. Next you'll tell me some of them can tie their shoes without instructions."

"I mean it, Stone. Rogers is going to be looking for reasons to reassign you. Your closure rate keeps him at bay for now, but he's been wanting to shake things up in Homicide."

She nodded, knowing he was right but unwilling to acknowledge the warning verbally. The thought of having to justify her methods to Rogers made her jaw clench tighter than the department's budget.

"That was good work on the burglary connection," Harrison added. "Your memory's wasted on dead bodies."

"Dead bodies don't complain about my bedside manner," Emma replied. "And they never ask about my weekend plans."

Harrison laughed, a short bark that echoed in the empty room like a single clap in a cathedral. "True enough. Still, consider branching out. There's talk of a joint task force with the FBI. Might be a good opportunity."

Emma remained seated as Harrison walked to the window, his silhouette framed against the Anchorage skyline. "There's something else you should know about this case up north," he said, his tone shifting to the one he used for sensitive briefings. "The body was found on Bureau of Land Management territory."

"Federal jurisdiction," Emma noted, immediately understanding the implications.

Harrison nodded. "And it gets more complicated. The land directly adjacent belongs to that survivalist group, the Alliance. They've been on federal watch lists for years. Nothing actionable, but enough concerns about stockpiling, paramilitary training, potential extremist connections to keep the FBI interested."

"So they're using a suspicious death as an excuse to get closer to the Alliance," Emma surmised, her distaste for jurisdictional politics evident in her tone.

"It's not that simple," Harrison countered. "The victim was a geology graduate student conducting research in areas surrounding the Alliance property. The FBI believes there may be resource-related motivations behind his death."

"Resources?" Emma's interest was genuinely piqued despite her resistance. "What kind?"

"That's part of what they want you for. Your background in resource crime investigations makes you valuable to them. That and your..." Harrison hesitated, searching for the diplomatic phrasing.

"My what?"

"Your ability to see patterns others miss. Your intuitive approach." Harrison turned from the window to face her directly. "The federal agent they're sending is reportedly brilliant but extremely analytical. By-the-book type. They need someone who can bridge the gap between methodical investigation and intuitive leaps."

Emma raised an eyebrow. "They want to partner me with some Bureau robot?"

"They requested you specifically," Harrison emphasized. "This could be a significant opportunity, Emma. Federal connections, high-profile case experience, the kind of credentials Rogers can't easily dismiss when my replacement is finalized."

She remained skeptical. "What's this agent's name?"

"Steele. Jeremiah Steele. Counterterrorism background with recent transfer to resource crimes and domestic extremism. Highly regarded within the Bureau."

"Sounds thrilling," Emma replied dryly, though the case details had admittedly captured her interest. A suspicious death, potential resource motives, and a survivalist compound all presented intriguing investigative angles.

"The joint task force would operate under FBI oversight but with local knowledge integration," Harrison continued. "You'd maintain your APD status while gaining federal case experience. It could position you perfectly for whatever comes after my retirement."

Before Emma could respond, Harrison's phone rang. He glanced at the screen and stood. "Think about it. Changes are coming whether you like it or not. Better to choose your own path than have Rogers decide it for you."

Emma remained seated as he left, turning his words over in her mind like a particularly puzzling piece of evidence. The FBI wanting her seemed unlikely, she'd gone out of her way to avoid interagency politics with the same determination that teenagers avoid vegetables. But with Harrison leaving, any port in a storm might be worth considering.

She gathered her notes and headed back to her desk, ignoring the curious looks of the other detectives. Ellis was already on the phone, his expression shifting from skepticism to surprise as he presumably followed up on her Blue Harbor Security lead. Score one for the Ice Queen.

Emma settled at her computer, the familiar isolation of her corner desk providing momentary comfort, like slipping into well-worn slippers. Change was coming, that much was clear. The question was whether she could navigate it without compromising the barriers she'd so carefully built, barriers that kept her focused, effective, and most importantly, free from the messy entanglements of workplace friendships.

The memory of her father's voice echoed unbidden in her mind: "Even the sparrow finds a home, Emma." She'd always hated that particular Bible verse, the implication that everyone should seek shelter, safety, connection. She'd spent a lifetime proving she needed none of those things. Well, maybe sometimes. Possibly when there was a spider in her apartment.

But as she watched Ellis hang up the phone and reluctantly approach her desk with the enthusiasm of someone headed for a root canal, Emma wondered if Harrison was right. Maybe it was time to choose a different path, before someone else chose it for her, a path that might include the occasional unnecessary conversation with a living, breathing colleague. Heaven help her.

CHAPTER 2:
Childhood Shadows & Agent Steele

Emma Stone drove slowly through the streets of Eagle River, the late afternoon sun casting long shadows across the road. Spruce Haven Assisted Living emerged ahead, a modern building incongruously nestled among the towering birch. Emma parked in her usual spot and sat for a moment, gathering her resolve as she did each week before these visits.

Inside, the familiar scent of antiseptic and artificial potpourri greeted her. She nodded at the receptionist, who knew her well enough not to attempt conversation beyond a pleasant smile.

"He's having a good day," Nurse Marlene said, intercepting Emma in the hallway. "Remembered my name this morning."

Emma nodded, grateful for the update but unwilling to get her hopes up. "Has he eaten?"

"Most of his lunch. Left the carrots, as usual." Marlene's smile was kind. "The piano tuner came yesterday. Your father insisted they do it right away when he heard it was off-key."

A ghost of a smile crossed Emma's face. Some things never changed, even as her father's mind slowly unraveled.

She found him sitting by the window, his once-commanding presence diminished in the oversized armchair. At eighty-eight, Reverend Thomas Stone looked a decade older, his body betraying him even as his mind played its cruel tricks.

"Emma," he said, his face lighting up with recognition. Relief flooded through her, it was indeed a good day.

"Hello, Dad." She leaned down to kiss his cheek, noting the careful way he'd combed his thinning hair, the clean shirt. Even in decline, Thomas Stone maintained standards.

"Did you bring your mother?" he asked, and just like that, the relief evaporated. Not such a good day after all.

"Mom's been gone for twelve years, Dad," Emma said gently, taking the seat opposite him. "It's just me today."

Confusion flickered across his face, followed by a moment of clarity and then profound sadness. "Of course. I forget sometimes."

Emma reached for a safer topic. "How are you feeling today?"

"The good Lord sustains me," he answered automatically, the preacher's cadence returning to his voice. "Though I admit the vessel grows weaker."

Emma suppressed a familiar surge of frustration at the religious platitudes that had dominated her childhood. She'd learned to bite her tongue, to save her rebellious thoughts for after these visits.

"The nurses say you're doing well," she offered instead.

Her father straightened in his chair. "I follow the regimen they've prescribed. Order and discipline are God's tools for a righteous life."

Order and discipline. The cornerstones of her upbringing in the reverend's household. Emma's mind drifted back to her teenage years, the endless rules, the strict curfews, the few approved activities and lack of high school friendships. Music had been her father's concession, though even that came with constraints. Church pieces only, hymns for Sunday service. Nothing contemporary that might "corrupt the spirit."

"I've been thinking about Mother lately," her father said, his gaze drifting to the window. "She always understood you better than I did."

Emma's attention snapped back. This was new, her father rarely acknowledged the tensions that had defined their relationship.

"She did," Emma agreed carefully. Her mother had been the buffer, the translator between father and daughter, until pneumonia had stolen her away a few years back.

"She told me once I was driving you away with all the rules," he continued, his voice fading. "Said you were like a wild bird, the tighter I held, the harder you'd fight."

Emma stared at him, unsure if this was a true memory or one of his mind's increasingly common fabrications. Her mother had indeed said something similar once, but never in her father's presence as far as Emma knew.

"I remember the night you left," he said suddenly, clarity returning to his eyes. "Eighteen years old, standing at the door with that ratty duffel bag, telling me you'd rather struggle on your own than live another day under my thumb."

Emma felt a flush of heat on her cheeks. She remembered that night all too well, the culmination of years of silent rebellion and carefully hidden defiance.

"I was stubborn," she admitted.

"Like me," he replied, a hint of pride in his voice. "You got that from me. Your mother said we were too alike to ever get along, both of us absolutely convinced of our own rightness."

Emma smiled despite herself. Her mother had been perceptive.

Her phone buzzed in her pocket, a text from Ellis about the burglary case. Emma ignored it.

"I went to hear you play once," her father said, his eyes fixed on some distant point beyond the window. "At that place downtown. The Blue Note."

Emma froze. "What?"

"Three years ago, before…" he gestured vaguely at the assisted living facility. "I didn't tell you. Just sat in the back. You were playing something complicated. Jazz, I suppose. People were watching you. Respectful."

Emma struggled to process this revelation. The Blue Note was her refuge, a quiet, upscale jazz bar where she occasionally played when the pressure of work became too much. Bernie had heard her once and offered her an open invitation to play whenever she needed, no questions asked. It was her secret, her escape valve.

"Why didn't you say anything?" she finally asked.

"Pride," he admitted, a word that had rarely crossed his lips. "Couldn't bring myself to admit you'd found your own way. That maybe my way wasn't the only path."

An aide appeared at the doorway. "Time for your medication, Reverend Stone."

Her father straightened, the brief moment of connection receding. "Already? Well, we must be obedient to the schedule." The minister's voice was back, performing righteousness even now.

"I'll come again sometime next week."

He nodded, already distracted by the approaching medication cart. "Bring your mother next time."

Emma paused, then nodded, accepting that clarity was always temporary now. "I'll try."

Outside in her car, Emma sat motionless, turning over her father's revelation. He had heard her play, had seen her in the one place she truly felt free. The thought was unsettling, a breach of the carefully maintained boundary between her past and present.

Her phone buzzed again with another text from Ellis confirming her hunch about Blue Harbor Security had paid off, the caretaker now a person of interest in the burglary case.

Emma started the car, pushing thoughts of her father aside as she pulled onto the highway back to Anchorage. Work awaited, and with it the structure and control she craved. Tonight, though, she might stop by The Blue Note. After a day like today, she needed the release that only music could provide, jazz with its improvisation and freedom within structure, the perfect rebellion for a preacher's daughter who'd never quite escaped her upbringing.

Freedom had a price, isolation, loneliness, the constant vigilance required to maintain her independence. But as the mountains loomed ahead, massive and indifferent to human concerns, Emma reminded herself that the price was worth paying.

The alternative was unthinkable. No matter how beautiful the cage was, it was still a cage.

* * *

Jeremiah Steele was the new man in town and wasn't entirely certain he'd made the right decision to move to Alaska. But he'd been in Anchorage all of two months and was ready to dive into a case. He flipped through the file methodically, making annotations in precise, measured handwriting. The clock on his office wall read 7:32 AM, making him one of the first agents in the Anchorage FBI field office. He preferred the quiet of early mornings, time to think without interruption, to organize his approach before the day's chaos began.

The reports from Talkeetna had been crossing his desk for three weeks now. Individually, they might have been dismissed as typical small-town occurrences. Collectively, they formed a pattern that piqued his analytical mind. A missing hiker, unusual activity around the river basin, reports of increased traffic to and from a known survivalist compound.

And now, a body.

The deceased, identified as Marcus Chen, 27, avid outdoorsman and geology enthusiast, had been found with injuries "inconsistent with an accidental fall," according to the preliminary ME report. The local State Trooper had requested assistance by FBI, citing limited resources and the potential connection to federal land.

Steele created a fresh spreadsheet on his computer, inputting the data points with meticulous attention to detail. Each event received its own row, categorized by date, time, location, and witness reliability. Patterns emerged through organization, this was the principle that had guided his fifteen-year career with the Bureau.

His phone rang, the screen displaying "Katherine Steele." He allowed himself a moment of resignation before answering.

"Jeremiah Steele," he said, his tone professional despite the caller.

"Jerry, it's me." Katherine's voice was clipped, efficient. After ten years of marriage and three of divorce, they had reduced their communication to the essential. "I'm finalizing the sale of the lake house. I need your signature on the paperwork by Thursday."

There was an uncomfortable pause while Steele made a note in his planner. "I'll call the realtor's office tomorrow."

"Fine." A pause. "Will you be keeping any of the furniture? I've got a buyer for the dining set if you don't want it."

"Take it all," he said, his attention already drifting back to the Talkeetna file. "I have no use for it. It isn't worth shipping to Alaska."

"Typical," Katherine muttered. "All these years and your apartment probably still looks like a hotel room."

Steele didn't respond to the bait. Their marriage had ended largely over what Katherine called his "emotional unavailability" his inability to connect with her beyond the surface level of their lives together. The final straw had been his reaction to her miscarriage. While she had crumbled, he had retreated to work, approaching their loss as a problem to be managed rather than a grief to be shared.

"Is there anything else?" he asked, maintaining his neutral tone.

"No." Another pause. "Take care of yourself, Jerry."

The line went dead before he could respond, not that he would have had much to say. Katherine had been right about most things. His apartment was indeed spartan, more a place to sleep than a home. His father, a career military intelligence officer, had instilled in him early the virtue of detachment. "Emotional entanglements cloud judgment," Colonel Steele had repeated throughout Jeremiah's childhood. "Maintain perspective. Attachment is vulnerability."

His father's lessons had served him well in counterterrorism and organized crime investigations. They had proven less successful in his personal life.

A knock at his door pulled Steele from his thoughts. Special Agent Diana Hickock, he'd already checked, stood in the doorway, a folder in hand.

"Morning, Steele. Got the toxicology report on the Talkeetna victim."

Steele nodded for her to continue.

"Clean. No drugs or alcohol. But there's something interesting, soil samples from his boots and clothing contain unusual mineral deposits. Gold, primarily."

Steele raised an eyebrow. "Gold?"

"Preliminary analysis suggests high-grade ore. The kind of concentration that might be commercially viable." She handed him the report. "Considering he was a geology student, it raises questions."

Steele added this information to his spreadsheet, a new data point that shifted the pattern. "The location of the body, how close to the survivalist compound?"

"About five miles. But it's on the same tributary. If there's gold in that stream…"

Steele nodded, making the connection. "Then our victim may have stumbled onto something valuable. Something worth killing for."

He pulled up the file on the survivalist group. Known as the "Alliance," they had established their compound seven years ago, led by a former military officer named James Barrett. Their manifesto, published online, spoke of self-sufficiency and preparation for societal collapse. Nothing overtly criminal, though their isolation and paramilitary training exercises had kept them on law enforcement's radar.

"What do we know about their finances?" Steele asked.

Diana shrugged. "Not much. They're pretty self-contained. Grow their own food, generate their own power. Members tithe their outside income to the group. Barrett was an investment banker before he went off-grid, so he presumably has resources."

Steele stared at his monitor, mentally connecting the data points. A geology student discovers gold near a survivalist compound and ends up dead. The local State Trooper, overwhelmed and underfunded, requests federal assistance. And all of it centered around Talkeetna, a small town primarily known as a base for Denali expeditions.

"We need someone on the ground," he said finally. "Someone who can blend in, observe without attracting attention."

"I'll put together a list of agents with undercover experience," Diana offered.

Steele shook his head. "Not undercover, exactly. More… informal investigation. Talkeetna's small. Strangers are noticed. But tourists are expected in Talkeetna."

He turned to his computer, typing quickly. "There's a detective with the Anchorage PD who might be a good fit. Homicide division, high closure rate, reputation for observation and recall. I read about her in last month's interagency briefing."

Diana peered over his shoulder at the personnel file that appeared on screen. "Detective Emma Stone? You want to bring in local PD?"

"Joint task force," Steele corrected. "Her captain mentioned she has a photographic memory. Useful skill for gathering intelligence without obvious documentation. And having two agents walk into a town that size would attract attention. A man and woman traveling together reads as a couple on vacation."

"You want to pose as a couple?" Diana sounded skeptical. "No offense, Steele, but you're not exactly known for your warmth."

Steele ignored the jab. "Professional necessity. We need to understand what's happening in Talkeetna before committing more resources. If there's gold involved, the motive becomes clearer, but we need evidence linking the survivalists to the murder."

"And you think this Detective Stone is the right partner for this?"

Steele studied the file, noting Stone's impressive case closure statistics and the comments about her preference for working alone. A kindred spirit, perhaps.

"I think she has the right skills and the right profile. We need someone detail-oriented who can maintain professional distance."

Diana looked unconvinced. "Captain Harrison is retiring this month. Stone will be reporting to Deputy Chief Rogers, who's not known for interagency cooperation."

"Then we'll need to move quickly." Steele closed the file and stood, gathering his notes. "I'll speak with Assistant Director Crawford about making the formal request. If there's gold in that stream, Ms. Stone and I need to be in Talkeetna before anyone else connects the dots."

As Diana Hickock left, Steele returned to his spreadsheet, adding the new variables and recalculating probabilities. The case was taking shape in his mind, organized, logical, each piece fitting into a framework he could understand.

People were messy, unpredictable, driven by emotions he often struggled to comprehend. But data didn't lie. Evidence followed patterns. And murders, in his experience, always came down to one of three motives: passion, power, or profit.

If gold was involved, profit seemed the most likely driver. And profit-motivated crimes were, in many ways, the easiest to solve. Follow the money, find the killer.

What remained unclear was how Detective Emma Stone would factor into the equation. Partnership required trust, communication, skills he had never fully mastered. But the case took priority over personal comfort.

Steele made a final note in his planner: "Contact APD re: Det. Stone." Then he closed the file, his mind already mapping out the investigation's next steps with characteristic precision.

CHAPTER 3:
The Blue Note

The Blue Note was Emma Stone's refuge on evenings when cases weighed too heavily. The small jazz bar tucked into a quiet corner of downtown Anchorage offered something essential, anonymity among strangers, with only the piano as her confidant. Bernie Holloway, the owner whom everyone affectionately called "Mr. B," had discovered her playing late one night when she thought the place was empty.

What amazed Bernie wasn't just that Emma could play, but how she played. He'd watched in fascination as she listened to a recording of Bill Evans' "Waltz for Debby" streaming from the bar's speakers, her head tilted slightly as if dissecting invisible architecture. Within minutes of the song ending, her fingers found the keys and reproduced not just the melody, but Evans' specific harmonic voicings, his delicate touch, even the subtle rhythmic displacement that made his interpretation distinctive.

"How did you do that?" Bernie had asked, approaching cautiously as she finished.

Emma had looked up, startled to discover she wasn't alone. "What do you mean?"

"Play it exactly like the recording. Note for note."

She'd shrugged, as if her ability was unremarkable. "I hear patterns. Musical structures are like... blueprints. Once you understand the architecture, you can rebuild it."

What Emma didn't explain, couldn't explain, really, was how music revealed itself to her in layers. First came the melody line, clear and obvious. Then the harmonic foundation, chord progressions that followed logical mathematical relationships. But beneath those surface elements, she heard something deeper, the emotional framework that gave the music its true meaning.

Bernie had tested her that night, playing various jazz standards from his collection. Thelonious Monk's angular "Round Midnight," the complex harmonies of "Giant Steps," even obscure pieces by lesser-known artists. Each time, Emma listened with that characteristic tilt of her head, her green eyes focused on some internal processing that Bernie couldn't fathom. And each time, she reproduced the music with startling accuracy, though never as mere mimicry.

Her versions carried something extra, a personal interpretation woven into the familiar structures. Where the original recording might emphasize technical precision, Emma found emotional resonance. Where another pianist relied on speed and complexity, she discovered intimate spaces between the notes. She didn't just play the songs; she inhabited them, transforming familiar melodies into personal statements.

"That piano's been waiting for fingers that understand it," Bernie had told her that first night, his voice gravelly from decades of cigarettes before he'd quit. "Play whenever you need to, Detective. Good for business, good for the soul."

Emma's musical gift had developed despite her father's restrictions, not because of them. Reverend Stone had permitted only hymns and classical pieces, music he deemed "spiritually appropriate." But Emma's ear was indiscriminate, she absorbed musical information from every source, filing away progressions from overheard radio songs, harmonic structures from television commercials, rhythmic patterns from the ambient sounds of daily life.

During her teenage rebellion, she'd discovered jazz through a pair of headphones and a used CD collection, music that spoke to her need for both structure and freedom. Jazz followed rules but encouraged breaking them, respected tradition while demanding innovation. It was the perfect musical language for someone caught between her father's rigid expectations and her own fierce independence.

Now, years later, The Blue Note provided the sanctuary her childhood home never had. Here, she could take a song she'd heard only once and transform it into something entirely her own, letting her emotions speak through chord progressions and melodic variations that no sheet music could capture.

The other patrons had no idea they were witnessing something extraordinary, a detective whose photographic memory and pattern recognition skills, so valuable in solving crimes, revealed themselves most purely through music. Emma could memorize case files with ease, but she could memorize Coltrane solos with joy.

Bernie understood he was hosting something special, though he wisely never made a show of it. Emma Stone was a musical prodigy who happened to carry a badge, not a cop who dabbled in piano. At The Blue Note, surrounded by sympathetic strangers and the forgiving acoustics of an old building, she could finally let her true self breathe through eighty-eight keys.

What neither Emma nor Mr. B had anticipated was Randall Bauer. Randall discovered The Blue Note, and Emma, six months ago. A successful real estate developer with an expanding empire of Anchorage properties, Randall approached life with the calculated precision of someone who assessed value in everything and everyone. Tall, impeccably dressed, with salt-and-pepper hair that enhanced rather than aged him, he projected the confidence of a man accustomed to closing deals.

From his first evening hearing Emma play, Randall claimed the corner table near the piano as his territory. He arrived precisely at eight on nights when Emma typically performed, ordered a single malt Scotch neat, and watched her with undisguised appreciation. His knowledge of jazz was genuine, his comments about her technique insightful. If his interest had remained musical, Emma might have welcomed the conversations.

"Your interpretation of that Debussy piece was remarkable," he said one evening, approaching as she gathered her notebook of charts. "I have a collection of rare jazz recordings from the '50s I think would inspire you. Perhaps over dinner tomorrow?"

"Thank you, but I'm not dating for now," Emma replied with practiced politeness.

Randall countered smoothly. "This is about the love of music Purely cultural appreciation."

His persistence became a predictable rhythm, each refusal met with undiminished confidence that eventually she would accept. What troubled Emma wasn't his interest but his approach, the way he discussed her playing as if evaluating an acquisition, the subtle expectation that her resistance was merely negotiation. Randall Bauer collected properties, fine art, and rare wines. Emma recognized the same proprietary gleam when he watched her play.

"He means well," Mr. B commented one quiet night, wiping glasses behind the bar. "But men like Bauer don't understand that not everything valuable is for sale."

"As long as he respects boundaries," Emma replied, though something in Randall's determined pursuit suggested a man unaccustomed to boundaries he hadn't established himself.

For now, Emma maintained her sanctuary at The Blue Note, her polite but firm rejections of Randall's invitations, and her carefully separated worlds. The piano remained her confidant, her music the one vulnerability she allowed herself in public. The persistent real estate developer was simply another complication to navigate, one she handled with the same composed detachment that defined her professional life.

What Emma couldn't know was how her careful compartmentalization would unravel with her assignment to Talkeetna and partnership with Steele, or how Randall Bauer's determination would complicate her life in ways she never anticipated.

CHAPTER 4:

The Retirement Party

The Anchorage Police Department's recreation room had been transformed for the evening with blue and white streamers, a sheet cake bearing an edible badge, and a modest open bar that would undoubtedly be the most popular station of the night. Emma Stone lingered near the entrance, already plotting her escape route. Captain Harrison's retirement party was a mandatory appearance, but nobody had specified how long she needed to stay.

She smoothed the unfamiliar fabric of her navy cocktail dress and wished, not for the first time, that she'd wore her usual pantsuit instead. The dress had been an impulse purchase, a rare concession to femininity that she was already regretting. At least she'd kept her sensible low heels, Alaska's unpredictable April weather demanded the practicality of layers and options.

"Stone! You actually came." Detective Ellis appeared at her side, holding a beer. "And in a dress, no less. The world truly is ending."

Emma gave him a tight smile. "Harrison deserves the respect. He's been good to all of us."

"True enough." Ellis nodded toward the captain, who was holding court near the punch bowl. "Rogers is already measuring the drapes, you know. Word is he's bringing in his own team for Homicide."

Emma had heard the rumors but refused to give Ellis the satisfaction of a reaction. Her future at APD was uncertain, but she wouldn't discuss it at a party, especially with Ellis.

"Excuse me," she said, moving toward the bar. A scotch would make the next hour more bearable.

"Detective Stone," Harrison called, waving her over. "Just the person I wanted to see."

Emma changed course, approaching her captain and the small group surrounding him. She recognized most of the faces, senior officers, a deputy mayor, the district attorney, but one stood out as unfamiliar.

"Emma, meet Special Agent Jeremiah Steele, FBI," Harrison said, gesturing to the stranger. "Steele, this is Detective Emma Stone, our finest in Homicide."

Emma assessed the FBI agent with a professional eye. Tall, probably a few inches over six feet, with the kind of physique that spoke of regular gym visits. Dark hair cut in a conservative style, a strong jawline, and eyes that were cataloging her just as methodically as she was examining him. His suit was expensive but understated, his posture military-straight.

"Detective." Steele extended his hand, his grip firm and brief. "Captain Harrison speaks highly of your investigative skills."

"Agent Steele." Emma kept her tone neutral. "I wasn't aware the FBI had an interest in our department."

"Interagency cooperation is valuable in our line of work," Steele replied, his expression giving away nothing. "Particularly in a state with so much federal land and such limited resources."

There was something almost automated about his delivery, as if he were reciting from a Bureau handbook. Emma fought the urge to roll her eyes.

"And what does this 'cooperation' look like exactly? The FBI swoops in, takes over, and local law enforcement gets relegated to coffee runs and paperwork?" She couldn't keep the edge from her voice, memories of previous federal interventions still rankling.

"Effective interagency operations utilize complementary skill sets," Steele explained, his tone remaining infuriatingly even. "Local knowledge combined with federal resources and specialized training. Shared jurisdiction permits expedited warrants, expanded search authorities, and cross-boundary investigation continuity.

When executed properly, success rates increase by approximately thirty-two percent."

Emma stared at him, momentarily caught between irritation at his textbook response and an unexpected, unwelcome flutter in her stomach. Despite his rigid demeanor, or perhaps because of it, there was something undeniably attractive about him. The sharp jawline, the focused intensity in his eyes, the confident posture, all combined into a package that her brain unhelpfully categorized as extremely appealing.

She immediately felt foolish for the observation. Handsome or not, Steele represented everything she disliked about federal agents, by-the-book, procedure-obsessed, probably viewing local detectives as provincial talents in need of proper guidance.

Get a grip, she scolded herself silently, annoyed by her own reaction. *He's just another suit with a badge and an inflated sense of importance.*

Yet as she formulated her next salvo in what was rapidly becoming a territorial dispute disguised as small talk, Emma couldn't quite silence the treacherous thought that working closely with Agent Steele might prove distracting in ways that had nothing to do with jurisdictional conflicts.

"Splendid statistics," she replied coolly, compensating for her unwanted attraction with additional frost in her tone. "Though I imagine they look better in PowerPoint presentations than they play out in the real world."

Harrison coughed, a poor disguise for a laugh. "Stone has a unique perspective on police work. Nearly fifteen years on the force, five in Homicide with our highest closure rate."

"Impressive," Steele acknowledged, though his tone suggested mere politeness rather than genuine admiration. "I reviewed your file. Your observational skills are particularly noted."

Emma raised an eyebrow. "You reviewed my file? I wasn't aware I was being evaluated."

"The Bureau maintains comprehensive databases on potential assets," Steele said matter-of-factly. "Joint task forces often require specific skill sets."

"I'm not an 'asset,' Agent Steele. I'm a detective." Emma felt her hackles rising. "And I don't recall applying for any task force."

Harrison intervened smoothly. "That's actually what I wanted to discuss with both of you. Emma, Agent Steele is investigating some unusual occurrences in Talkeetna that may connect to a homicide. The FBI has requested your assistance specifically."

Emma shot Harrison a look that clearly communicated her displeasure. "My caseload is full, Captain."

"Deputy Chief Rogers has already approved the reassignment," Harrison said, the slight emphasis on Rogers' name a reminder of Emma's tenuous position once Harrison retired. "It's an opportunity, Emma."

Steele, apparently oblivious to the undercurrents, continued as if the matter were settled. "We leave for Talkeetna on Monday. The operation requires discretion, we'll be posing as tourists to avoid drawing attention."

Emma nearly choked on her scotch. "Excuse me? Posing as what?"

"Tourists," Steele repeated, his expression suggesting he found her reaction excessive. "Talkeetna is a small community. Two law enforcement officers asking questions would be conspicuous. A couple visiting from Anchorage would not."

"A couple," Emma echoed, looking to Harrison for support and finding none. "Captain, with all due respect...."

"It's a solid tactical approach," Harrison said, though his eyes held an apology. "And it's only for a week or two while you decide what you think about the situation."

Emma felt cornered, a sensation she despised. Working with a partner was bad enough, but posing as a couple with this human machine? And in Talkeetna of all places, where the population was small enough that maintaining a cover story would require constant vigilance.

"What exactly is this case?" she asked, reluctantly accepting that she might not have a choice.

"We should discuss the details privately," Steele said, glancing meaningfully at the partygoers nearby.

"There's a body," Harrison added quietly. "Found near a known survivalist compound. Circumstances suggest foul play, but jurisdiction is complicated by the location. The FBI wants a light touch until they understand what they're dealing with."

Emma considered her options. If Rogers was already approving her reassignment, refusing would give him ammunition to sideline her permanently once Harrison left. And despite her irritation with Steele's approach, a murder investigation outside the usual APD politics held a certain appeal.

"Fine," she conceded with poor grace. "But I'll need all the case files before Monday. And separate accommodations."

"We've reserved a two-bedroom rental," Steele said. "The case files are already prepared for your review. I can have them delivered to your office tomorrow."

His efficiency was both impressive and annoying. Emma had the distinct impression he'd been certain of her agreement before she'd even given it.

"One more thing," Harrison said, lowering his voice further. "This is sensitive. If there's a connection to the survivalist group, it could become politically charged. Rogers wants this handled quietly."

"Of course he does," Emma muttered.

Steele checked his watch, a gesture Emma suspected was habitual rather than necessary. "I should go. Detective Stone, I'll contact you tomorrow with the logistical details. Captain Harrison, congratulations on your retirement."

With a nod to them both, he departed, moving through the party with the same efficient purpose that seemed to characterize everything about him.

"He grows on you," Harrison said, noting Emma's expression.

"Like a fungus, I'm sure." Emma took a large swallow of scotch. "Is this really necessary, Captain? Partnering me with Mr. Roboto from the FBI?"

Harrison's face grew serious. "Rogers was looking for a reason to reassign you to desk duty, Emma. This keeps you in the field, working a case that matters. Steele specifically requested you based on your case record."

"Lucky me."

"He's good at what he does," Harrison continued. "One of their best analysts. Methodical, thorough. And remember, evidence might be inadmissible if chain of custody is broken by jurisdictional disputes. We need to work together."

"And about as personable as a filing cabinet," Emma added.

Harrison laughed. "You're not exactly known for your warm and fuzzy nature either, Detective. Maybe that's why he thought you'd work well together."

Emma couldn't argue with that assessment. She preferred working alone precisely because most partners wanted more personal connection than she was willing to offer. At least Steele seemed equally disinterested in friendship. She understood that FBI brought expensive federal resources like helicopters, and specialized teams while State Troopers knew the terrain better. This would need to be a team effort.

"Fine," she said again. "But when this is over, I want your recommendation for the lieutenant's exam. If I'm going to survive Rogers, I need rank on my side."

"Deal." Harrison raised his glass to hers. "Consider it my retirement gift. Now go mingle for at least fifteen more minutes before you sneak out. It's my party, after all."

Emma managed a genuine smile for her mentor. "Yes, sir. Fifteen minutes of mingling, and not a second more."

As Harrison moved away to greet new arrivals, Emma contemplated the unexpected turn her career had just taken. A temporary assignment in Talkeetna, partnered with an FBI agent who had already managed to irritate her within minutes of their introduction, playing at being a couple while investigating a potential murder.

She drained her scotch. If nothing else, the next two weeks promised to be far from boring.

* * *

The Blue Note was quieter than usual when Emma slipped in after Captain Harrison's retirement party, still wearing her navy cocktail dress. She needed the release that only the piano could provide, especially tonight, with the news of her unexpected assignment to Talkeetna still settling uneasily in her mind.

Bernie looked up from behind the bar, his weathered face breaking into a smile. "Detective Stone. Wasn't expecting you tonight."

"Needed to play, Mr. B," she replied, already moving toward the piano in the corner. "Mind if I stay a while?"

"Always welcome, but I should tell you, we're shutting down for renovations starting Monday. Plumbing issues can't be ignored anymore." Bernie gestured apologetically at the ceiling. "Should be about three weeks before we reopen."

Emma felt a pang of disappointment. Her sanctuary temporarily closed just when a new partnership and case would likely increase her need for it. "I'll get my fill tonight, then."

She settled at the piano, letting her fingers find the keys without conscious thought. The music flowed from some place beyond calculation or plan, melancholy jazz that matched her unsettled mood. She lost herself in the playing, barely registering when Bernie placed a glass of water on the piano's edge or when the door chimed with a new arrival.

It was the familiar scent that alerted her, subtle notes of sandalwood and something distinctly expensive. Randall Bauer had arrived.

"Exquisite as always," he said when she finished the piece, standing closer than necessary. "I heard about the renovation. Three weeks without hearing you play seems... unacceptable."

Emma reached for her water, creating space between them. "The pipes don't care about our preferences, unfortunately."

"Perhaps this is the universe suggesting a different venue," Randall smiled, perfect teeth gleaming in the low light. "My penthouse has a baby grand that's criminally underused. You could play there whenever you like."

"That's generous, but no thank you," Emma replied, her tone polite but firm.

Something flickered behind Randall's eyes, a momentary crack in his sophisticated veneer. "Then perhaps your number? We could meet for coffee when you have time."

"I appreciate the interest, Randall, but I'm actually leaving town for a case. I'll be gone for a while."

"A case? Anything interesting?" His recovery was smooth, but Emma caught the tightening of his jaw.

"Just work." She began gathering her things, signaling the conversation's end.

"At least let me call you. Check in on your investigation."

"That's not possible. Goodnight, Randall."

As she left, Emma didn't see the transformation that overtook Randall's face, the way his carefully cultivated charm collapsed into something hard and possessive. He watched her walk away, fingers tightening around his glass until his knuckles whitened.

Bernie, observing from behind the bar, felt a chill at Randall's expression. He'd seen that look before, a man who viewed rejection not as a final answer, but as an obstacle to overcome by any means necessary.

"She's just private," Bernie offered cautiously.

Randall's smile returned, a perfect mask sliding back into place. "Everyone has boundaries, Bernie. But boundaries can be redrawn." He finished his drink in one swallow. "They always can."

CHAPTER 5:
The Assignment

The Anchorage FBI field office occupied the top three floors of a nondescript office building downtown. Emma Stone made her way through security, pointedly ignoring the visitor badge that identified her as "APD Liaison" rather than "Detective." Small power plays were the FBI's specialty.

The conference room where the briefing was scheduled was easy to find, it was the only one with actual people in it at 7:30 on a Saturday morning. Emma had deliberately dressed in her most professional pantsuit, a subtle correction to the cocktail dress impression from the retirement party. If she was going to be forced into this partnership, she would at least establish herself as a detective, not a prop.

Steele was already there, of course, arranging files on the conference table with military precision. He acknowledged her with a nod but didn't interrupt his task to greet her. Three other agents were present, including a woman in her mid-thirties who introduced herself as Special Agent Diana Hickock.

"Detective Stone, thank you for joining us," Diana said, her handshake firm. "Agent Steele speaks highly of your observational skills."

Emma doubted that very much, but she kept her expression neutral. "I understand there's a body in Talkeetna."

"Straight to business. I like that." Diana gestured toward a seat. "We're waiting on Assistant Director Crawford, then we'll begin."

Emma took a position across from Steele, who was now studying a topographical map of the Talkeetna area with intense concentration. He'd spread out several satellite photos, marking them with colored pushpins. From her vantage point, Emma could see they corresponded to GPS coordinates noted in the file he'd sent over yesterday.

The door opened and a man in his fifties entered, his presence commanding immediate attention. "Let's get started," he said without preamble. "Detective Stone, I'm Assistant Director Crawford. Welcome to the task force."

Emma nodded, noting how the other agents straightened in their chairs. Crawford was clearly not someone who tolerated inefficiency.

"Three weeks ago, Marcus Chen, 27, geology graduate student from UAF, went missing during a solo hike near Talkeetna," Crawford began as Diana distributed folders to everyone at the table. "His body was discovered five days later by a local guide. Cause of death was initially reported as a fall, but the autopsy revealed evidence of blunt force trauma inconsistent with an accidental fall."

Emma opened her folder, scanning the autopsy photos with a professional eye. The body had been found at the base of a rocky slope, but as Crawford indicated, the injuries didn't match a simple fall. The pattern suggested the victim had been struck from behind before falling.

"What was a geology student doing hiking alone in that area?" she asked, noting the location on the map.

Steele answered without looking up from his own notes. "The area is known for unique geological formations. Chen's research focused on alluvial deposits in subarctic regions."

"Alluvial deposits," Emma repeated. "As in gold?"

That got Steele's attention. He looked up, a flicker of surprise crossing his otherwise impassive face. "Yes. Among other minerals. How did you know?"

Emma shrugged. "Gold mining is Alaska's history. Graduate students don't trek into remote areas unless they're looking for something specific."

Crawford nodded approvingly. "That's exactly what we think happened. Lab analysis of soil samples from Chen's clothing and equipment showed high concentrations of gold particulates. We believe he may have discovered a significant deposit."

"And someone killed him for it," Emma concluded. "Who knew about his research?"

"His doctoral advisor, a few colleagues at the university," Diana said. "We've interviewed them all. Nothing suspicious. His field notes from previous expeditions mentioned potential sites along this tributary", she pointed to a blue line on the map, "but nothing conclusive."

"What about the locals?" Emma asked. "Gold fever is a real thing in Alaska. If rumors were circulating about a student finding a new deposit…"

"That's where it gets complicated," Crawford said. "The area where Chen was found is approximately five miles from a known survivalist compound. The Alliance has occupied that land for seven years. They're off-grid, self-sufficient, and generally keep to themselves."

Crawford continued, "In Talkeetna, survival knowledge creates a sharp divide between locals and outsiders. Year-round residents possess intimate familiarity with seasonal changes in river currents, which slopes accumulate dangerous snow loads, and where treacherous ice forms earliest in fall. They've memorized safe passage routes that circumvent dangerous wildlife territories and know precisely when certain areas become inaccessible due to seasonal conditions."

Another agent, whom Emma hadn't been introduced to, pulled up a series of photos on the screen at the front of the room. "The Alliance was founded by James Barrett, former investment banker turned doomsday prepper. Their manifesto focuses on preparation for societal collapse, self-reliance, and what they call 'reclaiming American freedoms.' About forty members, including families. They operate on private land but have been known to use the surrounding state and federal lands for hunting and training exercises."

Emma studied the photos of the compound, a collection of cabins and larger structures arranged around a central clearing, solar panels visible on several roofs, a greenhouse, what appeared to be a shooting range.

"Any history of violence?" she asked.

"Nothing confirmed," Crawford answered. "They're anti-government but haven't crossed into militia territory as far as we can tell. They file their paperwork, pay their taxes. Barrett has made significant land purchases in the area over the years, always through proper channels."

"But?" Emma prompted, sensing the unspoken concern.

"But they're intensely private," Steele said, finally joining the conversation fully. "They've had confrontations with hikers who've strayed too close to their property. Nothing violent but threatening enough that the incidents were reported to local authorities."

"And Chen's body was found near their land," Emma concluded.

"On federal land, technically," Crawford corrected. "But yes, close enough to raise questions. The local State Trooper requested FBI assistance given the jurisdictional complications and limited resources."

Emma leaned back in her chair, processing the information. "So, you want to investigate this survivalist group without tipping them off that they're suspects in a potential homicide."

"Precisely," Crawford confirmed. "Which brings us to your assignment. Agent Steele has proposed a covert initial investigation. You and he will pose as tourists staying in Talkeetna, gathering intelligence on both the town's awareness of Chen's activities and the Alliance's movements."

Emma looked directly at Steele. "I work better alone, Agent Steele. And I suspect you do too."

Steele met her gaze unflinchingly. "I do. But this operation requires complementary skill sets. Your background in homicide investigation and your observational abilities pair well with my analytical approach and federal resources."

"And two tourists attract less attention than two obvious law enforcement officers," Emma acknowledged, though reluctantly.

"We've arranged accommodation at the Susitna River Lodge," Diana said, sliding another folder toward Emma. "Two-bedroom cabin, weekly rental. Your cover story is that you're a couple celebrating your anniversary, taking a scenic vacation before the summer tourist season begins."

Emma barely suppressed a grimace. "Married? That's going to require some acting."

"I'm not thrilled with the romantic pretense either, Detective," Steele said, his tone making it clear he found the arrangement equally distasteful. "But it's the most efficient cover."

"Actually," Emma countered, "friends would be more believable. Less expectation of public affection, more freedom to separate and gather information independently."

Crawford shook his head. "Friends don't typically share accommodation in a town with multiple hotels. The anniversary provides a reason for your interest in romantic activities like scenic flights and guided excursions, which will give you access to areas near the Alliance compound without suspicion."

Emma looked to Steele for support, but he merely shrugged, apparently having already lost this argument.

"This assignment is not optional, Detective Stone," Crawford said, his tone softening slightly. "Your department has already approved the temporary reassignment, and your captain specifically recommended you for your ability to notice details others miss. We need those skills."

Emma knew when she was beaten. Harrison had made it clear this assignment was her shield against Rogers' plans to sideline her. And despite her reservations about working with Steele, the case itself was intriguing.

"Fine," she conceded. "But I want it on record that I think this cover story creates unnecessary complications."

"Noted," Crawford said dryly. "Agent Steele had the same objection. Perhaps you two are more compatible than you think."

Neither Emma nor Steele dignified that with a response.

"Your primary objectives," Crawford continued, "are to establish whether Chen discovered gold on or near Alliance property, determine if anyone in the Alliance knew about his activities, and assess whether they had motive and opportunity to kill him. Secondary objective is to gather intelligence on the Alliance's current activities and potential threats."

"Rules of engagement?" Emma asked.

"Observation only at this stage," Crawford emphasized. "No direct confrontation with Alliance members unless absolutely necessary for maintaining cover. If you find evidence linking them to Chen's death, we send in a full team. This is reconnaissance."

Steele began gathering his materials with the same precision he'd shown in arranging them. "We'll need to establish a communication protocol. Daily check-ins would be conspicuous in a vacation setting."

"Agreed," Crawford said. "We've arranged for secure communications through a modified weather app on your phones. Details are in your packets. Emergency extraction if needed."

Emma flipped through the rest of her folder, noting the thoroughness of the operational details. Whatever else she might think of the FBI, they were certainly comprehensive in their planning.

"We leave Monday morning," Steele said, addressing Emma directly. "I suggest we use tomorrow to align our cover stories and review the case materials separately. The drive to Talkeetna will provide time to establish a working rapport before we arrive."

Emma nearly laughed at his clinical approach to what most people would consider basic human interaction. "A working rapport. Of course."

Crawford stood, signaling the end of the briefing. "Detective Stone, Agent Steele, I expect professionalism and results. Your different approaches should be complementary, not conflicting. Are we clear?"

"Yes, sir," they answered simultaneously, then exchanged startled glances at the unexpected unison.

As the meeting broke up, Emma gathered her materials, already mentally preparing for the assignment. A murder investigation disguised as a romantic getaway, partnered with the human equivalent of a spreadsheet. At least the case itself was interesting, gold, survivalists, and a murder in the wilderness had all the elements of an Alaskan thriller.

Steele approached as she was leaving. "Detective. One more thing."

Emma paused, raising an eyebrow in question.

"We should pack for variable weather conditions. Talkeetna in April can range from spring thaw to winter storm within hours."

Of all the things he could have said, about the case, their cover, their working relationship, he chose to offer advice on packing. Emma wasn't sure whether to be annoyed or amused.

"I've lived in Alaska my entire life, Agent Steele. I think I can manage to pack accordingly."

He nodded, apparently oblivious to her sarcasm. "Good. I'll pick you up at 7 AM Monday. The earlier we arrive, the more time we have to establish our presence before nightfall."

As Emma watched him walk away, his posture military-straight even in casual movement, she wondered what she'd gotten herself into. A couple of weeks in a remote cabin with Agent Steele, pretending to be a happily married couple while investigating a potential murder.

Harrison owed her more than a recommendation for the lieutenant's exam. He owed her a bottle of very expensive scotch.

CHAPTER 6:
Arrival In Talkeetna

The two-hour drive from Anchorage had been largely silent. Steele focused on the road with the same intensity he seemed to bring to everything, while Emma stared out the window, watching the landscape transform from urban sprawl to pristine wilderness. The Chugach Mountains had given way to rolling forests, and now, as they approached Talkeetna, the Alaska Range dominated the horizon.

"There it is," Emma said, breaking the silence as Denali appeared, its massive peak gleaming white against the clear blue sky. Even after a lifetime in Alaska, the mountain still took her breath away.

"Twenty thousand three hundred and ten feet," Steele recited without looking away from the road. "The tallest mountain in North America. From Talkeetna, Denali rises majestically, its towering 20,310-foot peak dominating the landscape despite being over 100 miles away. Have you seen it on clear days, when the "Great One" creates an amazing silhouette against the sky? It draws the eye like a magnetic force."

Emma suppressed a grin. At least he let his passion out for one of nature's most awe-inspiring sights. "It's beautiful," she said pointedly.

Steele's glance lingered on the mountain, then he nodded. "It is impressive."

Dense forests of spruce and birch trees blanket the landscape surrounding Talkeetna, creating a verdant backdrop against the distant mountain views. The convergence of three powerful glacial rivers, the

Susitna, Talkeetna, and Chulitna, formed a dramatic natural feature at the edge of town, their waters rushing with distinctive colors as they merge to form the "Big Susitna River."

The road curved, and suddenly the turn off to Talkeetna appeared before them. A mile or two more and a collection of colorful buildings nestled among towering spruce trees, the kind of picturesque Alaskan town that appeared on postcards and tourism websites. Main Street was lined with weathered wooden storefronts, their signs hand-painted and rustic. Despite being a hub for mountaineers and wilderness enthusiasts, the April timing meant the town was relatively quiet, caught in the lull between winter activities and the summer tourist season.

The weathered structures house local shops, eateries, and the famous Fairview Inn, where visitors and locals alike gathered. Beyond this historic core, more modern developments spread outward, though still maintaining a frontier town character. The juxtaposition of rustic pioneers' cabins alongside newer constructions created a unique aesthetic that honored both Talkeetna's past and present.

"Population eight hundred seventy-six," Steele said as they drove slowly down the main street. "Primary industries are tourism and outdoor recreation services."

"Do you always narrate census data?" Emma asked, unable to keep the chuckle from her voice.

Steele seemed genuinely puzzled by her question. "Context is important for the investigation."

"So is blending in," she reminded him. "Tourists gawk at scenery, not recite demographics."

To her surprise, Steele nodded. "Point taken. I'll adjust my approach."

They parked in front of a two-story log building with a hand-carved sign reading "Susitna River Lodge." The front porch was lined with rocking chairs, and window boxes waited for the summer flowers that would eventually fill them. It looked like every Alaskan B&B Emma had ever seen, charming, rustic, and deliberately playing to tourists' expectations of frontier living.

Inside, the lodge was warm and inviting, with a massive stone fireplace dominating the common area. Antique snowshoes and old mining tools decorated the walls, alongside framed photographs of Denali in various seasons. The reception desk was a repurposed general store counter, behind which stood a woman in her sixties with silver hair pulled back in a practical braid.

"Welcome to Susitna River Lodge," she said warmly. "You must be the Steeles. I'm Martha Cartwright, owner and innkeeper."

Emma felt a jolt at hearing herself referred to as "Mrs. Steele" but managed to maintain her cover with a practiced smile. "Yes, that's us. I'm Emma, and this is my husband, Jeremiah."

Steele placed his hand lightly on the small of Emma's back, the gesture so unexpected she nearly flinched. "It's our anniversary," he said, his voice suddenly warmer than she'd heard it before. "Five years."

Martha beamed. "Well, congratulations! You've picked a perfect time to visit. The crowds haven't arrived yet, but the weather's turning beautiful." She pulled a large ledger toward her and began the check-in process. "Now, I've got you in the Fireweed Cabin. It's our honeymoon cabin, actually, very private, with a lovely view of the mountains."

Emma and Steele exchanged a quick glance. "Honeymoon cabin?" Emma asked, working to keep her tone light.

"Oh, it's perfect for an anniversary too," Martha assured her, misinterpreting her concern. "King-sized bed, private hot tub on the deck, fireplace. Very romantic."

"We had requested a two-bedroom accommodation," Steele said, his professional tone slipping back into place.

Martha frowned, consulting her reservation book. "That's odd. I have you down for the Fireweed. Let me check my emails." She tapped at a computer that looked at least a decade old, squinting at the screen. "Oh, I see what happened. You were originally booked for the Cottonwood Cabin with two bedrooms, but there was water damage last week from a burst pipe. I sent an email about the change..." She looked up apologetically. "I'm so sorry if that wasn't clear."

Emma resisted the urge to look accusingly at Steele, who was undoubtedly already calculating how this change would impact their operation.

"Is there anything else available?" Steele asked. "My wife sometimes has trouble sleeping, so we occasionally need separate rooms."

It was a reasonable cover story, but Martha was already shaking her head. "I'm afraid not. We're hosting a small photography workshop this week, and all our other cabins are booked. The Fireweed does have a very comfortable pull-out sofa in the living room, though."

Emma forced a smile. "That will be fine. We'll make it work."

Martha looked relieved. "Wonderful. And as an apology for the mix-up, breakfast will be on the house for your entire stay." She handed them an old-fashioned key with a wooden tag. "Fireweed is the last cabin on the left path. Dinner is served in the main lodge from six to eight if you'd like to join us, though the cabin has a fully equipped kitchen if you prefer privacy."

As they walked back to the car to retrieve their luggage, Emma muttered under her breath, "Did the FBI not confirm the accommodations?"

"Agent Hickok handled the arrangements," Steele replied, equally quietly. "This is an unfortunate complication, but not insurmountable."

"Easy for you to say. You're probably getting the bed."

To her surprise, Steele shook his head. "I require minimal sleep. The sofa will be sufficient."

The Fireweed Cabin was, as promised, picturesque and private, set slightly apart from the other cabins and backed by a grove of spruce trees. Inside, it was every bit as romantic as Martha had described, a spacious main room with a stone fireplace, a small but well-appointed kitchen, and a bedroom visible through an open door, dominated by a large bed covered in a handmade quilt. Large windows offered stunning views of the mountains, and a deck wrapped around two sides of the cabin, complete with the promised hot tub.

"Well," Emma said, standing awkwardly in the center of the room, her duffel bag still slung over her shoulder. "This is cozy."

Steele was already assessing the space with his analytical eye. "The layout provides adequate privacy despite the single bedroom. We can establish a schedule for use of shared spaces."

Emma rolled her eyes. "Relax, Steele. I'm not going to jump you in your sleep."

For the first time, she saw what might have been embarrassment flicker across his face. "That wasn't my concern. I merely meant to acknowledge that this arrangement is not what either of us anticipated."

Emma dropped her bag on a chair and moved to the windows, taking in the view. "Let's just establish some basic boundaries and get on with the investigation. I take the first shower in the morning, you get it in the evening. Bedroom door stays closed when either of us is changing. And under no circumstances do we discuss this awkward setup with anyone in town."

Steele nodded. "Agreed. We should head into town soon, establish our presence and make initial observations."

"Give me ten minutes to freshen up, and we can grab a late lunch somewhere public," Emma said, already moving toward the bathroom with her toiletry bag.

Twenty minutes later, they were strolling down Talkeetna's main street, playing the part of tourists admiring the quaint buildings and spectacular mountain backdrop. Emma had changed into less formal attire, jeans, hiking boots, and a warm fleece, while Steele looked slightly out of place in his button-down shirt and khakis. She made a mental note to suggest he invest in less FBI-standard casual wear if they were going to be convincing as a vacationing couple.

They stopped at a brewpub called the Denali Brewing Company, choosing a table near the window with a good view of the street. A few locals were scattered around the rustic interior, nursing beers and chatting quietly. The lunch crowd had already come and gone, leaving the place relatively empty.

A waitress approached with a friendly smile. "Welcome to Talkeetna! Just passing through or staying a while?"

"Staying for a couple of weeks," Emma replied warmly. "It's our anniversary."

"Well, congratulations! I'm Kelly. First time in Talkeetna?"

Steele nodded. "We've been to Alaska before but never made it up this way."

"You picked a good time. Another month and you won't be able to move down Main Street for all the tourists." Kelly handed them menus. "Any big plans while you're here?"

"We're hoping to do some hiking," Emma said. "Maybe a flight-seeing tour if the weather holds."

"The trails around here are amazing. Though be careful if you're heading out alone. Stick to the marked paths." A shadow seemed to cross Kelly's face briefly.

Emma seized the opening. "Is it dangerous?"

Kelly shrugged, her expression carefully neutral now. "Just the usual Alaska wilderness concerns. Bears will be waking up soon, weather can change quickly. You know how it is."

"We heard something about a hiker who had an accident recently," Steele said, his tone casual but his gaze sharp.

The change in Kelly's demeanor was subtle but unmistakable. Her smile became fixed, her posture slightly more rigid. "Yeah, that was unfortunate. Young guy from the university. But he was way off the regular trails, in a really remote area."

"How awful," Emma said, watching Kelly closely. "Was he hiking alone?"

"From what I heard. Look don't let that worry you. The marked trails are perfectly safe, and there are plenty of guided options if you want some local expertise." Kelly's tone made it clear she wanted to change the subject. "Our special today is halibut tacos, and all the beers are brewed right here."

Emma and Steele placed their orders, and as Kelly walked away, they exchanged meaningful glances.

"She tensed up immediately," Emma murmured.

Steele nodded slightly. "The topic is sensitive. Notice how she emphasized he was 'way off the regular trails', distancing the incident from tourism areas."

"Small towns depend on visitors. A suspicious death is bad for business."

Their conversation paused as an older man approached their table. His weathered face and calloused hands spoke of a lifetime of outdoor work, and his flannel shirt and canvas pants were worn but clean.

"Welcome to Talkeetna," he said gruffly. "Martha said we had some anniversary folks staying at the lodge. I'm Jim Cartwright, Martha's husband."

Emma smiled at him. "Nice to meet you. The cabin is beautiful."

"Built it myself, twenty years ago." There was pride in his voice. "Martha said there was some confusion with the booking. Everything working out alright?"

"Perfectly," Steele assured him. "The view alone is worth any inconvenience we've encountered."

Jim nodded approvingly. "Good attitude. You folks interested in some fishing while you're here? River's running high with the spring melt, but there are some good spots for rainbow trout."

"That sounds wonderful," Emma said. "We'd love local recommendations."

"Come by the front desk tomorrow morning. I'll mark up a map for you." Jim glanced around the pub, then lowered his voice slightly. "Word of advice, stick to the areas I mark. Some places around here, folks value their privacy. Especially these days."

With that cryptic comment, he nodded goodbye and headed toward the bar, where he joined a group of men who'd been watching their interaction with undisguised curiosity.

"Well, that was interesting," Emma murmured as Kelly returned with their drinks.

"Jim giving you the local tour guide spiel?" Kelly asked with an affectionate eye-roll. "He knows every inch of these woods. If he tells you where to fish, you'll come back with dinner, guaranteed."

"He mentioned some people value their privacy around here," Steele said casually. "Anyone we should be particularly careful not to disturb?"

Kelly's eyes flicked briefly toward Jim's group at the bar, then back. "Oh, you know how it is in small towns. Everybody's got their territory. But mainly he's probably talking about the folks up at the Alliance compound. They keep to themselves, and they prefer others do the same."

"Alliance compound?" Emma asked innocently.

"Just a back-to-the-land group living off-grid up the valley. Self-sufficient types." Kelly's tone was deliberately casual, but Emma caught the warning underneath. "Nothing to worry about if you stick to the tourist areas."

Despite being a popular tourist destination, Talkeetna maintained a profound sense of isolation. The town was accessible primarily via a single spur road that branches off from the Parks Highway, with the railroad providing an alternative connection to the outside world. Beyond the town's modest boundaries, wilderness quickly took over, dense forests, unmarked trails, and challenging terrain create natural barriers that separated Talkeetna from the wider world. During winter months, heavy snowfall would further limit access, enhancing the feeling that Talkeetna stood as a small outpost of civilization surrounded by Alaska's vast, untamed wilderness.

As Kelly moved away to serve another table, Emma met Steele's gaze across the table. Without speaking, they both recognized that they'd stumbled upon their first significant information. The Alliance was known to the locals, and there was clearly an unspoken agreement to steer tourists away from their territory.

And somewhere in that territory, a young geology student had discovered something worth killing for.

Kelly had just delivered more coffee when Emma's phone vibrated against the wooden table. She frowned at the unfamiliar Anchorage number, hesitated, then answered.

"Detective Stone."

"Emma, it's Randall Bauer. Don't hang up."

The smooth voice sent an immediate chill through her. Emma's expression tightened, though she maintained her composure with practiced control.

"How did you get this number?" she asked, her voice deliberately neutral, aware of Steele's analytical gaze now fixed on her.

"Your colleague Officer Mitchell was very helpful when I mentioned I needed to discuss a property listing near your precinct," Randall replied, satisfaction evident in his tone. "He thought you might be interested in the investment opportunity."

Emma made a mental note to have a serious conversation with Mitchell when she returned to Anchorage. "I'm working a case, Mr. Bauer. This isn't a good time."

"You left so suddenly," Randall continued as if she hadn't spoken. "Bernie mentioned you'd be gone for a while. I thought we could discuss the renovations at The Blue Note, perhaps make plans for when you return."

Steele raised an eyebrow, clearly noting her discomfort. Emma shifted slightly, turning toward the window.

"That won't be possible. I'll be focused on this case for the foreseeable future."

"Where are you staying?" Randall asked, his tone casual but probing. "Perhaps I could…"

"Mr. Bauer," Emma interrupted firmly, "I'm not able to discuss my whereabouts or plans. Please don't call this number. I'll be out of town for a while."

From the background, Steele's voice carried clearly as he asked Kelly about local hiking trails. There was a moment of telling silence on the line.

"You're not alone," Randall observed, his voice taking on a harder edge. "Work colleagues, I assume? Or something more personal, Emma?"

"This conversation is over."

She ended the call and immediately blocked the number, her fingers moving with swift precision across the screen. When she looked up, Steele was studying her with that careful assessment she was beginning to recognize.

"Problem?" he asked simply.

"Nothing relevant to the case," Emma replied, tucking her phone away. "Just someone who doesn't understand professional boundaries."

Steele nodded, not pressing further despite the obvious questions in his eyes. "Your tone turned my blood to ice. I'm glad that wasn't me on the other end." He winked.

It was his way of trying to make her feel better without overstepping, acknowledgment of her capability while still showing support. Emma found herself unexpectedly appreciative of his approach.

"I've handled worse," she said, then added with grim certainty, "but I'll need to have a conversation with Officer Mitchell when we return to Anchorage."

As they returned to discussing the case, Emma pushed thoughts of Randall to the back of her mind. The unwelcome call would be dealt with later, right now, a killer demanded her complete focus. Still, she knew Randall Bauer well enough to recognize that blocked calls alone wouldn't deter him. Some men saw rejection as merely the opening gambit in a longer game.

✳ ✳ ✳

One hundred miles away in his penthouse office overlooking downtown Anchorage, Randall Bauer stared at his phone screen displaying the dreaded "call failed" message. He set the device down with deliberate care, his manicured fingers drumming once against the mahogany desk before going completely still.

The rejection wasn't unexpected, Emma Stone had proven remarkably resistant to his usual approaches. What concerned him was the background voice he'd heard, clearly male, clearly comfortable enough with Emma to interrupt their conversation. In six months of careful observation, Randall had never seen her with a romantic partner. She was solitary by nature, predictable in her routines, accessible through her musical refuge at The Blue Note.

He walked to the floor-to-ceiling windows, hands clasped behind his back as he surveyed the city spread below. Randall had built his real estate empire through patience and methodical planning. Every acquisition required time, research, the identification of pressure points and opportunities. Emma Stone was simply his most challenging project to date.

The blocked number was a minor inconvenience. He had other phones, other approaches. More importantly, he had time. Whatever case had taken her out of town would eventually conclude. She would return to Anchorage, to her apartment, to her need for musical expression. And when she did, he would be ready.

Randall's reflection in the window showed a man in complete control, expensive suit perfectly tailored, expression calm and confident. But behind his composed exterior, something darker stirred, a possessiveness that had been carefully contained but never eliminated. Emma's continued resistance wasn't just frustrating; it was becoming personally insulting to a man accustomed to getting what he wanted.

He returned to his desk and opened the file he'd been compiling on Detective Emma Stone. Six months of discrete observation had yielded considerable information, her work schedule, her musical preferences, her father's condition at the assisted living facility. All useful data for someone patient enough to find the right approach.

The male voice on the phone represented a new variable. But variables could be managed, just like zoning boards and building permits and any other obstacle that stood between Randall and his objectives. He'd simply need to gather more information about Emma's current circumstances.

Randall smiled slightly as he closed the file. Challenges had never deterred him before. If anything, Emma's resistance made her more valuable, more worth the investment of time and resources required to acquire her.

Some acquisitions took months. Some took years. Randall Bauer had both patience and persistence in abundant supply.

CHAPTER 7:
The Investigation Begins

Morning light filtered through the cabin windows as Emma methodically applied her makeup. It wasn't her usual minimal workday routine, but rather the careful application of someone mindful of maintaining appearances. The mirror reflected a woman who looked relaxed and refreshed, a tourist enjoying her anniversary getaway, rather than a detective investigating a potential homicide.

"Fifteen minutes," Steele called from the main room where he'd been up since dawn, reviewing case notes and mapping their plan for the day. He'd slept on the pullout sofa as promised, rising before Emma had even stirred.

"Almost ready," she replied, applying a final touch of mascara. The transformation complete, she emerged from the bathroom to find Steele dressed in what appeared to be brand new hiking pants and a flannel shirt that still had creases from the packaging.

"You went shopping," she observed with mild surprise.

Steele nodded, looking slightly uncomfortable in the casual attire. "You suggested my usual clothing would draw attention."

"Good call," Emma admitted, grabbing her jacket. "You almost look like a real person now."

The Talkeetna State Troopers Office occupied a modest building just off Main Street, its weathered exterior blending with the town's rustic aesthetic. A single patrol vehicle was parked outside, alongside a mud-splattered pickup truck. The facade gave little indication that inside, a complex investigation was underway.

"Remember," Emma murmured as they approached, "we're federal consultants here to assist, not take over."

"I'm familiar with jurisdictional sensitivity, Detective," Steele replied, though his tone lacked its usual edge.

The Alaska State Troopers office in Talkeetna stands as a modest yet sturdy single-story log building at the edge of town, with the majestic Denali mountain range creating a dramatic backdrop on clear days. The parking lot holds a mix of rugged patrol SUVs emblazoned with the blue and gold Alaska State Trooper insignia alongside civilian vehicles with mud-splattered tires. A weathered wooden sign marks the entrance, almost hidden by overgrown spruce trees that have weathered decades of harsh winters.

Inside, the office combined practicality with the distinctive character of a remote outpost. The reception area featured well-worn wooden benches, walls adorned with safety notices, wildlife warnings, and a large topographical map of the surrounding wilderness areas marked with colored pins tracking ongoing investigations and search-and-rescue operations. The scent of strong coffee permanently permeates the air, emanating from an ancient coffeemaker that sits on a small table alongside a stack of chipped mugs.

Beyond the public area, the working space consisted of a handful of desks arranged in an open bullpen format, allowing the small team of troopers to communicate easily while handling the vast territory under their jurisdiction. Trooper Dave Holden's desk sat in the corner by a window that offered glimpses of the Susitna River, his space noticeably more organized than his colleagues' with case files arranged in precise stacks and a small potted plant struggling to survive in the limited sunlight. The walls were thin enough that conversations carried, creating an environment where privacy was scarce and team members know each other's business whether they wanted to or not.

A conference room that doubled as a break area held a large table often covered with maps, evidence photos, and takeout containers from the limited dining options in town. The room featured a dated whiteboard permanently stained with marker residue from years of case briefings, and a small kitchenette with a microwave that made suspicious noises when used.

The building's age showed in its creaking floorboards, occasional drafts that whistle through in winter, and the uneven heating that left some areas freezing while others overheat. Yet there was an undeniable sense of purpose and community in this outpost, a frontier spirit that suited Dave Holden's nature.

Trooper Dave Holden was a tall man with the lean build of someone who spent more time outdoors than behind a desk. His salt-and-pepper beard was neatly trimmed, and shrewd eyes assessed them as they entered the small reception area. The badge on his chest was worn at the edges, suggesting years of service.

"Agent Steele," he said, extending his calloused hand. "And you must be Detective Stone. Anchorage sent your credentials over this morning."

After brief introductions, Holden led them to a small conference room that appeared to double as a lunch area. A coffee maker gurgled in the corner, and the whiteboard on the wall was divided between case notes and a duty roster.

"Not exactly what you're used to in Anchorage," Holden said with a hint of defensiveness, "but we make do."

"It's more than adequate," Emma assured him. "We appreciate you reaching out for assistance."

Holden seemed to relax slightly. "Three full-time deputies including myself covering an area the size of Delaware. When something like this happens…" He shook his head. "Chen's death isn't the kind of case we deal with often."

"What made you suspect it wasn't an accident?" Steele asked, direct as always.

Holden pulled a folder from the stack on the table. "Initially, we thought it was. The body was found at the base of a steep slope, typical hiking accident scenario. But the ME in Anchorage found inconsistencies." He opened the folder, revealing autopsy photos. "The skull fracture that killed him didn't match the expected pattern for a fall. The angle suggests he was struck from behind with a blunt object before he went down the slope."

Emma studied the photos. The ME's assessment appeared correct, the fracture pattern indicated a deliberate blow rather than impact from a fall.

"And there were defensive wounds on his hands," Holden continued, pointing to close-ups of the victim's knuckles. "Consistent with trying to ward off an attack."

"What about the scene?" Emma asked. "Any evidence of a struggle at the top of the slope?"

Holden grimaced. "That's where it gets complicated. By the time we identified the exact location where he went down, we'd had heavy rain. Most physical evidence was compromised. We found his backpack twenty yards from the body, contents scattered. Camera strap but no camera, though his phone was still in his pocket."

"The report mentioned a local guide found the body," Steele said, scanning the file in front of him.

"Ray Sutton," Holden confirmed. "He operates a wilderness guide service in town. Was taking a client on a fishing expedition when they spotted Chen's body in the creek bed." He checked his watch. "Sutton should be here any minute. I asked him to come in when I heard you were arriving today."

As if on cue, the office door opened, and a wiry man in his forties entered. Dressed in typical guide attire, sturdy pants, flannel shirt, and a vest with numerous pockets, Ray Sutton had the weather-beaten face of someone who spent most of his life outdoors.

"Holden," he nodded, then eyed Emma and Steele curiously.

After the introductions, they settled around the conference table. Sutton seemed relaxed but alert, his gaze moving between the three law enforcement officers with careful assessment.

"I've already told Holden everything," he began, a hint of impatience in his voice. "Not sure what else I can add."

"We appreciate your time, Mr. Sutton," Emma said, deliberately softening her tone. "Sometimes fresh eyes notice different details. Could you walk us through what happened the day you found Marcus Chen?"

Sutton sighed but nodded. "I was guiding a client, banker from Seattle who comes up every spring. We were checking out a tributary of the Susitna that usually has good rainbow trout this time of year. Was heading to my usual spot when we saw something unnatural in the creek bed about thirty yards downstream." His expression darkened. "Realized it was a body pretty quick. Told my client to stay put and went to check."

"Was it immediately obvious that it was Chen?" Steele asked.

"No. Face was…" Sutton hesitated. "Face was pretty damaged from the fall and exposure. But I recognized the jacket, bright blue, technical material. Had seen a hiker wearing it in town a few days earlier." He shook his head. "Wasn't hard to put together that it was the missing university kid once I got a look at him."

"What did you do next?" Emma prompted.

"Used my satellite phone to call Dave," Sutton said, nodding toward Holden. "Stayed with the body until his deputy arrived, then got my client back to town. Poor guy's fishing trip was ruined, but he was understanding about it."

"Had you seen Chen in the area before his disappearance?" Steele asked.

Sutton paused, considering. "Saw him in town a couple times. The Mountain Brewer, talking to some of the locals. Seemed like a friendly kid, asking a lot of questions about the back country."

"What kind of questions?" Emma asked casually.

"Typical stuff at first, trail conditions, weather patterns. Then he got more specific, asking about stream formations east of Byers Peak." Sutton's eyes narrowed slightly. "That area's not on any tourist maps. When I asked why he was interested, he said something about his geology research."

Emma and Steele exchanged a quick glance. Byers Peak was less than three miles from the Alliance compound.

"Is that area unusual in some way?" Emma asked.

Sutton shrugged, but something in his posture had changed, becoming more guarded. "Just remote. Not much out there except woods and mountains. And the Alliance compound, of course. Agent Steele, your thermal imaging and satellite surveillance are impressive," Holden said, "but they won't tell you which creek beds flood during spring melt or which trails oldtimers been using for the past seven years."

"Technology provides objective data," Steele replied evenly. "Heat signatures don't lie, GPS coordinates are precise, and our equipment works regardless of weather conditions."

"Your heat signatures will pick up every moose, bear, and wolf in a fifty-mile radius," Holden countered. "My people can tell you exactly where a killer is likely to hole up based on thirty years of tracking fugitives in this terrain."

Steele paused, "You're suggesting local knowledge of the land trumps federal resources."

"I'm suggesting your fancy gadgets work best when they're pointed in the right direction by someone who knows where to look."

"And I'm suggesting that gut instincts and local folklore aren't admissible in court," Steele shot back.

Sutten's jaw tightened. "My 'folklore' has closed more cases than...."

"Stop." Emma stepped between them, her voice cutting through the escalating tension. "While you men measure whose approach is bigger, the killer is putting more distance between us and him."

The men looked at her, then at each other. Steele spoke first.

"Compromise. We use federal surveillance if we need it. You direct us to the most probable locations based on your terrain knowledge."

Holden nodded grudgingly. "Your toys watch the perimeter. My people move on foot through the areas the killer is most likely to use."

"Agreed," Steele said. "Time's wasting. Did you mention the Alliance to Chen when he asked about the area?" Steele pressed looking at Sutton.

"Sure did. Told him those folks value their privacy and it's best to give their land a wide berth." Sutton's gaze hardened. "Same advice I give all outsiders. The Alliance might be odd, but they've got rights to their property."

Emma noted his defensive tone. "Did Chen seem particularly interested in the Alliance?"

"Not especially. He was focused on the creek systems. Said something about alluvial deposits having 'unique properties' in that geological formation." Sutton shook his head. "Academic talk. I just told him to be careful. Those back creeks can rise fast with snowmelt."

"Where exactly did you find the body in relation to the Alliance property?" Steele asked.

"About three miles southwest of their boundary line, near where Mink Creek joins the larger tributary." Sutton's expression was carefully neutral now. "Where bureau and public land meet, but not that far from their hunting grounds."

Dave Holden cleared his throat. "I've already interviewed folks at the Alliance. They claim no knowledge of Chen or his activities. Said they hadn't seen any hikers near their property in the weeks before his death."

"But you don't believe them," Emma observed quietly.

Holden shifted uncomfortably. "Didn't say that. Just noting what they told me."

"Could you show us where exactly the body was found?" Steele asked, pulling out a topographical map from his folder.

Sutton leaned forward, studying the map for a moment before pointing to a spot where two blue lines joined. "Right about here. He'd fallen from this slope above the creek junction."

Emma studied the location, noting its proximity to the Alliance compound and the creek system that appeared to flow from higher elevation through their property and down toward the Bureau and public lands where Chen was found.

"What makes that particular creek unusual, Mr. Sutton?" she asked directly. "Why would a geology student be specifically interested in it?"

Sutton sat back, his expression carefully blank. "I'm not a geologist, ma'am. Couldn't tell you."

"But you know these woods better than most," Emma pressed gently. "You must have noticed something special about that area."

A long silence filled the room. Finally, Sutton sighed. "There've been stories about color in those creek beds. Especially after heavy rains when the water runs clear. Flashes of something catching the light."

"Gold," Steele said flatly.

Sutton's eyes flicked to him, then away. "Just old prospector tales. Been hearing them for decades. Nothing ever comes of it."

"But Chen might have taken those tales seriously," Emma suggested. "Given his research."

"Maybe." Sutton stood abruptly. "Look, I've got clients waiting. Unless there's something else?"

The Trooper nodded. "Thanks, Ray. We'll call if we need anything else."

After Sutton had left, an uncomfortable silence settled over the conference room. Holden finally broke it, his voice low.

"You need to understand something about Talkeetna. We live alongside the Alliance folks. They shop in our stores, their kids come to our school. They're odd, but they're part of the community."

"And if they're connected to Chen's death?" Steele asked.

Holden's expression hardened. "Then we'll handle it by the book. But treading carefully matters around here. These communities are fragile ecosystems."

"We understand," Emma assured him. "We're just gathering information at this stage."

After reviewing the remaining files and thanking the Trooper, Emma and Steele stepped back onto Main Street, maintaining their tourist facade as they strolled toward the Mountain Brewer Café where Chen had reportedly spent time.

"Sutton was hiding something," Emma murmured once they were out of earshot.

Steele nodded slightly. "His knowledge of the creek's properties seemed extensive for someone claiming ignorance."

"And the trooper is walking a delicate line," Emma added. "He needs outside help but doesn't want to upset the local balance."

"The creek is the key," Steele said decisively. "We need to see where Chen was working and where he died."

Emma glanced at the mountains looming in the distance, beautiful and dangerous in equal measure. "Looks like we need to book a guided hike," she said. "Preferably with someone who isn't Ray Sutton."

"Agreed." Steele's expression remained impassive, but Emma thought she detected a flicker of anticipation in his eyes. For all his analytical demeanor, the agent clearly enjoyed the chase.

The Mountain Brewer Café beckoned ahead, its windows steamed with warmth against the crisp spring air. Inside, they might find more pieces of the puzzle, what Chen had been asking about, who he'd spoken with, what he might have discovered that led someone to silence him permanently.

As they walked, Emma was acutely aware of eyes following them from shop windows and porches. In a town this small, news traveled fast. The investigation had begun, and already the delicate balance of Talkeetna was shifting in response.

CHAPTER 8:

Uncomfortable Quarters

The cabin's small kitchen filled with the aroma of pasta sauce as Emma stirred the pot absently, her mind still processing the day's information. At the counter beside her, Steele worked with surprising precision, his knife moving in rapid, even strokes as he julienned carrots into perfect matchsticks before moving on to bell peppers. His technique was flawless, the blade never left the cutting board, his fingers curled in proper position, each cut identical to the last.

"Where did you learn to do that?" Emma asked, watching him brunoise an onion with professional efficiency.

"CIA training," Steele replied without looking up from his work.

Emma's eyebrows shot up. "The CIA teaches cooking?"

"Culinary Institute of America," he clarified, the ghost of a smile playing at his lips. "Two years before Quantico. My father thought practical skills would make me more self-sufficient."

"Your father sent you to culinary school?" Emma couldn't hide her surprise. The methodical FBI agent was full of unexpected layers.

"Among other things. Auto mechanics, emergency medicine, firearms training, foreign languages." Steele began arranging the vegetables in the salad bowl with the same precision he brought to crime scene analysis. "Colonel Steele believed in comprehensive preparation for any scenario."

"Sounds exhausting."

"It was efficient," Steele corrected, though something in his tone suggested he agreed with her assessment. "Though I'll admit, most federal operations don't require perfect knife skills."

Emma watched him drizzle olive oil and vinegar with the measured pours of someone who understood ratios instinctively. "Do you actually enjoy cooking, or is it just another learned protocol?"

Steele paused, considering the question as if it had never occurred to him before. "I find the precision... satisfying."

"That's the most Steele answer possible," Emma said with genuine amusement, a soft chuckle escaping her lips.

"Not everything requires emotional complexity, Detective," he replied, but there was warmth in his voice now. "Sometimes a perfectly diced onion is simply a perfectly diced onion."

Emma added salt to the sauce, then tasted it thoughtfully. "My father would have called that prideful. He believed any skill that brought personal satisfaction was inherently sinful."

"And yet you became a detective and a musician. Both require considerable personal satisfaction in mastery."

She looked at him sharply, surprised by his insight. "I never thought about it that way."

"Perhaps rebellion was your path to finding what truly satisfied you, rather than what you were told should satisfy you."

The observation hung between them, more personal than their usual careful exchanges. Emma found herself studying Steele's profile as he finished the salad, noting how his guard had dropped slightly in the domestic setting.

"Your turn for revelation," she said. "What actually satisfies you, beyond perfectly diced vegetables?"

Steele was quiet for a long moment, his hands still. When he spoke, his voice was quieter than usual. "I'm still figuring that out."

After a brief uncomfortable silence, they managed to get the food to the table and the conversation continued on another train of thought.

"The timing of Chen's death corresponds with the period of heaviest rainfall last month," Steele said without looking up. "If gold deposits were exposed by the increased water flow, it would explain his presence in that particular location."

"It would also explain why no one found anything significant there before. Seasonal conditions might only reveal deposits at certain times."

"Exactly." Steele glanced up briefly. "The Alliance has been on that land for seven years. If there's substantial gold on their property, why haven't they mined it?"

"Maybe they didn't know it was there until recently," Emma suggested, draining the pasta. "Or maybe they did know and have been extracting it quietly."

"Without filing mining claims or permits? Risky."

Emma chuckled. "A group that's preparing for the collapse of society probably isn't too concerned about government paperwork."

Steele conceded the point with a slight nod. "Fair assessment."

They ate dinner at the small table, the silence between them growing increasingly uncomfortable. Emma found herself noticing details about Steele she hadn't before, the precision with which he cut his food, the way his eyes constantly scanned the room as if cataloging every object, the slight furrow in his brow when he was thinking deeply.

"You don't like silence, do you?" Steele observed suddenly.

Emma blinked in surprise. "What makes you say that?"

"Your discomfort increases proportionally to the duration of quiet periods. You shift in your seat, your breathing pattern changes, you find reasons to make noise, stirring your drink, tapping your fingers."

"Are you analyzing me, Agent Steele?" Emma asked, unsure whether to be annoyed or impressed by his observation.

"Professional habit," he replied. "Understanding behavioral patterns aids investigations."

"And what does my discomfort with silence tell you?"

Steele considered for a moment. "You're used to using conversation as a control mechanism. When it's quiet, you can't direct the interaction, leaving the outcome uncertain."

Emma stared at him, startled by the accuracy of his assessment. "That's…perceptive."

"Am I wrong?"

"No," she admitted reluctantly. "My father was a preacher who filled every silence with scripture. I learned early that keeping the conversation moving was safer than letting him fill the gaps."

Steele nodded as if filing this information away. "My father was the opposite. Military intelligence. He believed unnecessary words were security risks."

It was the most personal thing he'd shared since they'd met. Emma wasn't sure how to respond, so she busied herself clearing the dishes.

"I'll review the witness statements again tonight," Steele said, returning to his laptop. "There may be inconsistencies we missed."

And just like that, the moment of personal connection was gone, replaced by professional distance. Emma felt an unexpected pang of disappointment in her stomach.

"I'm going to shower," she announced, needing space from the confines of the small cabin and Steele's intense presence.

Later, unable to sleep despite the comfortable bed, Emma slipped out of the bedroom. The main room was dark except for the glow of embers in the fireplace. Steele was nowhere to be seen, perhaps he'd gone for a walk, or maybe he was actually sleeping on the pull-out sofa for once.

Emma pulled on her jacket and quietly left the cabin. The main lodge was dimly lit, a single lamp burning in the common room. To her surprise, an upright piano sat in the corner, its polished surface reflecting the soft light. She approached it cautiously, running her fingers lightly over the keys.

It had been weeks since she'd played. The Blue Note had been closed for renovations, depriving her of her usual outlet. Before she could reconsider, Emma sat at the bench and began to play, softly at first, then with growing confidence as she lost herself in the music.

She chose "Misty," letting the gentle, flowing melody wash away the tension of the day. The piece suited her mood, contemplative, searching, with moments of clarity breaking through complexity. As always, the music transported her, creating a space where her usual defenses could lower safely.

So absorbed was she in the playing that Emma didn't notice Steele's presence until she finished the piece. He stood in the doorway, a steaming mug in each hand, watching her with an expression she couldn't quite decipher.

"I didn't mean to interrupt," he said quietly, extending one of the mugs toward her. "Tea. You mentioned it helps you sleep."

Emma accepted the mug, surprised he'd noticed such a detail. "Thank you. I didn't realize anyone was listening."

"You play beautifully," Steele said, and for once, his tone wasn't merely polite or professional. There was genuine appreciation there.

"It helps me think," she admitted, taking a sip of the tea, chamomile with honey, exactly as she preferred it.

Steele sat in an armchair near the piano, maintaining a respectful distance. "Did it help? With thinking?"

"Maybe," Emma said. "There's something we're missing about this case. Something obvious that we're overlooking because we're focused on the Alliance."

"Such as?"

"I'm not sure yet. But Chen wasn't the only one who knew about the geology of that area. Sutton definitely knew more than he was saying."

Steele nodded thoughtfully. "His defensiveness when discussing the creek was notable."

"And he found the body," Emma added. "Convenient timing."

"You suspect him?"

Emma sighed, cradling the warm mug between her palms. "I don't know. It seems too obvious. But we should look into his background more thoroughly."

Steele was quiet for a moment, then asked, "How long have you played piano?"

The unexpected return to the personal caught Emma off guard. "Since I was five or six. My mom insisted. One of the few things from my childhood I actually kept."

"It shows. The technical proficiency combined with emotional expression is… impressive."

Coming from Steele, with his preference for data and analysis, the observation felt significant. Emma found herself wanting to know more about the man beneath the methodical exterior.

"Did you ever play an instrument?" she asked.

"Chess," he replied. "Not music, but my father considered it an acceptable pursuit. Pattern recognition, strategic thinking."

Emma smiled slightly. "That tracks."

They lapsed into silence, but unlike earlier, it felt almost comfortable.

"Dave Holden is worried about community tensions," Steele said finally. "If the Alliance is responsible for Chen's death, proving it could divide the town."

"And if gold is involved, it could get much worse," Emma agreed. "Gold fever is a real thing in Alaska. One confirmed discovery and this place could be overrun with amateur prospectors."

"Creating optimal conditions for additional conflict," Steele summed it up.

"Exactly." Emma finished her tea and set the mug aside. "We need to see that creek for ourselves. Tomorrow, I'll ask around about hiring a guide, someone other than Sutton."

"I've already identified three options," Steele said, predictably prepared. "The most promising is Lisa Tagaq. Native Alaskan, operates a small guiding business, knows the area well but isn't closely connected to the local politics."

"Sometimes your efficiency is actually useful," Emma conceded with a small smile.

Steele's expression softened fractionally. "A rare compliment, Detective. I'll make note of the occasion."

It took Emma a moment to realize he was making a joke, dry and subtle, but definitely humor. She laughed softly, surprised and slightly charmed by this glimpse of personality.

"We should get some rest," she said, standing from the piano bench. "Tomorrow will be a long day."

They walked back to the cabin together, the clear night sky ablaze with stars above them. The tension from earlier had dissipated, replaced by something approaching professional respect, perhaps even the beginnings of an actual partnership.

As they reached the cabin door, Steele paused. "You were right about the piano helping you think. Your observation about Sutton has merit. We've been focusing too narrowly on the Alliance."

"A good investigator follows all leads," Emma said, echoing one of Harrison's favorite sayings.

"Indeed." Steele opened the door, stepping aside to let her enter first. "Perhaps tomorrow we'll find what Chen discovered in that creek."

"And hopefully not meet the same fate," Emma added grimly.

Steele's expression turned serious. "I won't let that happen."

The simple declaration shouldn't have been reassuring, Emma was perfectly capable of handling herself, but something in his tone suggested that Steele's protection wasn't offered out of doubt in her abilities, but from a genuine sense of partnership. It was, she realized, the first time she'd worked with someone who might actually understand her approach to the job.

As she prepared for bed, Emma found herself thinking about Steele's reaction to her playing, the unguarded appreciation in his eyes, the way he'd brought her tea prepared exactly as she liked it, the unexpected hint of humor. Perhaps there was more to Agent Jeremiah Steele than spreadsheets and analytical precision after all.

And perhaps, just maybe, there was room for an actual partnership between them, at least for the duration of this case.

CHAPTER 9:

The Locals

Morning sunlight gilded Talkeetna's main street as Emma and Steele began their day with a purposeful stroll through town. Their cover as vacationing tourists provided the perfect excuse to explore businesses and engage locals in conversation.

"Remember," Emma murmured as they approached the first establishment, a homey diner called Twister Creek Roadhouse, "casual curiosity, not interrogation."

"I am capable of subtlety, Detective," Steele replied, though his stiff posture suggested otherwise.

The Roadhouse was bustling with breakfast patrons, a mix of locals and the photography workshop guests from their lodge. The aroma of fresh baked goods and coffee filled the warm interior, which was decorated with vintage Alaska memorabilia and faded photographs of mountain climbers.

A woman in her fifties with salt-and-pepper hair pulled back in a bandana greeted them from behind the counter. "Welcome to the Roadhouse! Grab any open seat, menus are on the tables."

They settled into a corner table with good sightlines to the rest of the room. Emma noted Steele's careful assessment of exits and windows, habits ingrained by years of fieldwork.

"That's Ruth McKinley," Emma whispered, nodding toward the woman who'd greeted them. "Owner according to the business listings we reviewed."

Steele nodded almost imperceptibly. "Three locals at the counter, work clothes, familiar with staff. Regular customers."

Ruth approached with coffee pot in hand. "Coffee to start? You must be the anniversary couple staying at Martha's place. Word travels fast here."

Emma smiled warmly. "That's us. I'm Emma, this is Jeremiah."

"Congratulations! How long?" Ruth poured coffee into their mugs without waiting for an answer.

"Five years," Steele replied with surprising smoothness. "Emma insisted on Alaska for the celebration."

"Always wanted to see Denali," Emma added, playing along. "The view from our cabin is incredible."

"You picked a good time, weather's clearing and the summer crowds haven't arrived yet." Ruth leaned in conspiratorially. "Any plans while you're here?"

"We're hoping to do some hiking," Emma said. "Maybe a guided trip? We heard there are some beautiful areas around here."

"Lisa Tagaq's your best bet," Ruth replied without hesitation. "Native-owned business, knows these mountains better than anyone. She does cultural and nature tours, her family's been in this region for generations."

"That sounds perfect," Emma enthused. "Is her office nearby?"

"End of the street, blue building with the raven painted on the sign." Ruth straightened as the bell over the door jingled. "Well, speak of the devil. Lisa! Got some customers for you!"

A woman in her early forties entered, dressed in practical hiking gear, her long black hair braided down her back. She approached with a confident stride and warm smile.

"Ruth trying to drum up business for me?" she asked, her voice melodic with a hint of amusement.

"These two want to explore our backyard," Ruth explained. "Anniversary trip."

Lisa extended her hand. "Lisa Tagaq. Congratulations on your anniversary vacation."

After introductions, Lisa joined them briefly to discuss potential hiking options. Emma observed her careful, intelligent eyes, straightforward manner, no obvious tension when discussing the trails around town.

"The south routes give you the best mountain views," Lisa explained, sketching a quick map on a napkin. "If you're interested in wildlife, the east trails offer better chances for moose and eagles."

"What about the streams?" Steele asked casually. "I read something about interesting geological formations in the area."

Lisa's expression flickered briefly, so quickly Emma might have missed it if she hadn't been watching closely.

"There's a waterfall about four miles out that's pretty popular with photographers," Lisa said neutrally. "The glacial runoff creates some beautiful blue pools."

"We heard about a university student who was studying the geology out here," Emma ventured. "Sadly had an accident recently?"

Lisa's expression sobered. "Yes, unfortunate situation. He was in areas most tourists don't visit, though. Challenging terrain."

"Were you familiar with his research?" Steele pressed gently.

"No, not really." Lisa stood, signaling an end to the conversation. "If you're serious about a guided hike, stop by my office later. I have an opening tomorrow morning."

After breakfast, they continued their canvas of Main Street, stopping at Denali Outdoor Outfitters, where the proprietor, a burly man named Mike Callahan, helped them browse hiking gear while sharing local gossip.

"You folks picked a good year to visit," Mike said as he rang up their purchases, a topographical map, water bottles, and hiking poles. "But, last couple of weeks we did have significant rainfall. The trails were pretty wet."

"We heard there was a hiking accident because of that," Emma commented, examining a display of hunting knives. "Young researcher, wasn't it?"

Mike's easy demeanor hardened slightly. "Chen. Yeah, terrible thing. Trooper says he slipped on a wet slope, but there's talk it might've been more complicated."

"What kind of talk?" Steele asked, maintaining his tourist persona despite his evident interest.

Mike glanced around despite the empty store. "Look, Talkeetna's a small place. We mind our business mostly. But Chen was asking questions about the mountain people, and then he turns up dead? Makes folks wonder."

"Mountain people?" Emma repeated innocently.

"The Alliance," Mike clarified, lowering his voice. "Survivalist group that set up camp about seven years back. Keep to themselves mostly, which is fine by everyone. Live-and-let-live is Alaska's unofficial motto."

"But you think they might be connected to this accident?"

Mike backpedaled quickly. "I'm not saying anything like that. Just repeating talk, is all. They're odd folks but never caused trouble. Buy supplies here sometimes. Professional, polite. Pay cash."

The bell above the door jingled, and Mike's demeanor changed instantly, becoming jovial. "Walt! Good to see you. What brings you to town?"

Emma turned casually, finding herself face to face with an older man sporting a thick head of gray hair. He wore practical outdoor clothing, quality gear that had seen considerable use, and carried himself with the quiet confidence of someone comfortable in wilderness settings.

"Supply run," the man answered, his voice deep and measured. "Need some replacement tent poles and water purification tablets."

"Got both in stock," Mike replied enthusiastically. "Let me finish up with these folks first."

Walter, Emma immediately connected him to the "Walt" Mike had greeted, nodded politely to them. "Visiting from out of town?"

"Anniversary trip," Emma explained, offering her practiced tourist smile. "Just picking up some gear for hiking."

"Beautiful country for it," Walter agreed, his pale blue eyes assessing them with subtle intensity that raised Emma's internal alarms. There was nothing overtly suspicious in his manner, yet she sensed a watchfulness behind his friendly demeanor. "Stick to the marked trails, though. Easy to get turned around out there."

"We're actually thinking of hiring a guide," Steele said. "Lisa Tagaq was recommended."

Something flickered in Walter's eyes. "Lisa's good. Knows the safe areas."

The emphasis on "safe" was slight but unmistakable.

"Walt's our local expert on wilderness survival," Mike interjected proudly. "Teaches classes sometimes at the community center. Used to work for the Forest Service before retirement."

Walter smiled modestly. "Just practical knowledge from years in the woods."

"Walt lives up near the Alliance community," Mike continued, seemingly oblivious to Walter's sudden stillness. "Independent type, like them, but more sociable."

"Only on supply days," Walter joked, though his eyes had cooled considerably. "Mike, I'll come back later when you're not busy."

Before they could engage him further, Walter nodded a polite goodbye and left the store.

"Known him long?" Emma asked.

"About six years," Mike replied. "Showed up after the Alliance was established. Keeps a cabin nearby but isn't officially part of their group. Good customer, knows his gear."

After leaving the outfitter, Emma and Steele continued down Main Street, maintaining their cover while processing the encounter.

"Interesting timing," Emma murmured as they entered the general store. "Walter appeared just as the conversation turned to the Alliance."

"His reaction to Lisa Tagaq was notable," Steele observed quietly. "Tension in his posture, pupil dilation."

"And he emphasized 'safe areas,'" Emma added. "Implying there are unsafe ones."

The general store offered everything from groceries to hardware, its shelves crammed with practical necessities for remote living. The elderly woman at the register introduced herself as Margaret Wilson, third-generation owner of Nagley's General Store.

"We used to be the only shop in town," she explained proudly. "Now we've got competition, but nobody beats our selection."

As they browsed, genuine interest in local honey and handcrafted souvenirs, Emma steered the conversation toward local history.

"Has Talkeetna always been a tourist town?" she asked.

"Goodness, no," Margaret chuckled. "Started as a mining settlement, then became a railway stop. Tourism really took off in the eighties when mountaineering got popular." She gestured to a faded photograph on the wall showing early prospectors standing beside a creek. "Gold brought the first settlers here. Not enough for a proper rush, but enough to establish the town."

"Is there still gold in the hills?" Steele asked casually.

Margaret's expression grew cagey. "There's always rumors. Nothing substantial in decades, though some folks still pan the creeks as a hobby."

The bell over the door jingled, and Emma turned to see Lisa Tagaq enter. She nodded in recognition before approaching Margaret with a supply list.

"Need to stock up before tomorrow's tours," Lisa explained. "Got a full day planned."

"Business picking up?" Margaret asked, accepting the list.

"Finally. Been a slow spring." Lisa glanced at Emma and Steele. "You two decide on a hike yet?"

"Actually, we were just heading to your office," Emma replied. "We're interested in seeing some of those geological formations you told us about."

A shadow crossed Lisa's face. "I should clarify, I don't guide in the eastern creek valleys. That's private property and protected watershed areas."

"Oh, we wouldn't want to trespass," Emma assured her. "Just looking for interesting landscapes. Maybe those blue pools you mentioned?"

Lisa relaxed slightly. "Those I can show you. They're on the approved trail system."

As Margaret gathered Lisa's supplies, Emma noticed a bulletin board near the register covered with community announcements. Among them was a flyer for a wilderness survival class taught by "Walter Kendrick, former Forest Service Ranger." The photo showed the same gray-haired man they'd met at the outfitter's.

"What can you tell us about this survival class?" Emma asked Margaret, pointing to the flyer.

"Walt's classes are popular with the summer residents," Margaret replied. "Practical skills, fire starting, edible plants, emergency shelter. He knows his stuff."

"Is he connected to the Alliance group we've heard mentioned?" Steele asked.

The atmosphere in the store shifted instantly. Margaret busied herself with Lisa's order, avoiding eye contact.

"Walt's his own man," Lisa said carefully. "He respects the Alliance's privacy, as we all do."

"I didn't mean to pry," Steele backpedaled smoothly. "Just trying to understand the community."

"Small towns work because people mind their boundaries," Margaret said pointedly, her earlier warmth diminished. "The Alliance folks keep to themselves, contribute to the economy when they need supplies, and don't cause trouble. That's all visitors need to know."

Message received, Emma thought. The Alliance was a topic locals preferred to avoid.

Their final stop was The Denali Draft House, a rustic bar at the end of Main Street. The interior was dim and cozy, wooden surfaces polished by years of use. This early in the day, only a few patrons occupied the barstools, likely regulars based on their comfortable postures.

The bartender, a man in his thirties with a neatly trimmed beard and forearms covered in nature-themed tattoos, welcomed them with a nod. "What can I get you folks?"

"Just coffee for now," Emma replied. "We're pacing ourselves, long day of exploring ahead."

"Smart move." He poured two cups from a carafe behind the bar. "I'm Jake, by the way. First time in Talkeetna?"

They chatted casually, with Jake offering tourist recommendations while Emma subtly steered the conversation toward local dynamics.

"We met an interesting gentleman earlier," she mentioned. "Walter something? Gray hair, seemed very knowledgeable about the area."

Jake's hands paused momentarily as he wiped down the bar. "Walt Kendrick. Yeah, he knows these woods better than most. Keeps to himself except when he comes to town for supplies or his occasional beer here."

"Mike at the outfitter mentioned he lives near some group called the Alliance?" Emma prompted.

Jake's expression closed slightly. "Look, not to be rude, but we don't gossip about neighbors here. Walt's a good customer, pays his tab, doesn't cause trouble. Same goes for the Alliance folks when they come to town."

"No offense intended," Steele interjected smoothly. "We're just trying to understand the community dynamics."

Jake softened slightly. "No harm done. It's just… Talkeetna's changing. More tourists every year, more outside attention. Some residents value their privacy more than others."

"Like the locals who've been here generations versus newcomers?" Emma suggested.

Jake shook his head. "More complicated than that. Lisa Tagaq's family has been here since before there was a town, but she welcomes tourism because it supports her business. The Alliance chose this area specifically for its remoteness, so they're more protective of their space. Walt falls somewhere in between."

"And where do you stand?" Steele asked.

Jake smiled wryly. "Me? I serve drinks to everybody and keep my opinions to myself. Best way to run a bar in a small town."

As they left the Draft House and continued their circuit of Main Street, Emma and Steele compared notes on their morning conversations.

"The town's protective of the Alliance," Emma observed. "Not out of affection necessarily, but respect for boundaries."

"Practical coexistence," Steele agreed. "But Walter Kendrick is the more interesting figure. Former Forest Service, lives near but not with the Alliance, teaches survival skills, watches newcomers carefully."

"And appeared at the outfitter precisely when we were asking about the survivalists," Emma added. "That's either remarkable coincidence or…"

"Or someone alerted him," Steele finished. "The question is why Walter Kendrick would want to observe two tourists asking questions about a student's accidental death."

"Unless it wasn't an accident," Emma said quietly, "and he knows exactly what happened to Marcus Chen."

They paused at the edge of town, gazing toward the mountains where the Alliance compound lay hidden among the trees. Somewhere in those woods, a creek bed held golden secrets worth killing for. And somewhere nearby, Walter Kendrick was watching, his friendly demeanor masking something Emma couldn't yet define, but her instincts told her he was more than just a retired ranger with a passion for wilderness survival.

"I think," she said carefully, "we should take Lisa up on that guided hike. See exactly what territory she's willing to show us, and what areas she's steering us away from."

Steele nodded, his analytical mind clearly reaching the same conclusion. "And perhaps learn more about Walter Kendrick's connection to the Alliance. The survival class flyer might provide an opportunity for direct contact."

"Good thinking." Emma started walking again, maintaining their tourist facade. "Let's book that hike and then see about signing up for a wilderness survival class."

CHAPTER 10:
Discovery at the Stream

T he decision came after a restless night of reviewing case files and topographical maps. Emma traced the creek's path with her finger for the dozent time, following the blue line from its source in the mountains down through the valley where Marcus Chen's body had been found.

"We need to see it for ourselves," she said, looking up from the map spread across their cabin's small dining table. "All the witness statements and crime scene photos in the world won't tell us what that stream is hiding."

Steele nodded, already reaching for his hiking gear. "Lisa Tagaq's tour yesterday was instructive for what she avoided showing us. That tributary system she steered us away from, that has to be where Chen was actually working."

"The question is why she didn't want us to see it," Emma replied, lacing up her boots. "And whether she's protecting the Alliance or something else entirely."

The morning air carried the crisp promise of spring as they hiked toward the coordinates from the State Trooper's case file. Emma had chosen a route that approached from the north, following what appeared to be an old game trail that wound through dense stands of spruce and birch. The path was barely visible, marked more by the absence of undergrowth than any deliberate clearing.

"Chen's roommate said he'd become secretive about his research locations," Emma said as they navigated around a fallen tree. "Started locking his notes away, researching mineral rights online. That's not the behavior of someone studying theoretical geology."

"It's the behavior of someone who found something valuable," Steele agreed, ducking under a low branch. "The question is whether he understood the danger that discovery would put him in."

They hiked in companionable silence for twenty minutes, the forest gradually opening as they approached the sound of running water. Through the trees ahead, Emma caught glimpses of moving water catching the morning sunlight.

"There," Steele said quietly, consulting his GPS. "According to the case file, Chen's body was found approximately fifty meters downstream from here, at the base of that rocky slope."

Emma surveyed the area with a detective's trained eye. The creek ran swift and clear, perhaps eight feet wide, carving its way through a landscape of moss-covered rocks and fallen logs. The banks were soft earth mixed with stone, showing the seasonal rise and fall of water levels.

"It's beautiful," she murmured, then caught herself. "But Chen didn't come here for the scenery."

"No," Steele agreed. "He came here following a theory about seasonal gold concentration. The question is whether his theory is found to be correct."

They approached the water's edge carefully, mindful of preserving any evidence that might remain from Chen's visit. Emma crouched near a section where the creek widened into a shallow pool, her gaze scanning the bottom.

"Steele," she called softly. "Look at this."

He joined her, following her pointing finger to where larger stones had been arranged in a subtle pattern across the creek bed. To casual observation, it might appear natural, but Emma's sharp eye caught the deliberate placement.

"Someone's been modifying the stream flow," she observed, wading carefully into the shallow water. "See how these rocks create a natural trap for heavier sediment? And here…" She pointed to smaller stones that had been cleared from the center channel. "This is a crude sluice system."

Steele photographed the arrangement from multiple angles. "Professional work but designed to appear natural. Someone with geological knowledge and mining experience."

They continued upstream, finding two more locations where subtle modifications had been made to the creek bed. Each showed recent disturbance, fresh scrape marks on the stones, disturbed moss patterns that indicated activity within the past week.

"Whoever's doing this is still active," Emma noted. "This isn't an abandoned operation."

As they rounded a bend in the creek, the landscape opened into a small clearing dominated by a distinctive granite outcropping. Here the water pooled deeper before continuing downstream, and the banks showed clear signs of human activity.

Emma knelt by the water's edge, running her fingers through the fine gravel and sand that had collected in the calmer water. After a moment, she opened her palm to reveal several tiny specks that gleamed unmistakably gold in the sunlight.

"Wow," she breathed. "Chen was right. There's actually gold here."

Steele's expression remained controlled, but she saw his eyes widen slightly. "Significant concentration?"

"Enough to make this worthwhile for someone with the right equipment and knowledge." Emma carefully transferred the gold flakes to a small evidence bag. "And if this deposit extends upstream onto Alliance property…"

"They'd have access to a valuable resource without filing claims or permits," Steele finished. "Completely off the books."

A prickling sensation across Emma's neck made her pause. The feeling of being observed was sudden and intense, triggering every instinct honed by years in law enforcement.

"We're not alone," she said quietly, not turning around. "Don't react obviously."

To his credit, Steele continued photographing the stream bed as if she'd merely commented on the weather. "Location?"

"Eastern ridge line, just at the tree line. Caught a reflection, probably binoculars or a scope."

"Distance?"

"Three to four hundred yards. Too far for positive identification, but close enough to see exactly what we're doing."

They continued their documentation for several more minutes, maintaining the pretense of casual interest while covertly gathering evidence. Emma followed a line of disturbed soil along the bank, noting how it led toward a flattened area partially concealed by overhanging branches.

"Steele," she called, her voice tight with discovery. "I think I found where Chen was actually attacked."

He joined her quickly at the concealed area. The grass was flattened in a pattern inconsistent with natural causes, and dark stains were visible on several rocks, stains that had been protected from rain by the overhead branches.

"Blood," Steele confirmed grimly. "This is where he was struck, then either fell or was pushed down to the creek where his body was found."

Emma reconstructed the scene in her mind. "He was working the stream, excited by his discovery, completely absorbed in documenting what he'd found. The killer approached from upstream, waited for the right moment, then struck."

"And removed Chen's field notebook containing evidence of both the gold discovery and potentially the killer's identity," Steele added.

The sensation of being watched intensified. Emma forced herself to continue the investigation methodically, but every instinct screamed that they were exposed and vulnerable in this remote location.

"We need to go," she said finally. "We've got what we came for, and whoever's watching us has seen enough to know we're not casual hikers."

They gathered their equipment and began the hike back toward town, deliberately choosing a different route to avoid potential ambush points. Emma felt the observer's attention following them for the first mile before gradually fading as they put distance between themselves and the stream.

"Walter Kendrick," Steele said once they were safely away from the creek. "Former Forest Service, extensive knowledge of geology and mining, living close enough to monitor this location regularly."

"And somehow connected to Marcus Chen's decision to change his research focus to this specific stream," Emma added. "The roommate mentioned an 'old-timer' who knew the area and gave Chen advice about access routes."

"The timing fits. Chen discovers gold, gets excited about the potential, starts researching mineral rights and property laws. But he doesn't realize he's stumbled onto someone else's operation."

As they emerged onto the main trail that would take them back to Talkeetna, Emma pulled out her phone to photograph the GPS coordinates of their route. "We need to get these samples analyzed, confirm the gold content and trace mineral composition."

"And we need to determine exactly how much of that creek system flows through or near Alliance property," Steele added. "If they're extracting gold without permits, it's a federal crime. If they killed to protect that operation…"

"Then we've got them," Emma finished. "The question is how to prove it without ending up like Chen and whoever else might have gotten too close to their secret."

They walked in contemplative silence for the remaining distance to town, both processing the implications of what they'd discovered. The creek held gold, enough to justify an ongoing extraction operation. Someone had been working that stream recently and regularly. Marcus Chen had found evidence of both the gold and the operation and had died for his discovery.

"There's something else," Emma said as they reached the outskirts of Talkeetna. "Whoever was watching us today, they let us complete our investigation. They could have intervened, scared us off, or worse. But they didn't."

Steele considered this. "They wanted to see what we'd find. Assess how much we know and how much of a threat we represent."

"Which means they're still deciding what to do about us."

"Or they're planning something for later, when we're not expecting it."

As they walked down Talkeetna's main street, Emma couldn't shake the feeling that their investigation had crossed a critical threshold. They now had evidence of both the gold operation and its connection to Chen's murder. But they also had the attention of killers who had already proven their willingness to eliminate threats.

The game had begun in earnest, and the stakes were measured in gold, secrets, and lives.

"Tonight, we analyze what we found," Emma said as they reached their cabin. "Tomorrow, we start figuring out how to get close enough to the Alliance to gather evidence without becoming the next victims."

"Agreed," Steele replied, but something in his expression suggested he was already calculating the risks of that approach. "Though I suspect they're going to make the next move before we're ready for it."

Emma looked back toward the mountains where the stream flowed, carrying its golden secret through wilderness that had already claimed one life. Somewhere in those peaks, Walter Kendrick was making his own calculations about two investigators who had seen too much and learned too much to be allowed to leave Talkeetna alive.

The discovery at the stream had given them the evidence they needed to solve Marcus Chen's murder. Now they had to survive long enough to use it.

CHAPTER 11

Under Watch

The late afternoon sun cast long shadows across Talkeetna's main street as Emma and Steele emerged from the Mountain Brewer Café. Their third day of investigation had yielded fragments, local unease about the deaths, careful deflections when they mentioned the eastern creek areas, and the growing certainty that the town was protecting something.

"We're being watched," Emma murmured, adjusting her jacket as they walked toward their rental car. "Gray-haired man, ten o'clock, partially concealed behind the hardware store."

Steele's gaze didn't shift, but his posture subtly changed. "Walter Kendrick?"

"Has to be. Same build, same watchful positioning we noted at the general store yesterday."

They maintained their tourist facade, pausing to admire a hand-carved sign advertising wilderness tours while Steele used the reflection in the shop window to observe their surveillance.

"He's not attempting concealment," Steele noted quietly. "Wants us to know we're being observed."

"Psychological pressure," Emma agreed. "Testing our reactions."

The distinctive pickup truck followed them back toward their cabin, maintaining distance but never losing sight. Walter wasn't just watching, he was tracking their movements, learning their patterns, possibly identifying their temporary residence.

"He's committed," Emma observed as they pulled into their driveway. "That's three hours of surveillance."

"Which means we represent a significant threat," Steele concluded. "The question is how much he knows."

They maintained casual conversation until they were inside with the door secured. Only then did their masks drop.

"Sweep for devices," Emma said immediately, reaching for the detection equipment Crawford had provided.

They worked in methodical silence. The cabin appeared clean, but something felt wrong. Emma paused in the bedroom, studying the space with her detective's eye for detail.

"Someone's been here," she called quietly.

Steele appeared in the doorway. "Evidence?"

"Subtle displacement. My suitcase is an inch further from the wall. Bathroom toiletries rearranged." Emma's jaw tightened. "Professional work, but they weren't expecting someone with a photographic memory."

They found additional evidence, a coffee mug turned slightly clockwise, case files restacked in different order, Emma's jacket moved from the chair back to hanging on the door hook.

"They documented everything," Steele concluded grimly. "Our materials, equipment, capabilities."

Emma checked the bedroom window latch. "This one's been manipulated. Entry point."

The violation of their private space created an unexpected intimacy between them. When Steele tested the window's strength, his shoulder brushed against hers in the confined space.

"Recent scratches on the metal," she noted, acutely aware of his proximity. "They came prepared."

For a moment, they remained motionless, processing the implications while intensely aware of each other's presence. The danger surrounding them seemed to amplify every sensation.

"Emma," he said quietly, her name carrying weight beyond professional address.

"I know," she replied, understanding the unspoken concern.

Then Steele stepped back, reasserting their careful distance. "We're compromised. They know our capabilities, our location. We know virtually nothing about theirs."

Emma moved to the dining table where their case materials were spread. "No more careful observation from a distance."

"The Alliance compound," Steele said, joining her. "We need intelligence from inside their operation."

Emma studied the topographical maps, her mind already calculating routes. "Approach as potential recruits rather than investigators."

"Our cover provides foundation," Steele agreed. "Disillusioned professionals seeking alternatives. After three days here, we could credibly claim growing interest in their community."

"Walter's surveillance actually supports the narrative," Emma realized. "His watching us could be protective assessment rather than hostile monitoring."

She stuffed surveillance equipment into her backpack. "We're going in. Tomorrow morning, while Walter thinks he's controlling the situation."

"Dangerous," Steele cautioned. "If they suspect our true purpose…"

"We handle it," Emma said firmly. "Together."

The simple declaration carried unexpected weight between them. Something had shifted in their partnership, professional respect deepening into something more personal and protective.

"Tomorrow," Steele decided. "We make contact with the Alliance directly."

Outside their cabin, night settled over the Alaskan wilderness. Somewhere in that darkness, Walter Kendrick was planning his next move, armed with intelligence about their investigation.

The game had escalated beyond subtle surveillance. Tomorrow would bring direct confrontation with secrets someone had already killed to protect.

CHAPTER 12

Inside the Alliance

Dawn light filtered through the cabin windows as Emma and Steele prepared for their most dangerous gambit yet. The previous night's discovery had transformed their careful investigation into an urgent race for information.

"GPS coordinates but no detailed layout," Steele said, checking his concealed recording equipment. "Satellite imagery shows structures but little about their security measures."

Emma adjusted her hiking clothes, practical gear that would appeal to survivalist sensibilities while concealing her service weapon. "They chose their location well. Natural barriers, limited approaches, excellent visibility."

They drove the winding forest roads in tense silence, both aware they were crossing from passive observation to active infiltration. The morning air carried spring's promise, but tension filled the vehicle as they approached potentially hostile territory.

The Alliance compound revealed itself through breaks in the tree line, log buildings arranged around a central clearing, solar panels gleaming on roofs, gardens separating structures. Smoke rose from chimneys as the community began its daily activities.

"Impressive organization," Emma observed. "They don't seem to be amateur survivalists."

"Military precision in the layout," Steele agreed. "Defensive positions, strategic infrastructure placement."

The checkpoint consisted of a simple wooden gate with a small guard post. A young man emerged as they stopped, friendly but alert, radio clipped to his belt.

"Good morning," he called. "Can I help you folks?"

"We're hoping to learn about your community," Emma replied with genuine enthusiasm. "We've heard you've created something special, sustainable living, self-sufficiency. We're interested in alternatives to conventional lifestyle."

The guard studied them carefully. "You're not journalists or government officials?"

"Just a married couple questioning whether there's a better way to live," Steele answered smoothly. "My wife's background in security, my experience in federal systems, we've both seen how institutions fail people."

Something shifted in the guard's expression, curiosity replacing caution. "What kind of federal work?"

"Analysis. Research. Watching good policies destroyed by political interference," Steele replied with convincing bitterness. "Eventually you realize the system's designed to benefit insiders, not serve the public."

The guard nodded slowly. "That's how most of us ended up here. Hold on."

He retreated to the guard post, speaking quietly into his radio. After several minutes, he returned with a woman in her forties, confident bearing, intelligent eyes.

"I'm Janet Cole," she introduced herself. "Welcome to the Alliance. Tom says you're interested in sustainable communities?"

"Very much so," Emma confirmed. "We've reached a point where we're questioning everything about conventional society."

Janet's smile was warm but assessing. "That's exactly what we've built here. Would you like a tour?"

They parked and followed Janet through the main gate. The compound was larger than their surveillance had suggested, fifteen buildings of varying sizes, solar arrays, greenhouse structures, rainwater collection systems.

"We could maintain operational self-sufficiency indefinitely," Janet explained as they walked. "Clean energy, sustainable agriculture, genuine community governance."

Children played in a central area under watchful adult supervision. A small group worked extensive garden plots. Others maintained equipment near a workshop complex.

"How long has the Alliance been established?" Steele asked.

"Seven years," Janet replied. "Started by James Barrett, our founder. Former investment banker who saw the system's corruption firsthand."

They approached the largest building, clearly administrative headquarters. As Janet prepared to lead them inside, a familiar figure emerged.

Walter Kendrick. Gray hair, weathered features, the same watchful eyes that had been observing them in town. He greeted Janet with casual familiarity before his gaze settled on Emma and Steele.

"Our visitors from town," he said, his voice carrying undertones Emma couldn't quite read. "Heard you folks were asking questions about sustainable living."

"Walter's been invaluable to our community," Janet explained. "Thirty years with the Forest Service. His knowledge of the land helped us establish everything you see here."

Walter's smile was measured, professional. "Always happy to help people seeking genuine alternatives to failing systems."

Emma felt Steele's subtle tension beside her. This was their primary suspect, standing three feet away, playing the role of helpful community elder.

"We're particularly interested in resource management," Emma said carefully. "How communities like yours handle… discoveries that might benefit the whole group."

Something flickered in Walter's eyes, caution, perhaps calculation. "The land provides for those who understand it," he replied slowly. "Modern society has forgotten how to recognize true wealth."

"What kind of wealth?" Steele pressed gently.

"Clean water, fertile soil, timber for building." Walter's gaze never left Emma's face. "Game for hunting, medicinal plants. Resources that sustain life rather than just generating profit."

Janet was nodding along, but Emma caught the slight emphasis Walter placed on certain words, a subtext meant for their ears specifically.

"Walter maintains his own cabin nearby," Janet continued, oblivious to the undercurrents. "Values his independence while contributing to community welfare."

"Separate residence?" Emma asked with deliberate innocence.

"About half a mile east," Walter replied. "Close enough to help when needed, far enough for privacy. I've always been something of a loner."

The tour continued through impressive facilities, workshop areas, communications center, medical clinic. Everything spoke of careful planning and significant financial investment. But Emma noticed Walter's constant presence, the way other members deferred to his opinions despite Janet's official leadership role.

As they examined the solar power installation, Walter moved closer to Emma. "You seem particularly observant," he said quietly. "Background in security, your husband mentioned?"

"Law enforcement," Emma confirmed. "Though I'm growing disillusioned with that world."

"Understandable. The system corrupts even those who enter with good intentions." Walter's voice carried sympathy that felt genuine. "Sometimes the only solution is complete separation from poisoned institutions."

They were interrupted by a commotion near the compound's eastern perimeter. Janet excused herself to investigate, leaving Emma and Steele alone with Walter for the first time.

"Impressive community," Steele observed. "Must require significant resources to maintain."

"Barrett had financial backing from his previous career," Walter replied smoothly. "But we've also developed... supplementary income streams. Sustainable ventures that support our independence."

"What kind of ventures?" Emma asked.

Walter's smile never wavered, but his eyes grew calculating. "Perhaps you'd like to see some of our more specialized operations? The ones Janet doesn't usually include in official tours?"

Emma felt her pulse quicken. This was it, Walter was testing them, potentially offering access to the illegal mining operation.

"We'd be very interested," she said carefully.

"Tomorrow morning," Walter decided. "Meet me at my cabin around nine. I'll show you how the land can truly provide for those wise enough to understand its gifts."

"That will be great. We appreciated your class," Emma replied. "Seemed like a natural next step to see how those principles apply in a community setting."

Kendrick nodded approvingly. "Oh, here's James Barrett, our founder and community coordinator.".

Barrett stepped forward, offering a firm handshake. His salt-and-pepper hair was neatly trimmed, and his clothing, though practical, was of obvious quality. Nothing about him suggested the wild-eyed extremist stereotype often associated with survivalist leaders. Instead, he projected calm competence and intelligent assessment.

"Walter speaks highly of your interest and aptitude," Barrett said, his voice carrying the refined accent of East Coast education. "We don't often open our doors to visitors, but he felt you might find value in our approach."

"We're honored," Steele replied. "What you've built here is remarkable."

Barrett's expression warmed slightly at the compliment. "It's a work in progress. Seven years of building, learning, adapting." His eyes took on an intensity that hadn't been there moments before. "But more than that, it's proof that another way is possible."

As they toured the impressive facilities, Barrett's commentary revealed layers of philosophy beneath the practical achievements.

"Most people assume we're here because we're afraid of government or society," he said as they examined the solar power installation. "The truth is more complex. I spent fifteen years on Wall Street, Emma. I saw how the system really works, how institutions that claim to serve the public actually exploit them."

His voice carried the conviction of personal experience. "I watched investment banks deliberately crash pension funds to profit from the chaos. I saw regulatory agencies staffed by former industry executives who protected their old employers while ordinary families lost everything. The 2008 crisis wasn't an accident, it was engineered theft on a massive scale."

Emma and Steele exchanged glances as Barrett continued, his measured tone making his radical words more unsettling.

"The Alliance didn't begin as a retreat from society," he explained, gesturing toward the thriving gardens and workshops around them. "It began as an attempt to create what society claims to be but never was, a place where resources serve community needs, where decisions benefit everyone, not just shareholders and political donors."

They paused at the greenhouse where vegetables grew in carefully tended rows. Barrett picked a tomato, examining it with satisfaction.

"In the outside world, this tomato would be grown with pesticides that poison groundwater, harvested by underpaid workers, transported thousands of miles burning fossil fuels, then sold at inflated prices to maximize corporate profit." He handed the tomato to Emma. "Here, it's grown sustainably, harvested by people who share in its value, consumed by the community that created it. Which system is more moral?"

"You're describing basic sustainability practices," Steele observed. "Not necessarily revolutionary."

Barrett's smile held a hint of sadness. "Mr. Steele, sustainability within a corrupt framework is just efficient exploitation. Real change requires stepping outside the system entirely." His gaze encompassed the entire compound. "What we've built here proves that human communities can function without the artificial scarcities and manufactured dependencies that keep people enslaved to institutions they don't control."

Through the trees, Emma glimpsed the cabin's exterior. Unlike the other Alliance buildings with their rustic charm, Kendrick's dwelling was starkly functional, almost military in its precision. A satellite dish and weather monitoring equipment suggested someone who valued information and communication.

Later, when Barrett was distracted by a minor equipment issue, Emma noticed the cabin door stood slightly ajar. Against protocol but driven by instinct, she slipped away from the group for a brief reconnaissance.

Inside, Kendrick's space revealed unexpected depths. The walls were covered with topographical maps marked in precise detail, but these weren't simple wilderness guides. Red X's marked locations throughout Alaska, each labeled with dates going back decades. Corporate mining sites, Emma realized. Every major environmental disaster in the state was documented with obsessive detail.

On his desk, a framed photograph showed a younger Kendrick in Forest Service uniform, standing beside an pristine mountain lake. The same lake appeared in a newspaper clipping pinned nearby, but the headline read: "Copper Mine Expansion Approved Despite Environmental Concerns." The lake in the grainy newsprint photo was brown with runoff, dead fish floating on the surface.

A leather journal lay open, the pages covered in Kendrick's unmistakable handwriting:

"Thirty years of fighting to protect what they claimed to value. Thirty years of being overruled by political appointees who sold our resources to the highest bidder. The Yellowstone Creek disaster could have been prevented. The Kenai Peninsula contamination was entirely predictable. But every time I filed reports, raised concerns, demanded proper environmental impact studies, I was told to 'focus on my assigned duties.'"

Emma photographed the page quickly before reading further:

"They forced my retirement to silence me. Called it 'philosophical differences' when I refused to approve the Chugach Mountain development. Sixty thousand acres of pristine wilderness handed to mining conglomerates who will strip it bare and leave poison in the groundwater. This is what 'public service' has become—serving corporate profits while destroying the public trust."

The final entry was more recent:

"The Alliance provides what government never could—genuine protection of natural resources. But protection requires vigilance. Some threats must be eliminated before they can cause irreparable damage. Chen would have brought industrial interests to this place. His 'research' was reconnaissance for future exploitation. Peterson was already contacting commercial mining consultants. I will not allow them to destroy another pristine watershed. Not again."

Emma heard footsteps approaching and quickly returned the journal to its position. As she slipped out the back door, she understood that Kendrick wasn't just a greedy opportunist. He was an environmental zealot whose decades of watching wilderness destroyed had driven him to murder anyone he perceived as a threat to "his" protected areas.

His illegal mining operation wasn't about personal enrichment, it was about maintaining control over resources he believed the government had failed to protect. In his twisted logic, killing was environmental conservation.

Emma caught up with the group and slipped in behind Steele.

"The government claims to protect public resources while selling mining rights to corporations that devastate landscapes for private profit. Banks claim to provide economic stability while creating boom-bust cycles that transfer wealth upward. The media claims to inform while manufacturing consent for policies that serve elite interests." His voice remained calm, but intensity burned beneath the surface. "Every institution has been corrupted beyond redemption."

"So, the Alliance represents complete separation?" Emma asked, genuinely curious despite her growing unease.

"The Alliance represents proof of concept," Barrett corrected. "Demonstration that humans can organize around cooperation rather than competition, sustainability rather than exploitation, truth rather than manipulation." He paused, watching children play in the central area. "Those children will grow up understanding that abundance comes from wise resource management, not from taking more than you need. They'll never accept the artificial scarcities that keep most people desperate and dependent."

Steele pressed gently: "And if the outside world refuses to adopt these principles?"

Barrett's expression hardened almost imperceptibly. "Then the outside world will collapse under the weight of its own contradictions, Mr. Steele. Our responsibility is to preserve an alternative for those wise enough to embrace it." His tone carried absolute conviction. "History is full of civilizations that chose corruption over sustainability. They all fell. We're simply preparing for that inevitability."

The tour continued, but Barrett's words hung in the air between them. This wasn't simple survivalist paranoia or anti-government sentiment. This was a comprehensive worldview that rejected the fundamental legitimacy of existing institutions, and the moral framework that might constrain actions taken in service of a "higher purpose."

As they reached the community hall, Emma realized they weren't dealing with a criminal who happened to lead a survivalist group. They were dealing with a true believer who saw himself as humanity's savior, surrounded by followers who genuinely trusted his vision of moral purity.

Which made him infinitely more dangerous than a simple opportunist would have been.

Barrett introduced them to several members as they walked, each with specific roles in the community. Janet Khan, a former nurse who now served as the compound's medical provider. Michael Dawson, an agricultural expert who managed their impressive food production system. Lily Barrett, James's wife, who coordinated education for the community's children.

Each person they met seemed genuinely committed to the Alliance's stated mission of sustainable self-sufficiency and preparation. None exhibited the paranoid hostility Emma had half expected from an isolated survivalist group. Instead, she observed a pragmatic community of individuals who had chosen an alternative lifestyle based on shared values.

"Most of our forty-three members came with specific skills," Barrett explained as they toured the greenhouse where fresh vegetables grew year-round. "Engineers, medical professionals, security specialists, teachers. We believe in practical preparation, not fear-mongering."

"How do you handle security?" Steele asked casually. "Being this remote must present challenges."

"Tyler oversees that aspect," Barrett replied. "We maintain awareness of our surroundings, but we're not paranoid. Most visitors are just hikers who've strayed from marked trails. We simply redirect them."

Emma noted the careful phrasing, not quite addressing how they "redirected" unwelcome visitors.

"And your relationship with the local community?" she inquired. "Talkeetna seems aware of your presence but cautious about discussing it."

Barrett smiled slightly. "Small towns thrive on live-and-let-live principles. We contribute to the local economy, respect boundaries, and maintain positive but limited interactions. It works for everyone."

The tour continued to the power generation station, an impressive array of solar panels, battery storage systems, and backup generators. Daniel Harris, their energy specialist and former electrical engineer, explained the self-sustaining system with evident pride.

"We're completely off-grid," he said. "Generate more than we need most of the year, which lets us store for winter months."

"What about communications?" Steele asked. "Do you maintain contact with the outside world?"

"Satellite internet, limited but functional," Harris explained. "We're not technophobes or hermits. We simply believe in controlling our technological dependencies rather than being controlled by them."

Throughout the tour, Emma maintained her role as interested potential recruit while carefully observing dynamics between members. Barrett clearly held authority, but it seemed based on respect rather than dominance. Walter Kendrick occupied an interesting position, not part of the formal leadership structure, yet deferred to by many members.

"Walter's cabin is just beyond those trees," Barrett mentioned as they passed a path leading away from the main compound. "He prefers a bit more solitude than most of us."

"But still part of the community?" Emma asked.

"Walter's contribution is unique," Barrett replied carefully. "His knowledge of the land, survival skills, and connections in town make him invaluable. He's family, even if he maintains his independence."

As they approached a workshop area, Emma noticed several members working with metal and wood. Among them was a man in his early thirties, focused intently on crafting what appeared to be a hunting bow.

"That's Eric Miller, our resident craftsman," Barrett explained. "Former architectural designer who now creates most of our tools and hunting equipment."

Miller looked up at the introduction, his expression shifting from concentration to friendly curiosity. As they exchanged greetings, Emma noted calluses on his hands consistent with regular manual labor. His demeanor was open and enthusiastic as he explained his current project.

"We try to make everything we need," he said proudly. "Reduces dependency on external supply chains."

"Very impressive," Emma replied, genuinely. "How long have you been with the Alliance?"

"Almost from the beginning," Miller said. "I was one of James's first recruits, we met at a sustainable living conference in Seattle. Never looked back." He gestured to the compound around them. "Why would I? Out here, my work has real purpose."

As they continued the tour, Emma and Steele were introduced to more Alliance members, each seemingly committed to the community's stated principles, none displaying obvious signs of involvement in illegal activities. If there was a conspiracy involving Chen's death and gold extraction, it wasn't evident in the general membership.

"What about financial sustainability?" Steele asked Barrett as they headed back toward the community hall. "A community this size must require significant resources."

Barrett nodded. "A fair question. Many members contributed initial capital from previous careers. We maintain investments managed by trusted associates outside the community. Some members still work remotely via satellite internet, and we sell excess produce and crafts in regional markets."

All plausible explanations, Emma noted, though none that necessarily accounted for gold as an income source.

As they reached the community hall, Barrett paused. "You've seen our physical infrastructure, but that's only part of what we've built. The true foundation is philosophical, a shared vision of resilience, sustainability, and community independence. Not rejection of society, but creation of a more deliberate alternative."

His words were measured, persuasive, the speech of someone accustomed to explaining his vision to potential recruits. Emma could understand the appeal. Despite her professional skepticism, she found herself impressed by much of what they'd seen.

"We'll be having lunch soon," Barrett continued. "You're welcome to join us, experience a bit more of daily life here."

"We'd like that," Emma replied.

As Barrett excused himself to attend to community matters, Kendrick approached them. "So, what do you think?" he asked, his pale blue eyes studying their reactions carefully.

"It's more developed than we expected," Steele answered truthfully. "The level of self-sufficiency is impressive."

Kendrick nodded, seemingly pleased by their response. "Most people have the wrong idea about us. They picture either militant extremists or incompetent hobbyists playing at survival. The reality is more practical."

"How did you get involved?" Emma asked, watching his expression carefully.

"I'd been living on my own nearby after retiring from the Forest Service," Kendrick explained. "When James established the Alliance, we crossed paths. Found we had compatible philosophies, complementary skills. They needed someone who understood the land; I appreciated having a community nearby while maintaining my independence."

His explanation aligned with their observations, yet Emma sensed there was more to the story. Before she could probe further, a bell rang from the community hall, signaling the meal.

"That's lunch," Kendrick said. "Come on, food's all grown or raised right here. You haven't lived until you've tried Janet's sourdough bread."

As they followed him toward the hall, Emma and Steele exchanged a subtle glance. The Alliance appeared to be exactly what it claimed, a self-sufficient community preparing for societal disruption. The members they'd met seemed earnest, committed, and unaware of any darker purposes.

Yet questions remained. The carefully restricted areas they hadn't been shown. Kendrick's separate residence and special status. Barrett's vague explanations of their financial model. And hovering over it all, the unsolved murder of Marcus Chen and the gold-laden stream just a mile or two from where they now stood.

If there was a connection between the Alliance and Chen's death, it wasn't evident in the general membership. The conspiracy, if it existed, was more selective, perhaps limited to Barrett, Kendrick, and possibly security chief Tyler Mackenzie.

As they entered the community hall, greeted warmly by Alliance members, Emma reminded herself of their purpose. They weren't there to be recruited, but to investigate a murder. No matter how impressive the community might be, someone had killed Marcus Chen to protect a secret, and that secret was still hidden beneath the surface of this seemingly idyllic settlement.

Janet returned and the official tour concluded, Emma and Steele maintained their enthusiastic tourist personas. But both recognized the significance of Walter's invitation.

They were being invited into the heart of the conspiracy, either as potential allies or as the next victims.

"Thank you for your time," Emma said as they prepared to leave. "This has been... enlightening."

"The beginning of wisdom is recognizing when change is necessary," Walter replied. His pale blue eyes held Emma's gaze for a moment longer than comfortable. "I look forward to our conversation tomorrow."

As they drove away from the compound, both remained silent until they were well beyond any possible surveillance range.

"He's testing us," Emma said finally.

"Gauging whether we're potential recruits or threats," Steele agreed. "Tomorrow's invitation could be our breakthrough."

"Or our death sentence."

They had achieved their objective, direct contact with their primary suspect and an invitation that might reveal the truth about the gold operation. But as the Alliance compound disappeared behind them, Emma couldn't shake the feeling that Walter Kendrick was playing a game several moves ahead of their own.

The investigation was about to enter its most dangerous phase, where one wrong word or gesture could transform them from investigators into victims.

CHAPTER 13:

The Renovation

Three days after his failed call to Emma, Randall Bauer sat across from Bernie Holloway in The Blue Note after closing time. The aging jazz club's flaws were more apparent in the harsh overhead lights, water stains on the ceiling, worn flooring near the bar, outdated fixtures that had once been charming but now just looked tired.

"Plumbing's just the start of it," Bernie sighed, running a hand through his thinning gray hair. "Contractor says the electrical needs updating too. I've been putting band-aids on this place for years."

Randall nodded sympathetically while his mind calculated square footage, property values, and potential. "You've mentioned wanting to move to a better location before. Ship Creek area is developing nicely."

"On my budget? That's a pipe dream." Bernie laughed humorlessly. "This renovation will drain my savings as it is."

Randall leaned forward, his expression shifting to what his business associates called his "closer face", confident, reassuring, with just the right touch of casual indifference. "What if it didn't have to be a dream, Bernie? The old Mariner Building on Ship Creek is available. Triple the space, waterfront location, parking that doesn't require a contortionist to use."

Bernie's eyes narrowed suspiciously. "And you know this how?"

"I acquired the building last month. Was planning to develop it into high-end offices, but..." Randall shrugged elegantly. "I've always had a soft spot for jazz, and I've made space available. The acoustics would be perfect."

"Perfect and perfectly unaffordable," Bernie snorted.

"Not with the right financing." Randall's voice dropped to a confidential tone. "I could offer a loan at two percent, well below market. No balloon payments, flexible terms. You could create the jazz club Anchorage deserves."

Bernie studied him, decades of bartending having honed his ability to spot ulterior motives. "Why would you do that?"

Randall smiled, the picture of beneficent success. "Let's call it cultural philanthropy. This city needs more venues for genuine artistic expression. And," he added with calculated honesty, "I appreciate talent when I hear it. Your pianist deserves a better stage."

Understanding dawned in Bernie's eyes. "This is about Detective Stone."

"This is about good business and good music," Randall corrected smoothly. "The fact that certain talented individuals might benefit is a happy coincidence."

Bernie hesitated, torn between suspicion and the dream he'd nursed for years, a proper jazz club in a location that could attract the crowds The Blue Note deserved.

"The offer expires when renovations on this location begin," Randall added, rising to leave. "Think about it, Bernie. Ship Creek. Water views. A real stage. A Steinway instead of that upright that needs tuning every other week."

He left his business card on the table, embossed with the Bauer Properties logo. As he walked out, Randall smiled to himself, already envisioning Emma's face when she returned from her case to find her sanctuary moved, transformed, and herself indebted, however indirectly, to his generosity.

He hadn't built his real estate empire by accepting rejection. If Emma Stone couldn't be pursued directly, he would simply reshape her world until all paths led to him. The Blue Note was just the beginning.

Detective Ray Mitchell sat in his unmarked car outside the renovated Blue Note, watching construction crews install new sound equipment through the floor-to-ceiling windows. The irony wasn't lost on him, he was surveilling a crime scene of his own making, watching his corruption take physical form in steel and glass.

His phone buzzed with a text from Randall.

Ship Creek location opening next month. Need you to handle any noise complaints from neighbors. Standard fee.

Mitchell's jaw tightened. "Standard fee" now meant $5,000 for what should have been routine police work. Six months ago, he'd sold Randall information about a drug raid for $500, rent money when his ex-wife's alimony payments were bleeding him dry. Now he was in so deep that refusing Randall's requests wasn't an option.

The transformation of The Blue Note wasn't just about Randall's obsession with Emma; it was the perfect vehicle for laundering money from his increasingly questionable business dealings. The renovation costs, officially listed at $2.3 million, provided clean paper trails for funds that originated from much darker sources.

"The construction loan documentation is perfect," Mitchell had assured Randall during their monthly meeting at an expensive downtown restaurant the week before. "City building permits, contractor invoices, everything's legitimate on paper."

What the paperwork didn't show was that half the renovation costs came from Mitchell's information-selling operation. Over eighteen months, Randall had paid him nearly $400,000 for police and FBI intelligence, advance warning about drug raids that allowed him to acquire properties before they hit the market, inside information about zoning changes that let him buy land cheaply before values skyrocketed, and detailed knowledge about which neighborhoods would see increased police attention.

But the worst part, the part that made Mitchell's stomach churn every time he thought about it, was what Randall had asked him to do regarding Emma Stone's cases.

"I need to know where Detective Stone is at all times," Randall had said during their first meeting after Emma had rejected his advances. "Her case assignments, her travel schedules, her current investigations. Everything."

Mitchell had hesitated. Selling information about drug dealers was one thing, those scumbags had it coming. But spying on a fellow officer, especially one with Emma's reputation for integrity, felt like crossing a line he might never be able to step back over.

"She's working a cold case review," Mitchell had finally said, the words tasting like ash in his mouth. "Something about missing persons in rural communities."

Randall's eyes had lit up with an intensity that made Mitchell deeply uncomfortable. "Which communities?"

That was when Mitchell realized he'd made a terrible mistake. Randall wasn't just obsessed with Emma, he was actively tracking her movements, trying to anticipate where she'd be and when. The information Mitchell provided was being used to orchestrate "accidental" encounters, unexpected meetings that Emma probably thought were coincidental.

Now, as Mitchell watched the construction crews at the Blue Note, he knew his corruption had evolved far beyond simple graft. He was enabling a stalker, and worse, he was about to help that stalker trap Emma in a web of financial obligation and manufactured debt.

"The beauty of the jazz club," Randall had explained during their last meeting, "is that legitimate entertainment businesses handle large cash transactions. Nobody questions why a successful venue might deposit $15,000 in cash on a good weekend. It provides the perfect cover for integrating our other revenue streams."

Mitchell had nodded, though he was increasingly uncomfortable with how far their arrangement had evolved. What had started as simple information trading had grown into systematic corruption that touched multiple investigations and affected real people's lives.

"Bernie doesn't know about the financial structure?" Mitchell had asked, though he already knew the answer.

"Bernie thinks he's a partner in a successful renovation," Randall had replied with cold amusement. "He has no idea that his signature on those loan documents makes him legally responsible for funds that would be very difficult to explain to federal investigators."

The implied threat was clear. If Mitchell ever tried to expose their arrangement, Bernie Holloway would be destroyed in the process, an innocent man who'd trusted Randall's generosity without understanding its true cost. And Emma, Mitchell realized with growing horror, was being set up as the emotional collateral. When she discovered her musical sanctuary was built on laundered money, she'd be devastated.

But Mitchell's corruption ran deeper than even Randall knew. Three weeks ago, he'd received a call that changed everything.

"Detective Mitchell? This is Special Agent Sarah Kahn with the FBI Financial Crimes Unit. I understand you've been working some interesting real estate cases lately."

Mitchell's blood had run cold. FBI agents didn't make casual phone calls about "interesting cases." They made targeted inquiries when they were building investigations.

"I'm not sure what you mean, Agent Kahn," Mitchell had said, trying to keep his voice steady.

"Oh, I think you do," Kahn had replied, her tone pleasant but unmistakably threatening. "See, we've been tracking some unusual property transactions in the Anchorage area. Properties that seem to change hands right before major developments are announced. Properties that are purchased by shell companies with remarkably good timing regarding city planning decisions."

Mitchell had said nothing, his mouth dry as desert sand.

"Here's what's going to happen," Kahn had continued. "You're going to keep doing exactly what you've been doing. But from now on, you're going to document everything. Every meeting with Randall Bauer, every piece of information you sell, every dollar that changes hands. Because, Detective Mitchell, you're now working for us."

The FBI had been investigating Randall Bauer for months, Kahn explained. Money laundering, bribery, corruption of public officials, and tax evasion. They needed someone on the inside, someone with access to Randall's operations. Mitchell's corruption, rather than ending his career, had made him the perfect double agent.

"Bauer's been running money through construction projects across Alaska," Kahn had said. "The Blue Note renovation is just the latest in a series of suspicious developments. We need to know how deep this goes."

Mitchell had realized then that his small-time corruption had made him a pawn in a much larger federal investigation into organized financial crimes.

Now, sitting outside the Blue Note, Mitchell knew he was caught in a web of his own making. He was spying on a fellow officer for a stalker, while secretly working for the FBI to catch that same stalker's money laundering operation, all while trying to keep his own head above water.

His phone buzzed again. Another text from Randall.

Emma returns from Talkeetna tomorrow. Want to know how her trip went. Standard arrangement.

Mitchell stared at the message, his stomach churning. Randall's obsession with Emma had nothing to do with his criminal activities, it was purely personal, which somehow made it worse. At least financial crimes had rational motives. Stalking was just sick.

Mitchell typed back. *Will handle it. Usual rate.*

But he also made a mental note to contact Agent Kahn. The FBI might not care about Randall's romantic obsessions, but Mitchell was increasingly worried about where that obsession might lead.

"Emma will love the new venue," Randall had said during their last meeting, his tone shifting to something more personal and unsettling. "A proper stage where she can showcase her talent, professional acoustics that do justice to her gift. When she sees what I've created for her, she'll understand the depth of my commitment."

Mitchell had suppressed a shiver at the possessive undertone. Randall's "gifts" always came with strings attached, and his interest in Emma Stone had grown from admiration into something that felt dangerously close to ownership.

Now, as Mitchell watched the workers install a custom lighting system designed to highlight a single pianist at center stage, he realized that Randall wasn't just building a jazz club, he was building a gilded cage. And Emma Stone was meant to be its only occupant.

The question was whether Mitchell could help the FBI catch Randall for his financial crimes before his obsession with Emma escalated into something truly dangerous. Because while Randall might not be a killer, Mitchell had seen enough domestic cases to know that rejected stalkers could become violent without warning.

And Emma had no idea what kind of web was being woven around her.

CHAPTER 14

Midnight Confessions

The cabin was quiet save for the gentle crackling of the fireplace. Emma sat curled in one corner of the sofa, cradling a mug of tea while Steele methodically organized their evidence at the dining table, photos from the stream site, notes from their visit to the Alliance compound, and samples they'd collected. The day's immersion in the survivalist community had left them both thoughtful, processing not just investigative leads but the uncomfortable parallels to their own lives.

"They're not what I expected," Emma admitted, breaking the contemplative silence. "Not the paranoid extremists from the training manuals."

Steele looked up from his notes. "Many started as idealists seeking alternatives to systems they found corrupt or unsustainable. Not unlike certain law enforcement officers I know."

Emma smiled faintly at his perceptiveness. "Noticed that, did you?"

"Your responses to their questions contained genuine conviction," Steele observed. "Particularly regarding disillusionment with bureaucratic systems."

"Because it wasn't all an act," Emma acknowledged, drawing her knees closer to her chest. "My father would have understood Barrett's philosophy perfectly, just with biblical justification instead of sociopolitical reasoning."

Steele set aside his notes and joined her by the fire, maintaining a respectful distance on the opposite end of the sofa. His usual rigid posture had softened slightly, a subtle shift she'd begun to recognize as his version of relaxation.

"You mentioned your father was a preacher," he prompted quietly.

Emma stared into the flames, weighing how much to reveal. Professional boundaries had always been her refuge, keeping colleagues at a safe distance. Yet something about this isolated cabin, the shared dangers they'd faced, and Steele's careful attention broke down her usual reticence.

"My father believed the world was corrupted beyond redemption," she began. "He preached about imminent judgment, the collapse of sinful society, the need to prepare for tribulation. We had a basement full of supplies, canned food, water purification tablets, medical kits. He taught me to hunt, to identify edible plants, to survive 'when the systems of man inevitably failed.'"

"Similar preparation, different justification," Steele noted.

"Exactly. When Kendrick talked about the land providing for those who understand it, I heard my father's voice." Emma shook her head. "The irony is, I became a cop partly to rebel against his worldview, to prove systems could work, justice could be served through established channels."

"And then discovered he wasn't entirely wrong," Steele suggested.

Emma met his gaze, surprised by his insight. "Yes. Not about the religious aspects, but about the fragility of institutions, the way power corrupts, how easily justice gets compromised by politics and expediency." She sighed. "It's a strange feeling, reaching adulthood only to discover your parent's paranoia wasn't completely unfounded."

"Complex legacy," Steele observed. When Emma raised an inquiring eyebrow, he elaborated: "Rejecting the framework while retaining the useful elements. Adaptation rather than complete dismissal."

"I suppose so," Emma agreed. "What about you? You mentioned your father was in military intelligence."

Steele's expression remained neutral, but Emma noticed a subtle tension return to his shoulders. "Colonel William Steele, United States Army Intelligence Corps. Thirty-two years of service, most of it classified."

"That must have been an interesting childhood," Emma prompted gently.

"Structured," Steele replied, choosing his words carefully. "My father approached parenting as another military operation, clear objectives, consistent discipline, measurable outcomes."

"Sounds warm and fuzzy," Emma said dryly.

The corner of Steele's mouth quirked upward, the closest thing to a smile she'd seen from him. "Emotional expression was classified as inefficient. Attachments were security vulnerabilities. Friends were potential compromise vectors."

Emma winced. "That explains a few things."

"My psychological profile, you mean." It wasn't a question.

"Your... precision," Emma clarified. "The way you process everything analytically."

Steele nodded, accepting the observation without offense. "My father's work shaped his worldview. He operated in environments where trust could be fatal, where relationships were often covers for intelligence gathering."

"Was he ever home?" Emma asked.

"Periodically. Enough to establish parameters and evaluate progress." Steele's voice remained even, but Emma sensed the depth beneath his measured words. "He missed my high school graduation because of an operation in eastern Europe. Sent a letter outlining career recommendations instead."

"That's harsh," Emma said softly.

"It was logical from his perspective," Steele countered. "He was preventing geopolitical destabilization. Personal milestones were secondary to national security."

Emma studied him, reading between the carefully constructed lines. "But it affected you."

Steele was quiet for a long moment, his gaze fixed on the dancing flames. "I learned that emotional distance was professional strength. That personal connections created vulnerabilities. That objective analysis was more reliable than subjective experience." He paused. "I excelled at Quantico because I'd been trained for it since birth."

"And your mother?"

"Died when I was eight. Cancer. My father reassigned me to my grandmother until he determined I was old enough for boarding school."

"Reassigned you," Emma repeated, the clinical terminology revealing volumes about Steele's upbringing.

"His exact words," Steele confirmed.

Emma set down her mug and shifted slightly closer to him on the sofa. "No wonder you understood what I meant about complicated parental legacies."

"Different methodologies, similar outcomes," Steele agreed. "Both of us shaped by fathers who saw the world through particular lenses and raised children accordingly."

"And both of us ended up in law enforcement despite, or because of, it," Emma added.

"The psychological literature suggests we often attempt to resolve childhood patterns through career choices," Steele observed.

Emma laughed softly. "Is that your way of saying we're both working through our daddy issues by carrying badges?"

Steele's expression remained serious, but something in his eyes softened. "A reductive but not entirely inaccurate assessment."

They fell silent, the fire crackling between them. Emma was struck by how much Steele had revealed, perhaps more than he had intended, given his usual reticence. The isolation of their assignment had created an unusual intimacy, breaking down professional barriers that might have remained intact in a normal investigative partnership.

"It's strange," she said finally. "I've worked with partners before, but never really knew them. Never wanted to, honestly."

"Tactical boundaries," Steele suggested. "Maintaining operational independence."

"That's a very Steele way of saying I kept people at arm's length," Emma replied with a small smile.

"Is that a compliment or criticism?" he asked, genuine uncertainty in his voice.

"Neither. Just an observation." Emma found herself studying his face, the strong jawline, the intelligent eyes that missed nothing, the controlled expressions that she was slowly learning to read. "You know, for someone raised to avoid connections, you're surprisingly good at listening."

"Analysis requires comprehensive data collection," he replied automatically, then paused. "But... thank you."

The moment stretched between them, something unspoken shifting in the air. Emma became acutely aware of how close they had drifted on the sofa, how the firelight cast warm shadows across Steele's features, softening his usual precision into something more accessible, more human.

"Steele," she said quietly, "I think we..."

The harsh ring of his secure phone shattered the moment. Steele reached for it immediately, his body language instantly reverting to professional alertness.

"Steele," he answered, listening intently. "Yes. When? I understand. Send the full analysis immediately." He ended the call and turned to Emma, all traces of their previous intimacy vanished. "That was the Anchorage lab. They've completed preliminary analysis of the stream samples."

Emma straightened, shifting mentally back to investigator mode despite the emotional whiplash. "And?"

"High-grade gold deposits, significantly above commercial mining viability thresholds. Distinctive mineral composition placing their origin definitively in the watershed connected to the Alliance property."

"Confirming Chen's discovery and our theory," Emma said, standing to pace the small room. "The Alliance, or at least some members, are extracting gold from public lands without permits or claims."

"The composition also matches trace minerals found under Chen's fingernails during the autopsy," Steele added. "Confirming he had direct contact with the site before his death."

Emma stopped pacing. "This gives us probable cause. We could bring in a full team now, execute search warrants on the compound and Kendrick's cabin."

Steele's expression grew thoughtful. "That approach sacrifices our current advantage. They don't know we've identified the gold connection. Tomorrow, Kendrick has offered to show us 'the land's treasures' without Barrett's supervision."

"You think he'll take us to the stream site?"

"It's a significant probability. He's assessing whether we're potential allies in whatever operation he's running, possibly separate from Barrett's knowledge."

Emma considered this. "So, we play along, gather more direct evidence linking Kendrick to both the gold extraction and Chen's death."

"Precisely. More tactical advantage than a frontal approach with warrants and teams."

The professional strategy made sense, yet Emma felt an undercurrent of concern that had nothing to do with the case. The moment that had been interrupted, the nearly palpable connection that had formed between them, now hung awkwardly in the air, neither acknowledged nor dismissed.

"We should prepare for tomorrow," she said finally, retreating to safer territory. "If Kendrick is testing us, we need to be ready."

Steele nodded, his focus entirely on the investigation once more. "I'll update the secure file with the lab results and prepare surveillance equipment for the hike."

As he moved back to the dining table to resume his methodical preparation, Emma remained by the fire, caught between professional necessity and personal awareness. Something had deepened between them tonight, boundaries crossed that couldn't easily be reestablished. They had shared parts of themselves rarely revealed, recognizing in each other the shadows of similar formative experiences.

And in that recognition, something dangerous had nearly happened, something that would complicate their partnership, their investigation, and their carefully maintained professional distance.

Perhaps the phone call had been fortunate timing after all, Emma thought as she watched Steele return to his precise documentation. They had a murderer to catch, a conspiracy to unravel. Personal revelations and almost-moments by firelight were distractions they couldn't afford, no matter how compelling the connection had felt in that suspended moment before the phone rang.

CHAPTER 15:

Golden Revelation

Morning light filtered through the cabin windows as Emma and Steele spread maps and documents across the dining table. The secure laptop displayed the detailed analysis from the Anchorage lab, confirming what they had suspected since finding the disturbed stream bed.

"Gold content averaging 15.3 grams per ton," Steele noted, scrolling through the technical report. "Well above commercial mining viability threshold."

"And the mineral composition is distinctive," Emma added, studying the geological analysis. "The specific combination of trace elements creates a unique fingerprint that matches perfectly with what was found under Chen's fingernails."

Steele nodded, connecting the evidence points with his characteristic precision. "Confirming he was actively handling material from that exact stream location before his death."

They had risen early, using the hours before their scheduled meeting with Kendrick to compile all available information about the land surrounding the Alliance compound. Property records, mining claims, geological surveys, anything that might help them understand the full scope of what they were uncovering.

"The Bureau of Land Management maps show the stream crosses three different categories of land," Emma said, tracing the blue line with her finger. "It originates on federal wilderness land, crosses the eastern edge of Alliance property, then continues onto state-managed public land before joining the larger river system."

"Where we found the evidence of gold extraction," Steele added, marking the location on the map. "Technically public land, but remote enough to avoid casual discovery."

Emma pulled up another document on her tablet. "No active mining claims registered for that watershed. Not by the Alliance, Kendrick, or anyone else."

"Making any extraction activity illegal," Steele concluded. "Unregistered mining on public land carries significant federal penalties."

"Plus, potential tax evasion if they're selling the gold without reporting the income," Emma added.

The picture was becoming clearer with each piece of evidence they assembled. The stream that flowed from federal land, across Alliance property, and through the public lands where Chen had died contained commercially viable gold deposits. Someone, likely Walter Kendrick, given his separate cabin near the watershed and his references to "the land's treasures," had discovered this resource and established a small-scale extraction operation.

"The question remains whether Barrett and the entire Alliance leadership are involved, or if this is Kendrick's independent operation," Steele observed.

Emma considered this carefully. "Barrett's evasiveness about their financial resources suggests at least awareness, if not active participation. But the dynamic between them yesterday, the way Kendrick distanced himself slightly from Barrett's vision, implies some separation of interests."

"A partnership with tension," Steele suggested. "Perhaps Kendrick discovered the gold, brought Barrett in as necessary cover, but maintains primary control of the operation."

"Which would explain his separate residence and special status," Emma agreed. "Not fully integrated into the community structure, but too valuable to exclude."

They turned to the timeline they'd constructed, presenting a chronological narrative of events.

"Kendrick retires from Forest Service, moves to area," Steele recited. "Approximately one year later, Barrett establishes Alliance compound nearby. Kendrick maintains separate residence but affiliated status."

"Add in the local guide Sutton's comment about 'old prospector tales' regarding color in the creek beds," Emma continued. "Suggesting rumors of gold in the area predated the Alliance's arrival."

"Kendrick's Forest Service background would give him geological knowledge, understanding of land management regulations, awareness of remote areas unlikely to be monitored," Steele analyzed. "Ideal skill set for identifying and quietly exploiting natural resources."

"And then Marcus Chen appears," Emma said grimly, tapping the young researcher's photograph. "Geology student studying alluvial gold deposits, specifically how seasonal rainfall affects concentration patterns."

"Following scientific evidence to the same creek Kendrick had been quietly working," Steele finished. "Becoming a threat to their operation if he documented the find academically or reported it officially."

Emma stood, needing to move as the theory solidified. "So, here's what we have: Kendrick discovers gold, establishes small-scale extraction operation. Alliance forms nearby, possibly with his encouragement, possibly coincidentally. He affiliates with them, gaining protection, community, and cover for his activities."

"The Alliance benefits from his knowledge and possibly a share of the gold proceeds," Steele continued, following her logical progression. "Providing financial support for their impressive infrastructure."

"Everything functions smoothly until Chen stumbles onto their operation," Emma added. "Excited by his discovery, he plans to document it scientifically. Kendrick realizes the threat and eliminates it, making it look like an accident."

"And removes Chen's field notebook containing evidence of both the gold deposit and potentially Kendrick's extraction activities," Steele concluded.

Emma returned to the table, studying the map intently. "If our theory is correct, and Kendrick follows through on his offer to show us 'the land's treasures' today, he's either testing us as potential allies…"

Steele glanced at Emma, "Or leading us into a potentially dangerous situation."

The implications hung in the air between them. They had solid evidence connecting the stream's gold deposits to Chen's death. They could call in backup now, execute search warrants, bring formal charges. But doing so would forfeit the opportunity to gather conclusive evidence directly linking Kendrick to both the illegal mining operation and Chen's murder.

"We proceed as planned," Emma decided. "Meet Kendrick, follow his lead, see exactly what he wants to show us. But we take precautions, communicate with the field office, track location, and coded check-ins."

"And extraction protocols if the situation deteriorates," Steele added, his expression revealing concern he rarely displayed.

Emma nodded, remembering their near-moment by the fire the night before. Despite their professional focus this morning, something had undeniably changed between them, a deepening connection that made the risks ahead more personal than either would typically allow.

"One more thing before we go," she said, pulling a final document from the stack. "I requested background on Kendrick's Forest Service career. Most was standard, commendations, promotions, typical career trajectory. But his retirement came after an internal investigation."

Steele's interest sharpened. "What kind of investigation?"

"Resource management discrepancies in his district," Emma explained. "Allegations of unauthorized timber harvesting, missing inventory from seized marijuana cultivation operations, discrepancies in confiscated wildlife products. Nothing proven conclusively, but enough smoke that retirement became his best option."

"Suggesting a pattern of exploiting natural resources for personal gain," Steele observed. "Using his position and knowledge to identify opportunities others would miss."

"Exactly," Emma confirmed grimly. "Which makes our theory even more plausible. This wouldn't be his first time bending rules around resource extraction."

Steele checked his watch. "We should prepare for the meeting. Nine o'clock at the Alliance gate."

As they gathered their tactical gear, concealed recording devices, emergency transponders, concealed backup weapons, Emma felt the weight of what lay ahead. Their investigation had uncovered a deadly secret hidden in the picturesque Alaskan wilderness. Gold, illegal mining, murder, and a former government official exploiting the land he had once been sworn to protect.

Whether Kendrick intended to recruit them into his operation or eliminate them as threats remained to be seen. But one thing was certain, their carefully constructed cover was about to face its most dangerous test.

CHAPTER 16:

Second Victim

Emma's phone rang just as she was lacing up her hiking boots for their meeting with Kendrick. The caller ID showed Trooper Holden's number, unusual for this early hour.

"Detective Stone," she answered, exchanging a concerned glance with Steele.

"You and your partner need to get down to the station," Holden said without preamble, his voice tense. "We've got another body."

Twenty minutes later, they stood in Holden's small office, their planned meeting with Kendrick temporarily postponed with a brief message about a "family emergency" requiring their attention in town.

"Dr. Alan Peterson, 52," Holden explained, spreading crime scene photos across his desk. "Local geologist, occasional consultant for the university. Found this morning by his wife when he didn't come home last night."

Emma studied the images, her stomach tightening at the similarities to Chen's case. Peterson's body had been discovered at the base of a ravine about two miles south of where Chen had died, in another remote area off the usual hiking trails.

"What was the cause of death?" Steele asked, examining the photos with clinical detachment.

"Blunt force trauma to the back of the head, followed by the fall," Holden replied grimly. "ME says the injury pattern is nearly identical to Chen's case."

"You're thinking the same killer," Emma said. It wasn't a question.

Holden nodded. "Two 'accidental' falls with suspiciously similar head injuries, both victims found in remote locations? This isn't coincidence."

"Did Peterson have any connection to Marcus Chen?" Steele inquired, already anticipating the answer.

"That's why I called you," Holden confirmed. "Peterson was one of the geologists who analyzed some samples Chen brought him informally, about a week before he died. And here's where it gets even more concerning," He slid a paper across the desk. "This was in Peterson's office. Preliminary analysis of soil samples, dated yesterday."

Emma scanned the document, her pulse quickening. The analysis described high-grade gold deposits with a distinctive mineral profile, identical to what their lab had confirmed from their own stream samples.

"Chen showed him samples from the stream," she said quietly. "And recently, Peterson was conducting his own follow-up analysis."

"Someone's eliminating people who know about the gold," Holden concluded, running a hand through his thinning hair. "The problem is, word about Peterson's death is already spreading. Two similar deaths in our small community, both looking like they were staged? People are talking serial killer."

"Which creates both problems and opportunities," Steele observed. "Public panic complicates the investigation, but also potentially forces our killer to be more cautious."

"Any witnesses?" Emma asked, returning to the crime scene photos. "Evidence at the scene?"

"Nothing conclusive yet," Holden admitted. "Peterson's wife said he mentioned meeting someone to discuss 'an interesting geological formation' he'd been studying. No name provided."

"Was his house or office disturbed?" Steele asked. "Any signs someone searched for his research?"

"Office was too organized according to his wife," Holden confirmed. "She said his files had been 'neatened up,' which wasn't his usual style. And his computer was wiped clean, factory reset. Whoever did this was looking for something specific."

Emma met Steele's gaze, both thinking the same thing. "Just like Chen's missing field notebook."

They spent the next hour reviewing the preliminary evidence from Peterson's death, the parallels to Chen's case becoming increasingly obvious. Both men had been studying the gold-bearing stream. Both had been killed in remote locations with similar methods. Both had their research materials either taken or destroyed.

"The killer is methodical," Steele observed as they stepped outside the Trooper's office for a private conversation. "Removing anyone with scientific knowledge of the gold deposit while staging deaths to appear accidental."

"But Peterson's death escalates things significantly," Emma replied, watching townspeople hurry past, their faces tense with the news already spreading through Talkeetna. "Two similar deaths creates a pattern even the casual observer can recognize."

Main Street had a different energy now, shopkeepers stood in doorways, exchanging worried conversations. A group of tourists huddled outside the guide office, gesturing anxiously as they apparently reconsidered their hiking plans. The carefree small-town atmosphere had been replaced by unmistakable tension.

"Trooper Holden is organizing a community meeting for this afternoon," Steele said. "Standard procedure to address public concerns and prevent panic."

"Which gives us a window to proceed with Kendrick," Emma decided. "I rescheduled our meeting for noon. If he's responsible for both deaths, his reaction to this news will be telling."

"Approaching him immediately after Peterson's murder is high-risk," Steele cautioned, concern evident in his usually impassive expression.

"It's also our best opportunity to observe genuine reactions," Emma countered. "He won't have time to fully process and mask his response. And if he's innocent, his insights on who else might have knowledge of the gold could be valuable."

They walked toward the café to regroup over coffee, both acutely aware of the stares and whispers following them, the outsiders who arrived just before the deaths began.

"We need to accelerate our timeline," Emma said once they were seated in a quiet corner. "Peterson's death changes everything. It confirms we're dealing with a killer who will eliminate anyone with knowledge of the gold deposit."

"Including us," Steele noted quietly. "If Kendrick connects us to the stream samples."

The implications hung between them. Their investigation had suddenly become significantly more dangerous. If Kendrick, or whoever was behind these deaths, realized they had identified the gold and connected it to Chen's murder, they could become the next targets.

"We should inform Crawford and request tactical support," Steele suggested. "Two confirmed homicides with linked evidence justifies a full response team."

Emma considered this, weighing operational protocols against investigative momentum. "After we meet with Kendrick," she decided. "His reaction to Peterson's death will either implicate or eliminate him as a suspect. If he's our killer, we need that confirmation before bringing in a team."

The café's usual morning chatter had been replaced by tense, hushed conversations. At a nearby table, a waitress was explaining to worried tourists that there was "nothing to fear if you stick to the marked trails and public areas."

"The community meeting will be revealing as well," Emma added. "Who attends, who doesn't, how different factions react to the news."

"Barrett will almost certainly be present," Steele noted. "As the Alliance's leader, he'll want to demonstrate community involvement and calm any suspicion toward his group."

"While Kendrick might avoid a public gathering," Emma concluded. "Especially if he's directly involved."

They finalized their approach for the meeting with Kendrick, adjusting tactics to account for Peterson's death. Instead of waiting for Kendrick to reveal the stream location, they would proactively mention Peterson's analysis of geological samples, watching for reactions that might confirm his involvement.

As they left the café, Emma noticed a familiar truck parked across the street, Walter Kendrick's vehicle, outside the general store. She nudged Steele, directing his attention to where the gray-haired man was loading supplies, his movements unhurried but purposeful.

"He's here in town already," she murmured. "Came in for supplies as if it's a normal day."

"Or gathering necessities before leaving the area," Steele suggested.

They watched as Kendrick finished loading his truck, exchanged brief words with the store owner, then drove slowly down Main Street. As he passed them, his gaze shifted briefly in their direction, neutral, revealing nothing, but unmistakably aware of their presence.

"He saw us," Emma noted. "No surprise or concern evident."

"Either excellent control or genuine innocence," Steele replied. "Impossible to determine from this distance."

They returned to the cabin to prepare for their noon meeting, both acutely aware that they were potentially arranging to meet a killer who had just claimed his second victim. The golden secret hidden in the stream had already cost two lives. The question now was how many more the killer would sacrifice to protect it, and whether Emma and Steele might be next on that list.

As they gathered their gear, Emma received a text from Trooper Holden confirming the community meeting at four o'clock. The time-line was tight, meet Kendrick at noon, potentially follow him to the stream location, then return for the town meeting where Barrett and other key players would be present.

"We stay together at all times," Steele said as they prepared to leave, his tone leaving no room for discussion. "No separation, even if Kendrick suggests it."

Emma nodded, recognizing the gravity of their situation. "Agreed. And continuous location tracking activated from this point forward."

They locked eyes briefly, the unspoken concern passing between them. Their investigation had uncovered a deadly secret, gold hidden in an Alaskan stream, a killer eliminating anyone with knowledge of its existence, and their own growing certainty that Walter Kendrick was somehow involved.

The next few hours would either confirm their suspicions or place them directly in the killer's path. Either way, the golden revelation had turned deadly, claiming a second victim and transforming their carefully planned investigation into a race against a killer who would stop at nothing to protect his treasure.

CHAPTER 17:
Under Pressure

The community center parking lot was filled with unfamiliar government vehicles when Emma and Steele returned from their abbreviated meeting with Walter Kendrick. Two black SUVs with tinted windows stood out starkly against the local pickup trucks and tourism vans, their very presence changing the atmosphere of the small town.

"Crawford moved quickly," Emma observed as they parked at the edge of the lot. "Looks like half the Anchorage field office is here."

"Peterson's death confirmed this is a federal case," Steele replied. "Two homicides linked to potential resource crimes on public lands triggered the rapid response protocol."

Inside the community center, the transformation was even more dramatic. What had been a rustic meeting space now buzzed with federal activity. A command post had been established in one corner, with communications equipment and laptop stations. Maps covered a large table in the center of the room, and agents in FBI windbreakers moved purposefully between workstations.

Assistant Director Crawford spotted them immediately. "Steele, Stone," he called, gesturing them toward a side room that had been repurposed as a secure briefing area. "Report."

For the next thirty minutes, they provided a detailed account of their investigation, the gold-bearing stream, the modifications indicating extraction activity, Kendrick's connection to the Alliance, and their theories about both deaths. Emma noticed Steele maintaining strict professional detachment, any hint of their personal connection carefully concealed behind Bureau protocols.

"And your meeting with Kendrick today?" Crawford prompted.

"Brief and inconclusive," Emma replied. "Once he heard about Peterson's death, he claimed a prior commitment with Barrett and rescheduled for tomorrow morning."

"His reaction to the news?"

"Controlled surprise," Steele analyzed. "Expressed appropriate concern, asked relevant questions about circumstances, but showed no excessive interest or avoidance behaviors."

"Either he's not involved, or he's exceptionally skilled at masking responses," Emma added.

Crawford nodded, absorbing their assessment. "The media's already here. Local reporters from Anchorage arrived about an hour ago, and we've had calls from national outlets. Two 'accidental' deaths in a remote Alaska town, potentially linked to gold? It's catnip to the press."

Emma grimaced. "That complicates everything. The killer will know we're treating these as homicides, not accidents."

"Which may cause him to accelerate plans or destroy evidence," Steele added.

"Or flee," Crawford noted grimly. "We've established discreet surveillance on Kendrick's cabin and monitoring on the Alliance compound, but media presence makes covert operations nearly impossible now."

Emma moved to the wall map, studying the markers indicating key locations. "The community meeting this afternoon will be crucial. With Peterson's death confirmed as murder, we'll see how different factions respond, particularly Barrett and the Alliance members."

"And Kendrick, if he attends," Steele added.

"You two maintain your cover for now," Crawford instructed. "Your connection with Kendrick and the Alliance is our best lead. The additional agents will handle evidence processing, surveillance, and perimeter control without revealing your involvement."

As they left the secure room, Emma noticed a news van parked outside the community center, a reporter preparing for a live broadcast.

"This will be all over Alaska by dinnertime," she murmured to Steele. "National news by tomorrow morning."

"Creating both pressure and opportunities," Steele replied as they slipped out a side door to avoid the cameras. "The killer must now operate with awareness of intensive investigation."

They walked down Main Street, maintaining their tourist cover while processing the dramatic escalation of the case. What had begun as a suspicious death investigation now involved multiple federal agencies, media attention, and a community on edge.

"We need supplies before the meeting," Emma said, nodding toward the general store. "And it gives us a chance to gauge the town's reaction."

Inside Nagley's General Store, the usual friendly atmosphere had been replaced by tense, hushed conversations. Margaret Wilson was explaining to a group of worried tourists that the trails around town were "perfectly safe with proper precautions."

"Just stick to the marked paths and go in groups," she advised. "No need to cancel your vacation plans."

Emma and Steele browsed casually, picking up bottled water and energy bars while eavesdropping on the local gossip.

"...saying it's the same killer," one older man muttered to his companion near the fishing supplies. "Peterson was a good man. Who'd want to hurt a rock scientist?"

"First that university kid, now Peterson," his friend replied. "Both of them poking around in the hills. Makes you wonder what they found out there."

Emma exchanged a meaningful glance with Steele. The connection between the victims' geological interests hadn't escaped local notice.

As they approached the counter to pay, the store door opened, and Walter Kendrick entered. He nodded to several locals before noticing Emma and Steele. If he was surprised to see them, he hid it perfectly.

"Thought you folks might have headed back to Anchorage with all this trouble," he said, approaching them with casual confidence. "Most tourists are cutting their trips short."

"We considered it," Emma replied carefully. "But it seemed premature to leave without understanding what's happening."

Kendrick nodded thoughtfully. "Smart. Though the authorities would probably prefer fewer civilians in their way."

"The community meeting this afternoon should clarify things," Steele said, watching Kendrick's reaction.

"Planning to attend?" Kendrick asked, selecting a few items from a nearby shelf. "Might be standing room only with all these new federal agents in town."

"We'll be there," Emma confirmed. "Will the Alliance be represented?"

Something flickered briefly in Kendrick's eyes, caution, perhaps, or calculation. "James will attend, certainly. The Alliance wants to help however possible. These deaths reflect poorly on our community, make outsiders nervous about the area."

His phrasing struck Emma as deliberately neutral, neither confirming nor denying his own planned attendance.

"Dr. Peterson was a geologist, right?" she asked, intentionally probing. "Similar to the first victim's background."

Kendrick set his items on the counter, his movements relaxed and unhurried. "Alan was knowledgeable about local formations. Consulted occasionally for land acquisitions, water surveys." He looked directly at Emma. "Curious mind, always studying rock samples and such. Some people develop unusual interests in local resources."

The subtle emphasis was unmistakable, a veiled reference that could be interpreted as merely conversational or distinctly threatening.

"Natural curiosity can lead people to unexpected discoveries," Steele responded, maintaining the seemingly innocent conversation while acknowledging the subtext.

Kendrick smiled slightly. "Indeed. Though in wilderness areas, it's wise to be cautious about where that curiosity takes you. Easy to get into dangerous situations when you venture off established paths."

He paid for his supplies, then turned back to them. "If you're staying in the area, perhaps we can reschedule our nature walk. There are aspects of the local landscape worth appreciating, with proper guidance, of course."

"We'd still be interested," Emma replied, matching his casual tone while recognizing the multiple layers of his offer.

"Good." Kendrick gathered his bag. "Safety in numbers these days. The wrong person alone in these woods could encounter… difficulties. I'd hate to see your anniversary trip end tragically."

With a nod that could have been friendly or warning, he left the store, the bell jingling in his wake.

Margaret Wilson exhaled slowly. "Walt's right about being careful. These deaths have everyone on edge."

"He seems concerned for the community," Emma observed, fishing for local perspective.

"Walt's always had a protective streak about this area," Margaret replied, bagging their purchases. "Knows these woods better than anyone. If there's a killer out there, Walt probably has his theories."

Outside, they watched Kendrick's truck head toward the edge of town, in the direction of the Alliance compound.

"That was a threat," Emma said quietly once they were alone. "Thinly veiled but unmistakable."

"Confirming he perceives us as potential threats," Steele agreed. "But carefully phrased to maintain plausible deniability."

"And his reference to 'unusual interests in local resources' suggests awareness of both victims' geological work," Emma added.

They walked slowly back toward their cabin, processing the encounter with Kendrick against the backdrop of the escalating investigation.

"His composure was notable," Steele observed. "Despite the federal presence and media attention, he approached us directly, controlled the interaction."

"Either extreme confidence or a calculated risk to assess our knowledge and intentions," Emma concluded.

As they reached their cabin, another news van drove past toward the community center, the vehicle emblazoned with a national network logo. The pressure was building from all sides, media coverage expanding, federal resources deploying, local community growing fearful, and Walter Kendrick watching their every move while delivering veiled threats about tragic ends to their "vacation."

The golden secret in the stream had transformed their undercover operation into something far more dangerous. Two men were already dead for discovering it, and Kendrick's warning had made it clear that he was prepared to protect that secret regardless of the growing attention.

The community meeting would bring all the key players together under intense scrutiny. Barrett representing the Alliance, local authorities led by Trooper Dave Holden, federal agencies coordinated by Crawford, and potentially Kendrick himself, all watched by media eager for sensational details about murder in the Alaskan wilderness.

And somewhere in that volatile mix, a killer would be calculating his next move, with Emma and Steele now clearly in his sights.

❉ ❉ ❉

FBI scrutiny of Alaska-based businesses meant increased attention on large cash transactions and recent property acquisitions, exactly the kind of oversight that could expose the money laundering scheme.

"We need to slow down the deposits," Mitchell warned during an encrypted phone call, his voice tight with anxiety. "The financial crimes task force is running background checks on anyone connected to major construction projects. Too much unexplained cash flow will trigger audit flags."

Mitchell's hands trembled slightly as he spoke. Agent Kahn had briefed him just that morning about the FBI's expanding investigation into suspicious real estate transactions across Alaska. Every word he spoke to Randall was being recorded, every financial detail documented for the federal case building against Bauer Properties.

"Absolutely not," Randall replied firmly. "The Blue Note's grand opening is scheduled for next week. Everything must proceed normally, or the delay itself will create suspicion."

Mitchell understood the real reason for Randall's insistence, and it had nothing to do with business strategy. Emma's return from Talkeetna was imminent, and Randall was determined to present her with his "gift" regardless of the risks. His obsession was overriding his business judgment in ways that threatened their entire operation, and gave the FBI exactly the kind of reckless behavior they needed to build their case.

"There's something else," Mitchell added reluctantly, knowing Agent Kahn would want him to probe this angle. "There's talk of expanded background checks on all personnel with access to sensitive case files. If they run a full financial audit on me..."

The irony wasn't lost on Mitchell. He was genuinely terrified of a financial audit, but not for the reasons Randall thought. While Randall's money sat in Mitchell's accounts as evidence of corruption, the FBI had documented every transaction. Mitchell's fear wasn't of being caught, it was of his cover being blown before they could nail Randall for the full scope of his crimes.

"Then you'll need to be very careful about how you explain your recent prosperity," Randall said coldly. "I suggest you think of creative ways to account for your improved circumstances that don't involve mentioning our business relationship."

The threat was implicit but unmistakable, and Mitchell felt a chill that had nothing to do with Alaska's weather. If his double agent status was exposed, Randall wouldn't hesitate to destroy him. But what Randall didn't know was that the FBI had already prepared Mitchell's cover story, complete with documented gambling winnings and a fictional inheritance that would explain his sudden financial improvement.

"Don't worry," Randall continued, his tone becoming almost paternal in a way that made Mitchell's skin crawl. "Once Emma sees what we've accomplished, once she understands the lengths I've gone to create something worthy of her talent, everything else will fall into place. The Blue Note represents our future together, detective. Your continued cooperation is simply ensuring that future remains possible."

Mitchell forced himself to respond with the appropriate mixture of greed and compliance that Randall expected. "Understood. I'll make sure nothing interferes with the opening."

But as soon as he hung up, Mitchell was already composing his encrypted report to Agent Kahn. Randall's obsession with Emma was making him sloppy, pushing him to take risks that would ultimately bring down his entire money laundering operation. The FBI just needed to be patient and let Randall's fixation on Detective Stone provide them with all the evidence they needed.

What worried Mitchell wasn't the federal investigation, it was what would happen to Emma when Randall's carefully constructed world began to collapse around him. Cornered criminals were dangerous, but cornered stalkers were potentially lethal.

CHAPTER 18:

The Chess Game

The community meeting had been a masterclass in small-town politics and carefully controlled information. Dave Holden provided just enough details to address public safety concerns without revealing the investigation's focus. Crawford maintained an authoritative federal presence while strategically withholding specifics. Barrett delivered a measured statement of cooperation on behalf of the Alliance, expressing appropriate concern while distancing his group from any connection to the deaths.

And Walter Kendrick, sitting quietly in the back row, had observed it all while contributing nothing.

Now, back in their cabin after the tense gathering, Emma paced the small living area, her mind racing with connections others hadn't yet made.

"He's playing us," she said finally, stopping to face Steele who sat reviewing case notes at the dining table. "Kendrick, he's three moves ahead in a strategic game."

Steele looked up, his analytical focus sharpening. "Explain."

"His behavior pattern is inconsistent with both guilt and innocence," Emma continued, grabbing the case files and spreading them across the table. "At the meeting, he stayed silent, nearly invisible, classic low-profile behavior for someone with something to hide. But this morning at the store, he deliberately approached us, drew attention to himself, even issued veiled threats."

"Contradictory reactions," Steele acknowledged, considering this.

"Not contradictory, strategic," Emma corrected. "He's controlling how different audiences perceive him. With us, he's confident, almost challenging, because he's assessed us as the primary threat. With the broader community and law enforcement, he's unremarkable, forgettable, just another concerned citizen."

Steele's eyes tracked her movement as she continued pacing. "You believe he's deliberately creating conflicting narratives."

"Yes, and it's working brilliantly," Emma affirmed. "Crawford and the federal team are focused on Barrett and the Alliance leadership because they're the visible power structure. Meanwhile, Kendrick, the actual threat, maintains his peripheral position, watching and adjusting."

She returned to the table, pulling out the autopsy reports for both victims. "Look at these again. Everyone's fixated on the similarities, blunt force trauma, remote locations, staged accidents. But there's a pattern in the differences that no one's connected."

Steele examined the reports with renewed attention as Emma highlighted specific details.

"Chen was killed at a creek junction heading upstream toward Alliance property," she pointed out. "Peterson was found in a ravine two miles south, well away from the primary gold site. Chen's death appeared opportunistic, he stumbled onto something and was silenced. Peterson's was methodical, targeted elimination after he began formal analysis."

She spread out a map, marking both locations. "Chen was killed where he made his discovery. Peterson was lured away from his findings to be eliminated. Different approaches tailored to different threats."

Understanding dawned in Steele's expression. "Suggesting the killer adapts tactics based on sophisticated threat assessment."

"Exactly," Emma said, her voice intensifying. "Not impulsive violence, but calculated risk management. Chen represented accidental discovery, eliminated where he posed immediate threat. Peterson represented methodical investigation, removed from his research environment after his knowledge was assessed."

Steele studied the pattern Emma had identified, mentally processing the implications. "Your analysis suggests a level of strategic thinking consistent with specialized training."

"Like a former federal officer with decades of wilderness experience," Emma confirmed. "Someone who understands evidence preservation, crime scene contamination, and investigative procedure."

She sat across from Steele, leaning forward intently. "Kendrick isn't just protecting a gold discovery. He's systematically eliminating threats while maintaining plausible deniability. And now he's evaluating us, deciding whether we're potential allies to recruit or threats to eliminate."

Steele was quiet for a moment, his expression contemplative. "Your intuitive pattern recognition identified what our analytical approach missed," he acknowledged.

Did Emma sense a rare admiration evident in his tone?

"My focus on consistent elements overlooked the strategic variation." Steele acknowledged.

Emma blinked, surprised by his direct recognition of her approach's value. "We see different parts of the same puzzle. Your systematic analysis establishes the framework; my intuitive leaps find the anomalies."

"A complementary methodology," Steele agreed. "More effective in combination than either approach independently."

The acknowledgment hung between them, another layer of connection building on their growing personal understanding. Emma felt a warmth that had nothing to do with the case and everything to do with genuine professional respect, something she'd rarely experienced from colleagues.

"If your assessment is correct," Steele continued, returning to the investigation, "Kendrick represents a significantly more sophisticated threat than we initially estimated. His approach to us suggests he's still evaluating, testing responses, and gauging knowledge."

"Which gives us an opportunity," Emma said, the outline of a plan forming. "We know what he wants, confidentiality about the gold. We know what he fears, exposure of his operation and connection to the deaths. We can use both to set a trap."

"You're suggesting we present ourselves as potential conspirators rather than threats," Steele deduced.

"Exactly. We reschedule the meeting he canceled, express specific interest in geological formations, hint at our own disillusionment with federal agencies," Emma outlined. "Make him believe we might be persuaded to join his operation rather than expose it."

"A high-risk approach," Steele noted, though his expression showed he was calculating probabilities rather than rejecting the strategy.

"But one that might lead him to reveal the gold operation directly," Emma countered. "If he believes we're considering his side, he might show us the extraction site himself, giving us definitive evidence connecting him to both the gold and potentially the murders."

Steele considered this, his analytical mind visibly working through scenarios. "We would need robust backup protocols. Crawford could position surveillance teams near the likely routes without revealing our role as active participants."

"And we'd need convincing motivation for our apparent willingness to consider illegal activity," Emma added. "Something that aligns with what he already knows about us."

"Our established cover provides foundation," Steele observed. "Disillusioned professionals seeking alternatives to corrupt systems. The discovery of gold could represent financial independence from those systems, a compelling narrative consistent with the personalities we've presented."

They spent the next hour developing the strategy, identifying potential risks and contingencies. Emma mapped the likely routes Kendrick might take, based on their knowledge of the stream's path and his cabin's location. Steele established communication protocols that would appear natural while maintaining contact with Crawford's team.

"The essential element is credibility," Steele emphasized. "Kendrick has extensive experience reading people. If he detects deception, the approach fails potentially catastrophically."

"Which means we don't fully pretend," Emma replied. "We incorporate genuine elements, our actual frustrations with bureaucratic limitations, real questions about resource management. The most effective undercover work blends truth with fabrication."

"Creating authentic responses under artificial circumstances," Steele agreed.

As they finalized the plan, Emma was struck by how seamlessly they now worked together, her intuitive leaps bridged by his logical framework, his analytical precision enhanced by her pattern recognition. What had begun as an awkward partnership of contrasting approaches had evolved into something unexpectedly effective.

"I'll contact Kendrick tonight," she decided. "Express continued interest in his 'nature walk' despite the recent events. Mention specific curiosity about local geological features. Make it clear we're not deterred by the deaths, perhaps even suggest they've heightened our interest in what the victims might have found."

"While I coordinate with Crawford to establish surveillance positions along likely routes," Steele added. "Covert enough to avoid detection but close enough for rapid intervention if necessary."

Emma nodded, then paused, meeting Steele's gaze directly. "This plan puts us at significant risk," she acknowledged. "If Kendrick suspects our true intentions…"

"He may decide we represent threats requiring elimination rather than potential allies," Steele finished, his typically impassive expression showing rare concern. "The statistical probability of violence increases substantially if our deception is detected."

The unspoken implication hung between them, they were potentially walking into the same danger that had claimed two lives already. A man who had methodically eliminated others who discovered his secret might do the same to them.

"We maintain constant awareness, multiple exit strategies, and continuous communication with backup teams," Emma said firmly. "This isn't just about solving two murders now, it's about preventing more. Kendrick has demonstrated he'll eliminate anyone who threatens his operation."

"Agreed," Steele said simply, his gaze holding hers. "The risk profile is justified by the potential threat containment."

But something in his expression told Emma that his concern wasn't purely analytical, that the potential danger to her registered on a personal level he rarely acknowledged. The connection they'd built over shared confidences, and mutual respect had created stakes beyond professional obligation.

As night fell over the Alaskan wilderness, Emma and Steele prepared for the most dangerous phase of their investigation. The trap was set. A carefully constructed narrative designed to appeal to Walter Kendrick's assessment of them as potential allies rather than threats. Their bait was their apparent interest in the same geological features that had led two men to their deaths. And their gambit depended entirely on Kendrick believing they might be corrupted rather than recognizing they were closing in on his secrets.

The chess game had entered its critical phase. Kendrick had been playing masterfully, eliminating pieces that threatened his position while maintaining strategic flexibility. But now Emma and Steele had recognized the true pattern of the board, and were making a bold move of their own.

The next day would determine whether they had outwitted a calculating killer or placed themselves directly in his path.

CHAPTER 19:

Growing Danger

Emma woke early, the Alaska sunlight already streaming through the cabin windows despite the early hour. They had contacted Kendrick the previous evening, rescheduling their "nature walk" for later that morning, and finalized coordination with Crawford's team. Everything was prepared for their strategic gambit.

As she emerged from the bedroom, she found Steele already up, examining something on the dining table with unusual intensity.

"What is it?" she asked, immediately alert to his tension.

Steele looked up, his expression grave. "This was slipped under our door sometime during the night."

Emma approached the table where a single sheet of paper lay. The message consisted of words cut from magazines and newspapers, arranged in a crude but chilling sentence:

TOURISTS SHOULD GO HOME BEFORE THEY BECOME PART OF THE LANDSCAPE

"Classic intimidation technique," Emma observed, studying the collage. "Deliberately primitive to avoid handwriting analysis."

"Effective in its simplicity," Steele agreed. "The phrasing echoes Kendrick's veiled threat about our trip ending 'tragically.'"

Emma examined the door and windows, confirming they remained secure as they had left them. "Someone approached the cabin without triggering any of our precautions."

"Suggesting professional skill or intimate knowledge of the property," Steele noted. "I'll document and bag it for evidence processing."

"This changes the timeline," Emma said, her mind racing through implications. "Kendrick could be moving from assessment to active deterrence."

"Escalating threat profile," Steele agreed. "We should consider postponing the operation."

Emma shook her head firmly. "That's exactly what he wants, to frighten us away before we get too close. This confirms we're on the right track."

After a tense breakfast, they prepared for their meeting with Kendrick, checking their concealed recording devices and emergency transponders. The threat had added a sharper edge to their preparations, the danger no longer theoretical but tangibly present.

"Crawford's team is positioned at three surveillance points along likely routes," Steele confirmed after a secure call. "Emergency response protocol established with seven-minute maximum deployment time to any location within the target area."

Emma nodded, adjusting her hiking boots. "Let's not need them."

They drove toward the Alliance compound in tense silence, both hyperaware of their surroundings. The morning was clear, the Alaskan landscape breathtaking in the golden light, creating a surreal contrast with the deadly stakes of their mission.

As they navigated a particularly steep section of road about three miles from town, Emma felt the steering suddenly go slack in her hands. The wheel spun freely, the vehicle lurching toward the steep drop-off on the right side.

"Brake!" Steele shouted, bracing himself against the dashboard.

Emma pumped the brake pedal, finding it unresponsive. "No brakes!"

Acting on instinct, she yanked the emergency brake while frantically downshifting to slow their momentum. The vehicle fishtailed violently, scraping against the mountainside on the left before spinning back toward the precipitous edge.

For one horrifying moment, the front right wheel slipped over the edge, the vehicle teetering precariously between safety and a devastating drop. Emma threw herself toward Steele's side of the vehicle, using their combined weight to shift the balance back toward the mountain.

The vehicle shuddered to a stop, its front right corner suspended over the cliff edge, held in place by little more than luck and physics.

"Don't move," Steele whispered, acutely aware that any shift in weight could send them over. "We need to exit my side."

With excruciating care, Steele eased his door open. "I'll go first, establish stable position, then assist you."

Emma assessed the vehicle's precarious balance. She could see his weight on the passenger side was keeping them from tipping. "Okay, you exit, then I'll slide out exactly as you clear the door."

Steele hesitated, clearly reluctant to leave her in the more dangerous position but recognizing the physics of the plan. With careful precision, he extracted himself from the vehicle, establishing a secure stance on solid ground.

"Now, Emma," he called, extending his hand through the open door. "Smooth, continuous movement."

Emma released her death grip on the steering wheel and began sliding across the seat, feeling the vehicle shift ominously beneath her. As her weight moved, the front end tilted further toward the abyss.

"Faster," Steele urged, his voice tight with controlled urgency.

She lunged the remaining distance just as the vehicle groaned and shifted dramatically. Steele's strong hands caught her, pulling her clear as the front wheels slipped further over the edge. In one fluid motion, he yanked her from the vehicle and against his chest, pivoting to place his body between her and the precarious drop.

For a breathless moment, they stood locked together, hearts pounding in synchronized terror as the vehicle teetered, then finally settled without plunging over.

"Are you hurt?" Steele asked, his voice hoarse, arms still protectively around her.

Emma shook her head, suddenly acutely aware of their physical proximity. "No. You?"

"Uninjured," he confirmed, though he made no move to release her. Instead, his grip tightened almost imperceptibly, as if confirming her solid presence against him.

The moment stretched between them, adrenaline and something more electric holding them motionless. Emma could feel Steele's heart hammering against her cheek, his typically controlled breathing uneven. This wasn't just professional concern, this was raw, personal fear for her safety.

Reluctantly, they separated, though Steele's hand remained on her arm as if unwilling to completely break contact. They moved carefully away from the vehicle, which remained poised in its precarious position.

"That was no accident," Emma said once they reached a safe distance. "The brake line and steering were both compromised."

Steele knelt to examine the thin trail of fluid leading back along the road. "Professional sabotage. The lines were cut in a way that would cause gradual failure once the system reached operating temperature."

"Meaning it was done while the vehicle was parked, designed to fail at maximum risk location," Emma concluded grimly. "This section of road was deliberately targeted, steep grade, sharp curve, significant drop."

"Kendrick," Steele said, the name itself an indictment. "The threat escalation matches his pattern, warning first, then direct action if the warning is ignored."

"He's eliminating perceived threats," Emma agreed. "Just like Chen and Peterson."

They called in the incident, and within minutes, Crawford's team arrived, securing the scene and documenting the sabotage. The evidence was irrefutable. Someone had deliberately tampered with their vehicle, intending to cause a fatal accident on this treacherous mountain road.

As a recovery team worked to secure the vehicle, Steele led Emma away from the activity, his expression unusually troubled.

"We need to abort the operation," he said without preamble. "The threat profile has exceeded acceptable parameters."

Emma stared at him in disbelief. "We can't back off now. This confirms Kendrick's involvement, he's escalating because we're getting close."

"He just attempted to kill us," Steele countered, uncharacteristic emotion bleeding into his voice. "The next attempt may succeed."

"Which is exactly why we need to continue," Emma insisted. "If we back off, he simply waits for another opportunity. Our best protection is completing this investigation and removing his freedom of action."

Steele shook his head, something raw and unfamiliar in his expression. "The operational risk is unacceptable."

"Since when do you make risk assessments based on emotion rather than analysis?" Emma challenged.

"Since the risk involves your safety," he replied without hesitation, then seemed startled by his own admission.

The naked honesty in his voice stopped Emma's next argument before it formed. For Steele, methodical, analytical Steele, to openly acknowledge an emotional basis for his position was unprecedented.

"Jeremiah," she said softly, using his first name for the first time. "I understand your concern. But backing off now makes us more vulnerable, not less. Kendrick knows we suspect him. He won't stop just because we stop pushing."

Steele held her gaze, internal conflict evident in his expression. "The statistical probability of success doesn't justify the potential cost," he said finally, his voice low and intense.

"What potential cost?" Emma pressed gently, sensing they were no longer discussing standard operational parameters.

"You," he said simply, the single word carrying weight beyond its brevity. "Losing you."

The admission hung between them, profound in its simplicity. Not "a partner" or "an asset" or any of the detached terms Steele typically employed. Just "you" personal, specific, irreplaceable.

Emma stepped closer, ignoring the activity around them. "That works both ways," she said quietly. "I'm not willing to let Kendrick go, knowing he'll eventually target you too. The safest approach is to finish this together."

Something shifted in Steele's expression, resignation mingled with resolve. "Then we adapt the plan. No separation. Continuous communication with backup teams. And we establish clear boundaries for risk assessment."

"Agreed," Emma said, relief washing through her. "We continue, but with enhanced precautions."

Crawford approached, interrupting their moment of connection. "Vehicle sabotage confirmed," he reported. "Professional work. We've arranged alternative transportation and increased security protocols."

They quickly revised their approach, adjusting timing and routes while maintaining the core strategy of engaging Kendrick directly. The sabotage attempt had elevated the stakes dramatically but also provided concrete evidence linking their investigation to the previous deaths.

As they prepared to depart with the new vehicle and enhanced security team, Steele drew Emma aside one final time.

"Statistics suggest that there is increased survival probability with partner awareness and protection," he said, his formal phrasing failing to disguise the depth of feeling behind the words. "Watch my back. I'm watching yours."

Emma nodded, recognizing this as the closest thing to 'be careful' that Steele's emotional vocabulary would allow. "Always," she promised.

In the past hour, their partnership had transformed yet again, personal concern now openly acknowledged alongside professional collaboration. The danger surrounding them had stripped away pretense, forcing recognition of feelings both had been carefully circumventing.

As they headed toward their rescheduled meeting with Kendrick, Emma was acutely aware that more than justice was now at stake. Whatever had been growing between them, trust, connection, perhaps something deeper, had emerged into the open, adding personal stakes to an already dangerous game.

Walter Kendrick, or someone unidentified, had escalated from threats to direct action, proving his willingness to eliminate anyone threatening his secret. But in doing so, he had unknowingly strengthened the resolve of the two investigators pursuing him, not just as professionals seeking justice, but as people unwilling to lose each other to his deadly machinations.

CHAPTER 20:

The Stream's Secret

Darkness finally settled over the Alaskan wilderness, bringing a preternatural silence broken only by the gentle gurgle of flowing water. Emma and Steele moved through the trees with practiced stealth, following the GPS coordinates they had marked during their previous visit to the stream. Crawford's team maintained position half a mile behind them, close enough for emergency response but distant enough to avoid detection.

After the sabotage attempt, they had adjusted their strategy. Instead of meeting Kendrick directly, a plan that now seemed foolishly dangerous, they had decided to gather conclusive evidence of the illegal mining operation first. Their cover story of mechanical problems with their replacement vehicle had bought them time and maintained the pretense that they were still planning to meet Kendrick the following day.

"Location approaching," Steele murmured, consulting the handheld GPS unit glowing dimly in the darkness. "Two hundred meters ahead."

Emma nodded, her night-vision enhanced by the specialized goggles Crawford had provided. The landscape appeared in ghostly green tones, revealing the contours of the forested slope leading down to the stream. They moved carefully, testing each step to avoid betraying their presence by snapping twigs or dislodged stones.

The stream came into view, its surface catching glimmers of moonlight filtering through the canopy. They paused at the tree line, scanning for any sign of human presence before proceeding toward the water's edge.

"No movement detected," Steele confirmed after a thorough survey. "Proceeding to primary investigation area."

They approached the section of stream where they had previously observed signs of disturbance, the location where natural rock formations created ideal conditions for gold deposits. In daylight, they had noticed subtle modifications to the stream bed. Now, with specialized equipment and under cover of darkness, they hoped to discover more conclusive evidence.

Emma moved slowly along the bank, her trained eye catching details that casual observers would miss. "Look here," she whispered, pointing to a nearly invisible line running from the water's edge into the surrounding brush. "Artificial construction."

Steele knelt beside her, examining what appeared to be a thin rubber tube partially buried in the soil. "Water diversion system," he confirmed. "Professional grade, designed for minimal visibility."

They followed the tube into the underbrush, pushing aside branches to reveal its path up the gentle slope away from the stream. After twenty yards, they discovered where it terminated, at a carefully concealed structure built into the hillside, disguised by natural materials and vegetation.

"This is sophisticated," Emma murmured, examining the camouflaged entrance. "Not amateur prospecting."

Using a specialized camera that detected heat signatures through solid surfaces, Steele scanned the structure. "No thermal signatures indicating current human presence," he reported. "Proceeding with entry investigation."

The concealed door was secured with a padlock, which Emma made quick work of with her specialized tool kit. They entered cautiously, Steele leading with his sidearm drawn while Emma covered their rear.

Inside, the small structure revealed its purpose immediately. A complex sluice system had been constructed, capable of processing significant amounts of stream material with remarkable efficiency. Specialized equipment for separating gold from sediment was arranged in a compact, portable configuration.

"This is commercial-grade equipment," Steele observed, photographing each component. "Designed for maximum yield with minimal environmental indicators."

Emma examined the separator tables and collection systems, noting the careful engineering. "This setup could process hundreds of pounds of material daily while appearing completely natural from any casual observation point."

"And based on the collection containers, they've been operating for months, possibly years," Steele added, indicating the organized storage system along one wall.

Emma opened one of the smaller containers, revealing a significant amount of gold dust and small nuggets. "This is easily worth thousands of dollars," she estimated. "And that's just one container."

They documented everything methodically, the equipment, the gold storage, the water diversion system, and the camouflage techniques. Each photograph and measurement added to the overwhelming evidence of a sophisticated illegal mining operation.

"The equipment bears no serial numbers or identifying marks," Steele noted. "Deliberately untraceable."

"But the design itself is distinctive," Emma countered. "Custom-built by someone with specialized knowledge."

As they completed their documentation, Emma noticed something they had initially overlooked, a small safe tucked into the corner of the structure, partially hidden behind equipment.

"That might contain documentation," she suggested. "Records, perhaps even connection to the deaths."

The safe proved more challenging than the padlock, but after several tense minutes, Emma managed to trigger the release mechanism.

"You are remarkably adept at picking locks," Steele said. "Where did you learn to do that?"

"A magician never reveals their secrets." Emma replied, smiling.

Inside, they found exactly what they had hoped for, a leather-bound notebook with handwritten records of extraction amounts, dates, and coded location markers.

"This looks like Chen's missing field notebook," Emma said, carefully photographing each page. "Repurposed for their operation after they took it from him."

Steele examined the handwriting. "Consistent with samples we have from Kendrick," he confirmed. "Direct evidentiary link."

Besides the notebook, the safe contained several USB drives, a small handgun, and various documents related to gold purity testing and private sales. Emma carefully documented each item, building their case piece by methodical piece.

"We have enough for warrants now," she said. "Direct evidence linking Kendrick to illegal mining, probable cause connecting him to Chen's death through the repurposed notebook."

"We should withdraw and coordinate with Crawford's team," Steele agreed, securing the evidence in their specialized collection bags.

They carefully reset the safe and prepared to exit, ensuring they left no obvious signs of their investigation. The operation had gone more smoothly than either had dared hope, solid evidence gathered without confrontation.

As they emerged from the structure, Emma froze. A faint sound from downstream had caught her attention, the distinctive crunch of boots on gravel.

"Someone's coming," she whispered, immediately taking cover behind a large boulder. Steele followed suit, positioning himself where he could observe the approach while remaining concealed.

Through their night vision goggles, they watched as a figure moved along the stream bank, following the same path they had taken earlier. The person moved with purpose and confidence, clearly familiar with the terrain. As the figure drew closer, they could make out details, male, approximately six feet tall, carrying a rifle and wearing what appeared to be tactical gear.

"Not Kendrick," Steele murmured. "Younger, different build."

"Security patrol," Emma suggested quietly. "Likely Alliance member."

The armed man paused near the structure, sweeping his flashlight across the area in a practiced pattern. For a heart-stopping moment, the beam passed directly over their position, but the boulder provided adequate concealment.

Apparently satisfied, the man approached the structure, checked the padlock, then continued his patrol along a route that suggested regular security rounds. He showed no surprise at finding the installation, clearly aware of its purpose and location.

"We need to follow him," Emma whispered once the guard had moved far enough away. "Establish connection to the Alliance compound."

"Negative," Steele countered firmly. "We have sufficient evidence. Additional pursuit increases exposure risk unnecessarily."

Before Emma could respond, the guard suddenly stopped, his posture changing to one of alert attention. He raised his rifle slightly, moving toward a different section of the stream bank.

"Someone else is out here," Steele observed tensely.

Through their goggles, they watched as a second figure emerged from the trees on the opposite bank. Even in the green-tinted night vision, the distinctive gray hair was immediately recognizable.

Walter Kendrick.

The guard's reaction was unexpected. Instead of acknowledgment or deference, he immediately raised his rifle to a ready position, challenging Kendrick's presence.

"That's far enough," the guard called, his voice carrying clearly in the night air. "This area is restricted."

Kendrick stopped, raising his hands slightly in a non-threatening gesture. "Easy, son. Just checking the equipment."

"No scheduled inspections tonight," the guard replied, suspicion evident in his tone. "Identify yourself."

Kendrick's posture changed subtly, surprise, then calculation. "Tyler sent me to check the yield records," he said, naming the Alliance security chief they had met during their visit.

"Tyler didn't notify me of any inspection," the guard responded, his rifle still trained on Kendrick. "And this area is under heightened security with the federal investigation. No unauthorized access."

Emma and Steele exchanged surprised glances. The guard clearly didn't recognize Kendrick, despite his prominent position with the Alliance. More significantly, he didn't appear to associate Kendrick with the mining operation at all.

"Look, there's been a miscommunication," Kendrick said, his tone shifting to one of authority. "I have standing access to this site. Check with Barrett if you don't believe me."

The mention of Barrett's name seemed to increase rather than alleviate the guard's suspicion. "Barrett doesn't oversee this operation," he replied coldly. "And I don't know who you are, but you need to leave. Now."

The standoff stretched for several tense seconds before Kendrick slowly backed away. "Just a mix-up," he said, his voice carefully controlled. "I'll sort it out with leadership."

The guard maintained his position until Kendrick disappeared back into the forest, then spoke quietly into what appeared to be a communications device on his shoulder. After receiving some response, he moved quickly to the structure, checked it thoroughly, then continued his patrol with increased vigilance.

Emma and Steele remained motionless until both men had moved well beyond their position, then carefully extracted themselves from their hiding spot.

"The guard didn't recognize Kendrick," Emma whispered as they began their cautious retreat toward their extraction point.

"More significantly, he displayed no awareness of Kendrick's involvement with the operation," Steele added. "Suggesting a compartmentalized structure with multiple unaware participants."

"The reference to Barrett not overseeing the operation implies separate command chains," Emma continued, her mind racing with implications. "Could Kendrick be running this independently, without Alliance leadership knowledge?"

"Or a splinter faction within the Alliance," Steele suggested. "Internal conflict over resource utilization."

They moved silently through the trees, processing this unexpected development. What had seemed a straightforward case of Kendrick and the Alliance protecting their illegal gold extraction had suddenly revealed additional layers of complexity. The confrontation they had witnessed suggested internal divisions and security protocols that even Kendrick couldn't navigate.

"We need to reassess," Emma said as they approached their rendezvous point with Crawford's team. "The power structure isn't what we thought."

Steele nodded, his expression thoughtful even in the darkness. "The operational dynamics have shifted. Kendrick may not be the ultimate authority we presumed."

As they reached the extraction team and reported their findings, Emma couldn't shake the feeling that they had uncovered only one layer of a more complex conspiracy. The stream had revealed its golden secret, but the true structure of who controlled it, and who had killed to protect it, remained murky.

What was clear, however, was that the situation was even more dangerous than they had initially assessed. Not just a rogue former ranger protecting his illegal mining operation, but potentially factions within the Alliance working at cross-purposes, with Kendrick caught somewhere in the middle.

As dawn approached and they returned to base with their evidence, one certainty remained, whoever controlled the gold extraction operation had already killed twice to protect it. And with internal conflicts now evident, the danger of additional violence was greater than ever.

CHAPTER 21:
Captured

The evidence gathered at the stream site had confirmed their suspicions about the illegal gold operation, but the unexpected confrontation between Kendrick and the guard had introduced new complications. As Emma and Steele debriefed with Crawford in the conference room at the Talkeetna Trooper's office, it became clear their investigation needed to expand in multiple directions simultaneously.

"The guard's reaction suggests a compartmentalized security structure," Steele explained, reviewing the surveillance footage they had captured. "He not only failed to recognize Kendrick but explicitly stated that Barrett doesn't oversee the operation."

Crawford studied the evidence with concern. "So, we have an illegal mining operation on federal land, potentially run by a faction within the Alliance rather than its official leadership."

"Or Kendrick is operating independently, using Alliance security protocols without their knowledge," Emma suggested. "Either way, the power structure is more complex than we initially assessed."

"Which means we need more information from multiple sources before moving to arrests," Crawford concluded. "Time is critical – the sabotage attempt indicates they know we're closing in."

After discussing options, they developed a strategy that would approach the problem from two angles simultaneously. Emma would return to the Alliance compound under the pretense of following up on their previous visit, gathering intelligence on internal power structures and potential factions. Meanwhile, Steele would dig deeper into Kendrick's background, searching for connections that might explain his current activities.

"I don't like separating," Steele said quietly as they prepared for their respective assignments. The memory of the sabotaged vehicle remained fresh, his uncharacteristic concern for Emma's safety still evident.

"It's the most efficient approach," Emma replied, though she shared his reservations. "We need answers quickly, and dividing forces covers more ground."

"Maintain hourly check-ins," Steele insisted. "Any deviation from schedule triggers immediate extraction protocol."

Emma nodded, touched by his concern despite the professional framing. "Same goes for you. Kendrick's already demonstrated willingness to eliminate threats."

The plan was set. Emma would contact Barrett directly, expressing continued interest in the Alliance's self-sufficiency models while observing internal dynamics. Steele would coordinate with analysts at the Anchorage field office, diving into Kendrick's history before his arrival in Talkeetna.

They parted at midday, each focused on their respective missions but acutely aware of the growing dangers surrounding them.

As Emma approached the Alliance compound for her follow-up visit, her detective instincts immediately registered the changes. Where previously she'd observed casual foot patrols with members moving between buildings in relaxed patterns, now she counted at least six individuals positioned at strategic points around the perimeter, their postures alert and purposeful. The friendly chaos of daily community life had been replaced by something more regimented; residents moved with efficiency rather than leisure, and she noticed several people carrying what appeared to be handheld radios clipped to their belts. The transformation was subtle enough that casual visitors might miss it, but Emma's trained eye catalogued each deviation from the baseline she'd established during their initial tour.

Most concerning was the positioning of the guards themselves. Rather than the random distribution she'd expect from a community going about normal business, they'd established overlapping fields of observation that covered all approach routes to the main buildings. Two men flanked the entrance to Barrett's administrative center, and she spotted another figure partially concealed near the communications equipment they'd glimpsed during their tour. The Alliance had shifted from welcoming community to defensive installation, suggesting they knew exactly why she'd returned and were prepared for federal intervention. Emma's pulse quickened as she realized she was walking into a compound that had transformed overnight from sanctuary to potential trap, with armed, coordinated security between her and any hope of easy retreat.

Tyler Mackenzie, the security chief, met her at the gate with noticeably increased vigilance. "Mrs. Steele," he greeted her, his gaze sweeping the surrounding area. "We were expecting both of you."

"My husband had some business in Anchorage," Emma explained smoothly. "But I was particularly interested in speaking with Sarah Khan about your medical self-sufficiency systems."

Tyler nodded, though Emma detected subtle tension in his posture. "James is expecting you. He's at the community hall."

As they walked through the compound, Emma noticed changes since their previous visit. Security patrols were more frequent and visible. Residents moved with purpose rather than the relaxed demeanor they'd displayed before. The community seemed on alert, not panicked, but definitely vigilant.

Something's triggered their defensive protocols, Emma thought, her mind automatically cataloging escape routes. The question is whether it's our investigation specifically, or federal attention in general.

James Barrett stood when they entered the community hall but didn't approach with his previous warmth.

"Emma, I must admit, I'm surprised you're still in the area given recent events."

"Actually, those events have made us more interested in communities that can function independently from broader social systems,"

Emma replied, watching his reaction carefully. "When institutions fail to protect citizens, alternatives become more compelling."

Barrett studied her for a moment, then smiled with what appeared to be genuine approval. "A perspective I share. Please, join me for tea while we wait for Sarah. She's just finishing her clinic hours."

In the community hall kitchen, Barrett prepared tea with practiced movements. Emma used the opportunity to probe gently for information while maintaining her cover.

"We haven't seen Walter Kendrick in town recently," she commented casually. "Does he have a wilderness class coming up?"

Barrett's hands paused almost imperceptibly. "Walter tends to keep to himself when there's increased attention on the area. Not comfortable with outsiders, especially law enforcement."

Interesting, Emma noted. He's distancing the Alliance from Kendrick without my prompting.

"Understandable, given the circumstances," Emma replied. "His cabin seemed quite separate from the main compound when you showed us around."

"Walter values his independence," Barrett said, his tone carefully neutral. "He's been a valuable ally to our community but has never fully integrated into our governance structure."

Emma noted the specific phrasing, ally rather than member, governance rather than leadership. The distinction felt deliberate, possibly even rehearsed.

"The Alliance seems to have very clear organizational systems," she observed. "Different roles, responsibilities."

Barrett handed her a steaming mug, his movements precise despite their casual conversation. "Structure is essential for self-sufficiency. Clear lines of authority, transparent decision-making processes."

"And resources?" Emma asked, taking a careful sip. "How do you manage those?"

Something flickered in Barrett's eyes, caution, perhaps, or calculation. "Equitably and sustainably. Every resource discovery, whether water, timber, or mineral, is documented and allocated according to community needs."

"Mineral resources?" Emma echoed with deliberate innocence.

Barrett's smile tightened slightly. "Theoretical example. Though this region has a rich mining history, of course."

He's testing me, Emma realized. Seeing how I react to the mention of minerals. This isn't casual conversation, it's an interrogation disguised as hospitality.

Inside the Alliance compound, Emma had noticed her phone losing signal shortly after her tour began. Initially dismissing it as typical remote area coverage issues, she became concerned when she couldn't reconnect even from higher ground. The dead zone seemed too complete, too convenient.

The building Barrett led her to was larger than most, with reinforced doors and what appeared to be a sophisticated security system.

"This is our administrative center," Barrett explained, entering a code on the keypad. "Where we manage community operations."

Inside, Emma found herself in what was essentially a command center: multiple computer stations, communications equipment, and large maps covering the walls. Most surprising were the detailed survey maps showing the surrounding wilderness, with the stream where they'd found the mining operation prominently marked.

This isn't just resource management, Emma thought, her training kicking in as she scanned the room. This is intelligence gathering. Military-grade.

Barrett watched her reaction carefully. "We believe in thorough resource mapping," he said smoothly. "One of our essentials."

Emma recognized the danger in her situation immediately. The room contained evidence directly linking the Alliance leadership to the gold extraction operation. More concerning, one wall displayed surveillance photos of various locations around Talkeetna, including their cabin and the Trooper's office.

"Very comprehensive," she commented, mentally mapping exit routes while maintaining her composure.

"We've been watching you and Agent Steele with great interest," Barrett said, dropping all pretense. "Your investigation techniques are quite impressive."

Emma's stomach dropped, but she maintained her cover. "I don't know what you mean. My husband and I are simply…"

"Please, Detective Stone," Barrett interrupted with a cold smile. "Let's not waste time with continued deceptions. We've been aware of your true identities since shortly after your arrival."

The door opened behind her, and Tyler entered with two armed guards. Barrett gestured for them to secure the exits while maintaining his eerily calm demeanor.

Steele was right, Emma thought, her mind racing through options. We should never have separated. His protective instincts weren't over-reaction, they were accurate threat assessment.

"Unfortunately, Detective, you've discovered aspects of our operation that we can't allow to be shared with your colleagues," Barrett continued, settling into a chair as if they were having a normal business meeting.

"You're making a serious mistake," Emma said, assessing her options. Three armed men, no immediate weapons within reach, the building likely monitored. "Federal agents know exactly where I am."

"The Alliance had nothing to do with those unfortunate incidents involving Mr. Chen and Dr. Peterson," Barrett replied, his tone disturbingly sincere. "That was Walter's independent initiative. A regrettable overreaction that's complicated our more legitimate enterprises."

Barrett's expression grew contemplative, almost professorial. "You know, Detective, when Walter first came to me with his discovery three years ago, I initially refused to consider it. The Alliance was founded on principles of legal self-sufficiency and ethical resource management."

He moved to the wall map, tracing the stream's path with his finger. "But Walter helped me understand something crucial about the nature of ownership and justice. This gold has been sitting in that stream for thousands of years, deposited by natural processes that predate any human claim to the land."

Barrett's voice took on the tone of a teacher explaining a complex moral principle. "The federal government claims ownership based on what?

Lines drawn on maps by politicians who never set foot in these mountains? Regulations written by bureaucrats serving corporate interests?"

Emma watched his face transform as he spoke, seeing the genuine conviction behind his rationalization. He actually believes this, she realized. This isn't just greed, it's ideology.

"Walter showed me the permits required to legally extract those resources," Barrett continued, his calm exterior masking growing intensity. "Months of environmental impact studies designed not to protect the land, but to delay independent operators while major corporations prepare their own claims. Application fees that exclude anyone without substantial capital. Regulatory frameworks that ensure only the already-wealthy can access public resources."

He turned back to Emma, his eyes bright with fervor. "The government wasn't protecting that gold for the American people, Detective. They were protecting it for themselves and their corporate partners. Walter's extraction operation was liberation, not theft."

"Liberation that required murder?" Emma challenged.

Barrett's expression darkened. "I told you, those deaths were Walter's decision, not mine. I believe in protecting our community and our mission, but violence was never part of my vision." His tone grew frustrated. "Walter's military background made him see threats everywhere. When Mr. Chen stumbled onto our operation, Walter acted unilaterally."

"But you didn't stop him," Emma pressed. "Why didn't you report the crime."

"Report it to whom?" Barrett's voice rose for the first time, revealing the depth of his ideological conviction. "To the same corrupt institutions that would use Chen's death as justification to seize our land and destroy everything we've built? To agencies that serve corporate interests while pretending to represent justice?"

He began pacing, his carefully maintained composure cracking. "You don't understand what we're preserving here, Detective. This isn't just about gold or even about our community. We're proving that humans can organize without the artificial hierarchies that have corrupted every civilization in history."

This is worse than simple greed, Emma thought. He's created a complete moral framework that justifies anything. That makes him infinitely more dangerous than a common criminal.

Barrett stopped directly in front of her, his intensity palpable. "The gold funds our independence from a system designed to keep people dependent and desperate. Every ounce we extract is one less resource the elites can use to maintain their stranglehold on human potential."

Emma saw clearly now that Barrett genuinely believed his own justifications. In his mind, the illegal mining wasn't theft, it was revolution. The cover-up wasn't obstruction of justice, it was protection of a higher moral purpose.

"Walter convinced me that sometimes we must work outside corrupt laws to serve true justice," Barrett continued, his voice returning to its earlier calm but carrying undertones of absolute conviction. "The Alliance provides something invaluable to humanity: proof that cooperation can replace competition, that sustainability can replace exploitation, that communities can govern themselves without external control."

"Even if that requires murder?" Emma repeated.

"Even if that requires difficult decisions," Barrett corrected, the euphemism revealing how completely he'd rationalized the violence. "Detective, you've seen what we've accomplished here. Clean energy, sustainable agriculture, genuine democracy. Everything your corrupted institutions claim to provide but never deliver."

He gestured toward the maps on the wall. "This gold operation funds something far more valuable than individual wealth, it funds hope for humanity's future. Walter understood that protecting this vision justifies actions that might seem extreme to those still trapped in conventional moral frameworks."

Emma realized she was facing something more dangerous than simple greed or even fanaticism. Barrett had constructed a complete philosophical system that transformed every illegal action into moral necessity, every crime into revolution, every victim into acceptable collateral damage for the greater good.

The true horror wasn't that he was lying to himself, it was that he absolutely believed every word.

The door opened behind her, and a security guard entered. His expression was grim as he addressed Barrett. "Perimeter teams report federal vehicles approaching the north access road."

Barrett nodded calmly. "It seems your partner has noticed your communication failure." He turned to Emma. "Unfortunately, Detective, you've discovered aspects of our operation that we can't allow to be shared with your colleagues."

Emma assessed her options rapidly. Three armed men plus Barrett. No immediate weapons within reach. The building likely monitored. Think, Emma. What would Steele do? He'd calculate probabilities, look for the logical weakness in their position.

"You're claiming Kendrick acted without Alliance authorization?" she asked, playing for time while studying her captors' positioning.

"Walter has been a useful but increasingly problematic partner," Barrett explained with surprising candor. "His discovery of the gold deposit was valuable, but his methods of protecting it have become a liability."

"A liability you're now planning to eliminate by using me as leverage," Emma concluded, understanding their strategy. "Buying time to dispose of evidence while federal forces focus on negotiation."

Barrett smiled appreciatively. "Your reputation for perceptiveness is well-earned, Detective." He turned to Tyler. "Secure her in the contingency room. Maintain communication blackout protocols."

As the guards moved toward her, Emma knew her window for action was closing. The "divide and conquer" strategy had backfired spectacularly, instead of gathering intelligence safely, she had walked directly into confirmation of the conspiracy while becoming a hostage in the process.

Steele was right about everything, she thought as Tyler's hand closed on her arm. His insistence on maintaining communication, his concern about separation, his uncharacteristic protectiveness. She had dismissed these as overreaction, but now she recognized them as the accurate risk assessment they were.

The communication breakdown hadn't just put their investigation at risk. It had put her life in immediate danger.

CHAPTER 22:
Escape Attempt

Emma assessed her situation with methodical calm despite her racing heart. The "contingency room" Barrett's men had locked her in was essentially a glorified storage closet: secure metal door, no windows, a single ventilation duct too small for escape. They had taken her phone, service weapon, and the emergency transponder disguised as a fitness tracker, leaving her with limited options.

But limited didn't mean none.

As soon as the door locked behind her, Emma began a thorough examination of the space. Metal shelving lined three walls, stocked with supplies: canned food, water purification tablets, medical kits, and other survival necessities. A tactical approach to preparedness that confirmed Barrett's meticulous planning extended to potential crises.

What caught her attention, however, were three heavy-duty plastic cases tucked behind stacks of emergency blankets. They were out of place among the neatly organized supplies, hastily stored rather than systematically arranged. Emma worked quickly to pull one free, recognizing the case design as specialized secure transport containers.

Emma forced herself to breathe slowly as the walls of the storage closet seemed to press inward with each passing minute. The space that had initially felt merely confining now triggered a visceral memory of her childhood punishments, hours locked in her father's study while he delivered sermons about obedience and divine correction. The familiar panic began at the base of her skull, a cold pressure that made her hands shake as she methodically examined every inch of her prison.

Not now, she commanded herself. Steele is depending on you to survive this. Use what Dad taught you, panic is the enemy of survival.

The ventilation duct above her head was barely eight inches wide, designed for airflow rather than human passage. Emma tested the metal grating anyway, finding it securely fastened with screws she had no tools to remove. The walls were solid construction with no gaps or weaknesses, and the floor was concrete poured directly over the building's foundation.

She traced the door frame with her fingertips, searching for any flaw in the construction that might provide leverage, but the Alliance builders had been thorough. The single overhead bulb cast harsh shadows that seemed to shift and dance as her breathing grew more labored in the increasingly stifling air.

Think like Steele, she told herself. What would his analytical mind find? What weakness are they assuming I won't notice?

Methodically, she began examining the storage supplies for anything that could serve as tools or weapons. Heavy cans could be projectiles, metal shelf brackets might work as lock picks, cleaning supplies could create distractions or barriers. Her father's survivalist paranoia, however twisted his motivations, had included practical skills she'd never imagined needing.

"Every prison has a weakness, Emma," she could hear his voice from years ago during one of his preparedness lectures. "The question is whether you're smart enough to find it before desperation makes you stupid."

The lock on the first case was substantial but not impossible. Using a metal shelf bracket she'd pried loose, Emma managed to trigger the release mechanism after several tense minutes. The lid opened to reveal precisely what she'd suspected: gold. Raw nuggets, processed dust, and small ingots, carefully separated and labeled with dates and locations.

"Kendrick's private stash," she whispered, understanding immediately. This wasn't Alliance inventory, this was personal supply being stored temporarily within the compound, hidden even from most Alliance members.

She quickly examined the other cases, finding similar contents plus something even more valuable: documentation. A small waterproof notebook contained handwritten records of extraction dates, amounts, and sale contacts. Most significantly, it included notes about "interference incidents" with dates that perfectly matched Chen and Peterson's deaths.

Direct evidence linking Kendrick to both the illegal mining and the murders.

As Emma photographed these crucial pages with the backup micro-camera concealed in her watch, standard FBI equipment Crawford had insisted upon, she heard voices approaching outside. Quickly returning everything to its original position, she moved to the most defensible position in the small room, the metal shelf bracket gripped tightly in her hand.

The door opened to reveal not Barrett or Tyler, but a younger woman Emma recognized from their previous visit: Melissa Wright, the Alliance's environmental specialist. She entered cautiously, carrying a tray with water and food.

"They told me to bring you this," she said, her voice low and tense. "They think I don't know what's happening, but I've suspected for months."

Emma maintained a defensive stance, ready to strike if this was a trap. "Suspected what?"

"That Barrett and Kendrick are using our community as cover for something illegal." Melissa glanced nervously at the door. "I joined the Alliance because I believed in sustainable living, not whatever they're hiding in those containers."

"You know about the gold?" Emma asked carefully, studying the woman's body language for signs of deception.

Melissa nodded, her fear appearing genuine. "I tracked unusual water quality changes in the eastern watershed, sediment patterns inconsistent with natural processes. When I reported it to Barrett, he dismissed my concerns and restricted access to that area." Her expression hardened. "Then that university student died, and Barrett and Kendrick had multiple private meetings."

Emma made a quick decision. This could be a trap, Melissa sent to gain her trust, or a genuine ally. The environmental specialist's background in water systems made her story plausible; she would naturally notice stream disruptions caused by mining activity.

"I'm a detective working with a federal agent investigating illegal gold extraction and two related homicides," Emma said directly. "I need to get this evidence out of the compound and warn my partner. Can you help me get out of here?"

Melissa's face went pale. "You don't understand what they'll do if they find out I helped you. Barrett isn't just our leader, he controls everything. Our housing, our food supply, our medical care. My sister lives here too, and she has a young daughter." She glanced nervously at the door, her voice dropping even lower. "Tyler's already suspicious of anyone who asks questions about the eastern operations. Last month, one of our members started questioning the increased security patrols, and suddenly his work assignments changed, his food rations got smaller. Barrett calls it 'community correction,' but it's punishment for disloyalty."

Emma leaned forward, recognizing the genuine terror in Melissa's eyes but pressing anyway. "Melissa, we believe Walter Kendrick has murdered two people, Marcus Chen and Dr. Peterson—to protect this operation. If Barrett and Tyler are covering for him, more people will die." She watched Melissa's face blanch at the mention of murder. "Those men died because they discovered what you've discovered about the water contamination. You're already at risk just for knowing about the environmental damage. Help me get evidence to the authorities, and we can protect you and your family. But if we do nothing, if we let this continue, how long before Barrett decides you know too much?"

The weight of professional certainty filled Emma's voice. "You've seen how they handle problems, Melissa. You know I'm right. If you don't help me, it will be worse for you and your family."

Melissa's hands trembled as she set the water tray down. After a long moment, she nodded. "I knew it was something serious when they increased security protocols." She lowered her voice further. "Tyler's mobilized the entire security team. They're planning to move something major tonight, equipment, documents, everything that could connect them to whatever's happening."

"Will you help me get out of here?" Emma asked.

Melissa hesitated, then nodded again, more firmly. "This isn't what I signed up for. But we need to move quickly, they check this room every thirty minutes."

She explained that Barrett and Tyler were occupied with the approaching federal agents, creating a potential window for escape through the compound's southern perimeter where security was thinnest. Melissa could provide distraction by triggering a minor environmental alert, a procedure she had authority to initiate.

"The maintenance tunnel leads from behind this building to the greenhouse complex," she explained, her voice barely audible. "From there, you can reach the southern fence line through the orchard. Security cameras have a three-second switching pattern, and if you time it right, you can slip through the blind spot."

Emma memorized the route, noting potential obstacles and alternate paths. The plan had risks, but staying put guaranteed she'd be used as leverage against the approaching federal team. She needed to escape and reconnect with Steele, sharing the critical evidence she'd discovered about Kendrick's direct involvement in the murders.

"Trigger the alert in five minutes," Emma instructed. "I'll move through the maintenance tunnel while security responds."

Melissa left with the untouched food tray, looking nervously determined. Emma prepared quickly, securing the micro-camera containing the crucial evidence and positioning herself by the door. If Melissa was setting her up, she'd know within minutes. If not, this was her only chance of escape.

Steele, I hope you've noticed I'm overdue for check-in, she thought. Because I'm about to need backup.

Exactly five minutes later, an alarm sounded from the direction of the water treatment facility. Through the thin walls, Emma heard rapid movement as security personnel responded to the environmental alert. Using the shelf bracket to trigger the simple interior lock mechanism, clearly not designed for holding prisoners, she slipped into the hallway.

The corridor was dimly lit, emergency lighting casting long shadows. Emma moved silently toward the rear exit Melissa had described, her law enforcement training kicking in as she navigated the building's layout. Every sense was hyperalert, the sound of boots on concrete floors above, radio chatter echoing from distant rooms, the hum of electrical systems throughout the structure.

She reached the rear door without encountering guards, finding it secured with a simple deadbolt rather than the electronic locks used on the main entrances. They weren't expecting internal threats, she realized. Their security is focused outward.

The door opened onto a narrow alley between buildings, moonlight providing minimal illumination. Emma pressed herself against the maintenance building's wall as a flashlight beam swept past, missing her by inches. Her heart hammered so loudly she was certain the guard could hear it over the distant alarm.

Through the thin wall behind her, she could hear Tyler's radio crackling with reports from other search teams, they were coordinating a grid pattern, systematically clearing each sector of the compound. She had perhaps thirty seconds before someone rounded the corner and spotted her position.

Move fast, move quiet, just like Dad taught you during those wilderness exercises, she reminded herself. Sound travels farther than you think in cold air.

The path to the greenhouse lay across fifteen feet of open ground, illuminated by a security light that hadn't been there during her previous visit. Emma waited for the guard's footsteps to fade, then sprinted across the exposed area, her soft-soled shoes barely making a whisper on the packed earth.

Just as she reached the greenhouse complex, voices erupted from the direction of the storage building. They'd discovered her escape sooner than expected. Behind her, she heard Tyler's boots pounding back toward the commotion, his radio alive with urgent chatter.

"She's out! All teams converge on the administrative sector. Lock down all perimeters."

Emma reached the greenhouse complex as floodlights blazed to life throughout the compound, transforming the Alliance from sleepy community into militarized fortress. The sudden brightness was disorienting, casting harsh shadows and creating dangerous pools of illumination she'd have to avoid.

She ducked between the glass structures, using their bulk to shield her from the searching beams, but her options were rapidly disappearing. Through the transparent walls, she could see armed figures moving with tactical precision, blocking the routes she'd planned to use. The fence line beckoned forty yards away through the orchard, but reaching it would require crossing open ground under direct observation from multiple guard positions.

They're better organized than I anticipated, Emma thought grimly. This isn't just community security, this is military-level response.

A shout from directly behind her sent adrenaline surging through her system, someone had spotted movement among the greenhouses. Emma dropped to a crawl, slithering between rows of young tomato plants as boots thundered past her hiding spot. The rich smell of earth and growing plants filled her nostrils as she pressed herself into the narrow space between growing tables.

Dirt clung to her clothes and hands as she lay motionless, praying the shadows would conceal her while searchers moved systematically through the structure. Above her head, a flashlight beam played across the greenhouse ceiling, its owner clearly aware that someone was hiding nearby but unable to pinpoint her exact location in the maze of plants and equipment.

Stay calm, she coached herself. They're rushing because of the alarm. Use their urgency against them.

The maintenance tunnel was where Melissa had described—a narrow concrete passage used for accessing utilities throughout the compound. Emma moved swiftly through the dimly lit space, her hands trailing along the walls for guidance in the near-darkness. The tunnel smelled of damp concrete and electrical systems, pipes and conduits running along the ceiling.

She emerged behind the greenhouse complex just as shouting erupted from the water treatment area. So far, Melissa had been truthful about the route and timing.

Emma navigated between the greenhouse buildings, using their bulk to shield her from the main compound. The orchard lay ahead, rows of young trees providing minimal cover between her and the fence line. This would be the most exposed portion of her escape route.

As she reached the orchard's edge, calculating the best path through the sparse cover, a voice called out behind her.

"That's far enough, Detective."

Emma spun to find Tyler Mackenzie standing twenty yards away, rifle raised to his shoulder. His expression was coldly professional, not angry, simply determined to complete his assignment.

"You won't make it to the fence," he said calmly, his weapon steady and aimed center mass. "Barrett wants you alive as leverage, but I'm authorized to use necessary force if you continue resisting."

Emma assessed her options in an instant. The fence was forty yards away across open ground. Tyler was a trained security professional at optimal firing range with a high-powered rifle. The odds of reaching cover before he could fire were virtually nonexistent.

But he wants me alive, she realized. That gives me options.

"The FBI knows about Kendrick's mining operation," she said, buying time while scanning for alternatives. "They have the stream location and evidence connecting him to both murders. Surrendering me won't change that."

"This isn't about Kendrick anymore," Tyler replied, his aim never wavering. "Barrett has his own concerns. Now turn around and walk back, or I'll shoot to wound and carry you back."

Emma noticed his precise wording, wound, not kill. Barrett needed her functional enough to be useful as a hostage. That limitation was her advantage.

In that moment, the compound's lights flickered briefly, an unexpected power fluctuation likely related to Melissa's diversionary tactic affecting the electrical grid. In the momentary distraction as Tyler's eyes involuntarily followed the fluctuation, Emma made her decision.

She dove sideways behind a wooden irrigation equipment shed as Tyler fired, the high-velocity round splintering wood where she'd stood milliseconds before. Her father's training kicked in, when caught in the open, create chaos and use it as cover.

Emma rolled behind the shed as Tyler chambered another round, her mind calculating angles and distances. With security alerted to her escape, her window was closing rapidly. She needed to create distance and confusion before reinforcements arrived.

Grabbing a heavy canister of fertilizer from inside the shed, she hurled it toward the greenhouse's propane heating system thirty feet away, then immediately sprinted in the opposite direction as Tyler fired again. The canister ruptured against the metal tank, creating a cloud of chemical dust and a loud metallic clang that temporarily obscured visibility and masked her movement.

Emma used the confusion to change direction entirely, circling back toward the eastern perimeter rather than the southern route Tyler would expect her to take. This area bordered the forest rather than open ground, offering better escape potential despite likely heavier security.

Misdirection, she thought as she moved. Make them think you're going one way while you go another.

Shouts echoed across the compound as security teams mobilized. Emergency alarms activated throughout the grounds as Emma pressed herself against a maintenance building, controlling her breathing as footsteps pounded past her position. The sound of multiple vehicles starting in the distance meant they were organizing vehicular pursuit—her time was running short.

When the immediate footsteps faded, she moved quickly along the building's shadow, approaching the eastern fence line. A security camera mounted on a nearby pole swept back and forth in a regular pattern, its housing equipped with night vision capabilities that would easily spot her approach.

Emma counted the timing, three seconds between sweeps, just as Melissa had described. But three seconds wasn't enough time to cross the exposed ground between her position and the fence.

I need a longer distraction.

She spotted a junction box for the electrical system mounted on the building's exterior. Using the metal shelf bracket she'd kept from the storage room, Emma pried open the cover and located the main power feed. A few strategic cuts with the bracket's sharp edge, and half the compound's lighting went dark.

In the confusion that followed, shouts about power failure, teams being redirected to check the electrical systems, Emma made her move. She crossed the exposed ground in a low crouch, reaching the fence precisely during the camera's sweep away from her position.

The barrier was eight feet tall with reinforced wire mesh designed to keep intruders out, not to keep prisoners in. Emma scaled it quickly, using the fence posts as leverage points and ignoring the burning pain as the sharp wire bit into her palms. Blood made her grip slippery, but her father's wilderness training had included rope climbing and obstacle courses that now served her well.

As she reached the top, shouts erupted from her left, another security team had spotted her silhouette against the sky. A spotlight swung in her direction as she launched herself over the fence, landing hard on the forest floor as the first shots rang out.

Emma rolled into the underbrush as bullets struck the ground where she'd landed, bark and leaves exploding around her. Without pausing, she pushed deeper into the forest, using the dense vegetation as cover while branches tore at her clothes and scratched her face.

Behind her, the Alliance compound erupted with activity, shouts, the sound of vehicles starting, the distinctive whine of ATVs being prepared for off-road pursuit. She had perhaps a ten-minute head start before organized pursuit began.

The pursuit had begun, but Emma Stone was no longer just a captive, she was a federal agent with critical evidence, alone in hostile territory but far from helpless. Her father's survivalist training, her law enforcement experience, and her determination to reach Steele would all be tested in the hours ahead.

The forest stretched out before her, dark and vast, hiding both sanctuary and danger in its depths. Somewhere in that wilderness, thirty federal agents were searching for her. She just had to stay alive long enough to find them.

Hold on, Steele, she thought as she disappeared into the Alaskan night. I'm coming home.

CHAPTER 23:
The Hunt

The moment Emma missed her second scheduled check-in, Steele knew something was wrong. He maintained his outward composure in front of the FBI analysts, but inside, alarm bells were sounding with increasing urgency.

"Try the emergency channel again," he instructed Agent Hickok, his voice betraying none of the concern churning beneath his professional facade.

Diana shook her head after the attempt. "Still no response. Could be equipment failure or signal interference at the compound."

Steele knew better. Emma was meticulous about communications protocol, if she wasn't responding, it wasn't by choice. He pulled up the satellite imagery of the Alliance compound, mapping potential approach vectors while calculating response times.

"Alert Crawford," he said, already reaching for his tactical gear. "Tell him we've lost contact with Detective Stone inside the Alliance compound. I'm initiating extraction protocol."

"Shouldn't we wait for confirmation before…" Diana began.

"Negative," Steele cut her off with uncharacteristic sharpness. "Two previous murders, a direct sabotage attempt, and now lost communications. The statistical probability of Detective Stone being in danger exceeds ninety percent."

Within thirty minutes, Steele had mobilized a response team and was enroute to the Alliance compound. His mind worked with clinical precision, analyzing every possible scenario while systematically suppressing the growing knot of fear in his chest. Fear was inefficient. Fear clouded judgment. Fear wouldn't help Emma.

But it persisted nonetheless, an unfamiliar emotion he couldn't fully process or dismiss.

Crawford met them at the staging area two miles from the compound entrance. "We've established a perimeter and initiated contact with Barrett," he reported. "He claims Stone left the compound an hour ago, declined their offer of lunch and headed back to town."

"That's a lie," Steele stated flatly. "She would have reestablished communication immediately upon leaving their signal-blocking range."

"I agree," Crawford said grimly. "We're treating this as a potential hostage situation. Barrett is stalling, claiming misunderstanding and offering to 'help search' for her."

Steele reviewed the tactical map, identifying the most likely locations within the compound where Emma might be held. The administrative building they hadn't toured during their previous visit was the logical choice, central, defensible, with sight lines to all approach vectors.

"I'll lead the primary entry team," he said, not asking permission but stating a fact.

Crawford studied him for a moment, noting the slight tension around Steele's eyes, the only outward sign of his internal state. "You're emotionally compromised, Steele. Standard protocol dictates..."

"I'm the most familiar with the compound layout and Detective Stone's operational patterns," Steele interrupted, his voice cool and logical despite the urgency building within him. "Tactical efficiency is optimized by my direct involvement."

Before Crawford could respond, the radio crackled with an urgent report from the eastern perimeter team. Gunshots had been heard from within the forest, approximately two miles from the compound fence line.

Steele was moving before Crawford finished relaying the information, grabbing night vision equipment and ordering the closest team to converge on the coordinates. The gunshots had come from the direction opposite their primary approach, which meant Emma was somehow no longer in the compound.

Either she had escaped, or someone had moved her.

Deep in the forest, Emma moved with calculated precision through terrain that grew more challenging with each step. The dense spruce and birch created a canopy that filtered the early morning light into scattered patches, perfect for concealment but treacherous for navigation. Her father's wilderness training, absorbed during those endless childhood lessons she'd once resented, now served as her lifeline.

"The forest will hide you if you understand its rhythms," she could hear his voice from decades past. "But it will kill you if you fight against its nature."

She had been moving for over an hour since her escape from the compound, using game trails and natural cover to put distance between herself and her pursuers. The sounds of organized search, ATVs, radio chatter, coordinated sweep patterns, had gradually faded behind her. But Emma knew this was only the beginning.

A twig snapped somewhere to her left, too deliberate to be natural. Emma froze, pressing herself against the rough bark of a large spruce, controlling her breathing as she listened to the forest around her. The normal sounds, wind through branches, distant bird calls, the rustle of small animals, continued undisturbed. But there was something else, a presence that didn't belong.

He's here.

Walter Kendrick emerged from behind a stand of birch trees fifty yards away, moving with the fluid silence of a lifetime outdoorsman. Unlike the Alliance security teams with their tactical gear and organized search patterns, Walter hunted with patient precision, reading the forest like text on a page.

Emma watched him examine the ground where she'd passed twenty minutes earlier, his weathered face intent as he studied disturbed moss and broken twigs. Even from this distance, she could see the methodical way he processed the signs, building a picture of her route and likely destination.

He's not just tracking me, she realized with growing unease. *He's thinking ahead, calculating where I'm going.*

Walter straightened, his pale blue eyes scanning the forest ahead. For a moment, his gaze seemed to settle on her hiding spot, and Emma felt her heart rate spike. But after a tense pause, he looked away, apparently satisfied with his assessment of her trail.

When he moved deeper into the forest, Emma waited several minutes before changing position. She needed to reach the federal perimeter, but Walter's tracking skills were forcing her away from the most direct route. Every step took her deeper into wilderness where his advantages would only grow.

As she picked her way carefully through a patch of dense undergrowth, Emma's mind drifted to the evidence she'd photographed in Barrett's storage room. Kendrick's handwritten records had revealed more than just gold extraction and murder, they'd shown the twisted logic of a man who saw himself as protector of the wilderness.

"Environmental enforcement," one entry had read. "Chen's academic study would have brought industrial attention to protected watershed. Elimination necessary to preserve ecosystem integrity."

The clinical language couldn't disguise the zealotry underneath. Walter Kendrick wasn't just a killer, he was a crusader who'd appointed himself guardian of the Alaskan wilderness, willing to murder anyone who threatened his vision of preservation.

A sound behind her made Emma turn. Walter stood thirty yards away, having approached with impossible silence while she'd been distracted by her thoughts. His hunting rifle was cradled in his arms, not immediately threatening but ready for use.

"Detective Stone," he called softly, his voice carrying easily in the still morning air. "You've led me on quite a chase."

Emma remained motionless behind the tree that concealed her, mind racing through options. She was too far from the federal perimeter to call for help, and Walter's woodcraft skills made escape unlikely in direct confrontation.

"I know you're there," Walter continued, his tone almost conversational. "The broken branch at knee height, the scuff mark on that moss-covered log. You're careful, but not careful enough for someone who's spent forty years reading these woods."

He's trying to draw me out, Emma realized. Testing to see if I'll panic or hold position.

"You know what's interesting about this forest?" Walter's voice took on the tone of a lecturer warming to his subject. "It's remained essentially unchanged for centuries. The same species, the same relationships, the same delicate balance that existed long before humans arrived with their greed and their machines."

Emma used his monologue as cover to shift position, moving silently to a more defensible spot behind a fallen log. The micro-camera on her wrist contained evidence that could destroy him, but only if she survived to deliver it.

"That young man, Chen, he didn't understand what he was really doing," Walter continued, and Emma could hear him moving slowly through the underbrush. "He saw gold and thought of profit, of academic recognition. He couldn't see the devastation that would follow, the mining trucks, the processing equipment, the poisoned streams."

There was genuine anguish in his voice now, the passion of a true believer confronting an incomprehensible world.

"I spent thirty years with the Forest Service watching them destroy what I'd sworn to protect. Every permit I was forced to approve, every environmental impact study I saw falsified, every pristine watershed handed over to corporations who saw only dollars per ton."

Emma carefully raised her head above the log, spotting Walter through a gap in the trees. He had stopped moving, his rifle now held at ready position as his eyes systematically scanned the area where she was hidden.

"The Cache Creek murders of 1939," Walter said suddenly, his voice taking on a different quality. "Do you know that story, Detective?"

Emma did know it, four miners killed in disputes over gold claims, a case that had haunted Alaska for decades. But she remained silent, recognizing that Walter was working toward something.

"Dick Francis and Frank Jenkins fought for years over those claims. Legal battles, court orders, public humiliation. And when it finally came to violence, four people died in a single day." Walter's voice grew quieter, more intense. "All for gold that poisoned the groundwater and left the landscape scarred for generations."

He resumed moving, but more slowly now, his attention divided between tracking and his internal narrative.

"History repeats itself, Detective. Chen would have brought the same destruction to this watershed. Peterson was already contacting commercial mining consultants. I've seen this pattern before, academic research becomes corporate reconnaissance, pristine wilderness becomes industrial wasteland."

Emma realized with chilling clarity that Walter wasn't just rationalizing his crimes, he genuinely believed he was a hero. In his twisted worldview, murder was environmental protection, silence was conservation.

"The gold will stay where it belongs," Walter continued, his voice now carrying the fervor of absolute conviction. "Hidden, protected, safe from the machines and the men who serve them. This forest has survived ice ages and fire, disease and flood. It won't be destroyed by human greed, not while I can prevent it."

The sound of his movement had stopped. Emma risked a quick glance and felt her blood run cold. Walter stood less than twenty feet away, his rifle raised and aimed directly at her position. His pale eyes held the calm certainty of a man completely convinced of his own righteousness.

"Stand up slowly, Detective," he commanded, his finger resting on the trigger. "Hands visible. You've caused enough disruption to this place."

Emma had no choice. She rose from behind the log, hands raised, the micro-camera on her wrist feeling impossibly obvious. Walter's gaze catalogued her condition, scratched, muddy, exhausted, but unbroken.

"You're remarkably resourceful," he acknowledged with what might have been respect. "Your escape from Barrett's compound was impressive. But this ends here."

"The FBI knows about the gold operation," Emma said, keeping her voice steady despite the rifle aimed at her chest. "They have the stream location and evidence connecting you to both murders. Killing me won't change that."

Walter's expression didn't change. "Perhaps. But it will prevent you from testifying about what you've seen. Without your firsthand account, they have only circumstantial evidence. Reasonable doubt, as you law enforcement types say."

He was right, and they both knew it. The micro-camera evidence would help, but Emma's testimony would be crucial for prosecution. Walter was calculating that eliminating her would create enough uncertainty to save him from conviction.

"You worked for the Forest Service for thirty years," Emma said, playing for time while scanning for escape routes. "You swore an oath to protect these lands for future generations. How does murder serve that mission?"

For the first time, uncertainty flickered across Walter's face. The question had struck something deeper than his surface rationalizations.

"You don't understand the forces at work," he replied, but his voice lacked its previous conviction. "Corporate interests, political corruption, regulatory capture. The system I served was designed to fail, designed to allow the destruction of everything I believed in."

Emma sensed an opening and pressed forward. "So you decided to become judge, jury, and executioner? To appoint yourself protector of the wilderness?"

"Someone had to," Walter snapped, his calm mask slipping. "Someone had to draw a line and say 'no more.' These mountains, these streams, this forest, they can't speak for themselves. They need someone willing to fight for them, whatever the cost."

The fervor in his voice was frightening in its intensity. Emma was facing a man who had transformed environmental concern into murderous zealotry, who saw himself as the sole guardian of natural systems that had existed for millennia without his protection.

"Chen was just a student," Emma said quietly. "Peterson was a local geologist. They weren't corporate raiders or environmental destroyers. They were scientists trying to understand the natural world."

"They were the advance scouts," Walter corrected, his rifle never wavering. "Academic research funded by grant money that traces back to mining interests. University studies that provide legal cover for resource extraction. I've seen this pattern dozens of times."

Emma realized she was arguing with someone whose worldview had been shaped by decades of watching environmental degradation, whose legitimate concerns had metastasized into paranoid conspiracy theories that justified anything in service of his cause.

A distant sound made both of them freeze, the mechanical whine of helicopter rotors approaching from the east. Walter's eyes narrowed as he processed the implications.

"Your federal friends are closer than I anticipated," he said with grim satisfaction. "No matter. A rifle shot will bring them running, but not quickly enough to save you."

As he adjusted his aim, Emma made a desperate calculation. The approaching helicopter meant Steele had mobilized extraction teams. If she could survive the next few minutes, help was coming.

"You're right about the system being corrupt," she said rapidly, playing to his environmental passion. "I've seen it too, corporate interests buying politicians, regulators who serve industry instead of the public. But killing people won't fix it."

"It fixed the immediate threat," Walter replied coldly. "Chen's death prevented academic study that would have led to industrial exploitation. Peterson's elimination stopped commercial mining consultations that would have brought heavy equipment to this watershed."

The helicopter was getting closer, but Emma could see Walter's finger tightening on the trigger. In seconds, he would fire and disappear into the forest before federal agents could respond to the gunshot.

In that moment of desperation, Emma heard another sound, the crack of a branch somewhere to Walter's left. His head turned involuntarily toward the noise, and Emma glimpsed a figure moving through the trees.

Steele had found them.

As Walter's attention divided between Emma and the new threat, she made her move.

The forest was a maze of shadows and obstacles as Steele led his team toward the reported gunfire location. They moved with disciplined speed, following tactical formation despite Steele's driving urge to race ahead. Procedure existed for a reason. Procedure maximized effectiveness. Procedure would help him find Emma.

When a second gunshot echoed through the trees, Steele immediately calculated trajectory and distance, closer now, perhaps a few feet ahead. He signaled the team to accelerate their advance, maintaining communications discipline while scanning the terrain with trained precision.

She's alive, he told himself with analytical certainty. If Kendrick wanted her dead, he wouldn't risk multiple shots that alert federal teams to his location. He's either trying to wound her or intimidate her.

The realization provided small comfort as Steele pushed through dense undergrowth, following the faint sounds of disturbance ahead. Every few minutes, he paused to listen for additional gunshots or calls for help, but the forest had returned to its natural quiet.

Through his earpiece, Crawford's voice provided updates: "Aerial surveillance shows movement in grid section seven-alpha. Single heat signature moving northeast toward the river confluence."

One signature, Steele noted with growing concern. Either they're moving together, or one is pursuing the other.

The eastern sky was just beginning to lighten when Steele spotted movement through the trees, a figure taking cover behind a fallen log as someone else disappeared into the denser forest. Even at this distance, he recognized Emma's distinctive movement pattern, the efficient economy of motion he'd come to know over their days together.

Relief flooded through him with such intensity it was almost physically painful.

But as he moved closer, Steele realized Emma wasn't alone. Walter Kendrick stood less than twenty yards from her position, rifle raised and aimed directly at where she was hidden. The former Forest Service ranger's attention was completely focused on his target, creating the opportunity Steele needed.

Moving with the silent precision of his tactical training, Steele approached from Kendrick's blind spot, using the natural cover of trees and undergrowth to close the distance. He could hear voices now, Emma and Kendrick engaged in some kind of conversation or negotiation.

She's buying time, he realized. Keeping him talking while looking for an opening.

Steele positioned himself behind a large spruce tree, drawing his sidearm while calculating angles and distances. He had a clear shot at Kendrick, but the range was at the edge of his pistol's effective accuracy. Miss, and Kendrick would have time to fire at Emma before Steele could close the distance.

Through the trees, he heard Emma say something about the system being corrupt, her voice carrying the careful neutrality of someone trying to defuse a dangerous situation. Kendrick's response revealed the depth of his environmental zealotry, the twisted logic that had transformed conservation into murder.

Steele waited for the perfect moment, knowing he would have only one chance. When Kendrick's attention seemed completely focused on Emma, he deliberately stepped on a dead branch, creating the sharp crack that made the gunman's head turn toward the new threat.

In that instant of divided attention, Emma moved.

She dove sideways as Walter's rifle swung toward Steele, the shot going wide and striking a tree trunk with a spray of bark. Steele emerged from cover, his own weapon drawn, but Kendrick was already moving with the fluid grace of a lifetime woodsman.

"Federal agent!" Steele shouted, his voice carrying through the forest. "Drop your weapon and surrender!"

Walter turned toward him with an expression of cold fury, working the bolt of his rifle to chamber another round. "Another servant of the system," he snarled. "How many of you will die to protect corporate interests?"

He raised the rifle toward Steele, but Emma had recovered from her dive and was now moving behind him. As Walter took aim, she launched herself at his legs, tackling him low and sending both of them crashing to the forest floor.

The rifle discharged harmlessly into the air as Walter and Emma struggled for control of the weapon. Steele rushed forward, but the combatants were too close together for him to risk a shot.

Walter was stronger, but Emma fought with the desperation of someone who'd already survived too much to give up now. She managed to tear the rifle from his grasp, sending it skittering across the forest floor, but Walter recovered quickly and reached for something at his belt.

A knife blade flashed in the morning light as Walter lunged at Emma. She rolled aside, the blade missing her by inches, and came up in a defensive crouch. Walter advanced with the confidence of someone who'd spent decades using edged tools in wilderness settings.

"Enough," Steele said quietly, his pistol now aimed directly at Walter's center mass from less than ten feet away. "Step away from Detective Stone. Now."

Walter paused, the knife still held in a threatening position, his eyes moving between Steele and Emma as he calculated odds. The sound of approaching helicopters was clearly audible now, federal reinforcements closing in on their position.

"You think you've won something here," Walter said, his voice carrying bitter resignation. "But this forest will be destroyed within five years. Commercial mining operations, processing facilities, contaminated groundwater. Everything I tried to protect will be poisoned for profit."

"Maybe," Emma replied, slowly rising to her feet while keeping distance between herself and the knife. "But that's not your decision to make. And murder isn't conservation."

Walter's expression shifted, the zealous certainty replaced by something like despair. "Thirty years," he whispered. "Thirty years of watching them tear apart everything beautiful, everything irreplaceable. I couldn't save the others, but I thought I could save this place."

For a moment, Steele saw not a dangerous fugitive but a broken man who'd spent his career watching his life's work undone by forces beyond his control. The tragedy was that Walter's passion for environmental protection was genuine, it was his methods that had become monstrous.

"Drop the knife, Walter," Steele said quietly. "It's over."

The helicopter sounds were very close now, and through the trees, Steele could see movement as additional federal agents approached their position. Walter heard them too, his shoulders sagging as he recognized the futility of further resistance.

The knife fell from his fingers, landing on the moss-covered ground with barely a sound. Walter raised his hands, the gesture of surrender that marked the end of his deadly campaign to protect the wilderness through murder.

"Agent Stone!" Steele called, abandoning protocol in his urgency to reach her. He pushed past the advancing team, eyes locked on her position as she carefully stood from behind the fallen log where she'd taken cover.

"Are you injured?" he asked as he reached her, scanning for any signs of harm or distress.

"Negative," she replied, though exhaustion was evident in her stance despite her professional response. "But I have critical evidence. Kendrick's records, documentation of the murders and the gold operation."

As the tactical team organized the arrest of Kendrick and secured the perimeter, Steele found himself unable to maintain the professional distance he'd cultivated throughout his career. The sight of Emma, alive, relatively unharmed, standing before him after hours of uncertainty, triggered something beyond his usual analytical framework.

"The extraction team encountered resistance at the compound perimeter," he reported, falling back on factual communication to mask the tumult of unfamiliar emotions. "Barrett is claiming diplomatic cooperation while denying all knowledge of any illegal activities."

"He's lying," Emma said decisively, proceeding to describe what she had discovered and the evidence she had secured, evidence that would break the case wide open. Her resourcefulness and courage in the face of extreme danger only intensified Steele's internal struggle.

As they stood in the growing dawn light, surrounded by the tactical team but somehow isolated in their shared experience, Steele found himself facing an unprecedented personal realization. The fear he had felt at Emma's disappearance, the relief at finding her safe, these weren't merely professional concerns for a valued colleague.

They were something he had never allowed himself to experience before.

The activity around them faded into the background as Emma finished her report, her eyes meeting his with a directness that suggested she too was processing something beyond the case.

She escaped a fortified compound and evaded both Kendrick and armed security teams, Steele thought, admiration breaking through his typically neutral analysis.

Emma smiled slightly despite her obvious exhaustion. "I applied your analytical approach to identify the optimal escape parameters."

"I believe your 'intuitive leaps' were the more relevant methodology in this instance," he replied, something almost like humor flickering in his expression.

Crawford approached with updated information about Kendrick's arrest and the compound situation, temporarily drawing their attention back to operational matters. When he moved away to coordinate with the tactical teams, Steele and Emma found themselves momentarily alone in a small clearing, the morning light strengthening around them.

"How did you find me?" Emma asked quietly.

"Probability analysis of likely escape routes based on terrain features and your training profile," Steele answered automatically, then paused. "And I... knew you wouldn't go toward the roads. You'd use the forest for cover, approach from an unexpected vector."

Emma studied him with those perceptive eyes that saw through his careful constructions. "That's not probability analysis, Steele. That's knowing me."

The distinction struck him with surprising force. He did know her, not just as a collection of data points and behavioral patterns, but as Emma. Stubborn, brilliant, intuitive Emma, who had somehow bypassed his carefully maintained emotional barriers.

"When you didn't check in..." he began, then faltered, unfamiliar with expressing such personal reactions. "The statistical models suggested multiple concerning scenarios."

"You were worried," Emma translated, stepping closer.

"'Worried' is an inadequate descriptor," Steele admitted. "I experienced... significant cognitive disruption. Inability to process alternative outcomes where you were not safely recovered."

A smile touched Emma's lips. "That might be the most romantic thing anyone's ever said to me."

"I don't have the appropriate vocabulary for this," Steele confessed, his usual precise language failing him. "My father didn't include emotional expression in his training curriculum."

"Mine included too much of the wrong kind," Emma replied softly. "Maybe we're both still learning."

The space between them seemed charged with unspoken recognition, of how far they had come since their awkward beginning, of the connection that had formed through shared danger and mutual respect, of feelings neither had intended to develop.

"Emma," Steele said, her name itself a departure from his usual formal address. "When I thought you were in danger, I experienced... a breaking point. A failure of my ability to compartmentalize."

"Is that a bad thing?" she asked, her expression open and unguarded in a way he rarely saw.

"I don't know," he answered honestly. "It's unprecedented in my experience."

Emma took another step closer, close enough that he could see the flecks of gold in her green eyes, the small cut on her cheek from her escape through the forest, the slight tremor of exhaustion in her hands.

"Sometimes unprecedented is good," she said quietly. "Sometimes it means discovering something valuable that was missing before."

The analytical part of Steele's mind calculated the professional implications, the potential complications, the statistical improbability of success given their different approaches to life and work. But for once, that analytical voice was overridden by something more immediate and compelling.

Without conscious decision, he closed the remaining distance between them, one hand rising to gently touch her face as though confirming she was really there, safe, alive. Emma leaned into his touch, her eyes never leaving his.

When their lips met, it wasn't the careful, measured action his logical mind might have planned. It was something elemental and necessary, a culmination of tension and relief, of professional admiration evolved into personal connection. Emma's arms wrapped around him, eliminating any remaining space between them as she returned the kiss with equal intensity.

For a man who had spent his life categorizing and analyzing every experience, this one defied classification. It simply was, immediate, essential, transformative.

When they finally separated, both slightly breathless, Steele found himself at a rare loss for words. Emma's smile held a mixture of wonder and understanding.

"That wasn't in the FBI partnership protocols," she murmured.

"An oversight in the manual," Steele replied.

A call from Crawford broke the moment, reality reasserting itself as the tactical situation demanded their attention. Kendrick was now in custody, the Alliance leadership was being detained for questioning, and the case required their professional focus.

But as they walked back toward the command post, something fundamental had shifted. The breaking point Steele had feared, the collapse of his carefully constructed emotional barriers, hadn't left him vulnerable as his father's teaching had always warned. Instead, it revealed a capacity he hadn't known he possessed.

The case would continue, the investigation would proceed with their usual methodical thoroughness. But beneath the professional surface, both knew that something rare and unexpected had emerged from the danger and tension of the past days, a connection neither had sought but both now recognized as invaluable.

The hunt was over. Walter Kendrick would face justice for his crimes. The golden stream would keep its secrets no longer. And two people who had spent their lives maintaining careful control had discovered the profound relief of letting someone else matter enough to risk everything for their safety.

In the growing Alaskan dawn, as federal agents processed the crime scene and prepared for the long journey back to civilization, Emma Stone and Jeremiah Steele had found something more valuable than gold hidden in the wilderness, they had found each other.

CHAPTER 24:

Confrontation

The aftermath of Emma's escape and Kendrick's capture had transformed the investigation from a deadly chase into methodical evidence compilation. What had begun as a suspicious death case had evolved into a complex web of illegal mining, murder, and conspiracy that reached beyond Kendrick to the Alliance leadership. Crawford had established a command center in the Talkeetna State Trooper's office, where Emma and Steele now assembled the complete picture from the scattered pieces they had gathered.

"Walter Kendrick's official Forest Service biography was heavily redacted," Steele explained, displaying the newly uncovered records on the conference room screen. "Our analysts managed to recover his complete employment history, including details that were deliberately obscured during his retirement process."

The assembled federal team studied the records with growing understanding. Kendrick hadn't simply been a Forest Service ranger—he had started his career as a mining engineer for several major extraction companies before joining the government agency.

"His specialized knowledge allowed him to identify resource potential that others would miss," Emma noted, connecting the pieces. "That's why Barrett partnered with him. Kendrick could locate valuable deposits on public land that weren't on any official surveys."

Agent Hickok added the financial analysis she had compiled. "Kendrick's bank records show irregular cash deposits beginning three years ago, shortly after the period of heavy rainfall that would have exposed the gold deposits in the stream bed. The amounts increased steadily, totaling over three hundred thousand dollars."

"But nowhere near the value of the extracted gold we documented," Steele observed. "Suggesting Barrett and the Alliance leadership were receiving the majority share."

The full picture of Kendrick's background revealed a man who had spent his entire career exploiting his knowledge of natural resources, first legitimately in the private sector, then through increasingly questionable means within the Forest Service, and finally through outright illegal extraction after his retirement.

"The Alliance provided perfect cover," Emma explained, indicating the maps showing the relationship between Alliance property and the gold-bearing stream. "Barrett established a seemingly legitimate survivalist community while Kendrick operated the extraction site on adjacent public land. The Alliance's security infrastructure protected both operations while denying knowledge or responsibility for any illegal actions."

"And most Alliance members had no knowledge of the illegal activities," Steele added, displaying the statements they had gathered from community members after securing the compound. "Barrett compartmentalized information, restricting awareness of the gold operation to a small inner circle including security chief Tyler Mackenzie."

As they assembled the evidence, Emma spread the photographs she had taken of Kendrick's private records found in the Alliance compound, the documents that provided the final damning connections.

"These entries correspond exactly to the dates of both Chen and Peterson's deaths," she highlighted, pointing to the notebook pages. "Kendrick documented them as 'resource protection incidents' with location coordinates matching where the bodies were found."

"Along with inventories of personal effects taken from each victim," Steele added. "Chen's field notebook, camera, and soil samples. Peterson's computer and analysis equipment."

Crawford studied the evidence with grim satisfaction. "This gives us beyond reasonable doubt for both homicides, plus the illegal mining operation and Barrett's conspiracy involvement."

Emma felt a complex mix of professional satisfaction and personal unease as she reviewed the evidence they'd compiled. The case was solid, airtight, even, but something about Kendrick's methodical documentation troubled her. These weren't the records of a man driven by greed alone.

"There's something else," she said, pulling out additional pages from Kendrick's notebook that she'd photographed. "These entries go back years, documenting environmental damage across Alaska. Mining operations, oil spills, illegal logging. He's been tracking corporate environmental crimes for decades."

Steele leaned forward, examining the meticulous records. "The scope is impressive. He documented violations that were never prosecuted, cover-ups that were never exposed, damage that was never remediated."

"It reads like the journal of someone who spent his career watching the system fail," Emma observed. "Every entry contains detailed evidence of environmental destruction, followed by notes about regulatory failures and political interference."

Crawford frowned. "You're suggesting Kendrick saw himself as some kind of environmental vigilante?"

"I'm suggesting his motivation was more complex than simple profit," Emma replied. "These records show a man driven by genuine environmental passion that metastasized into something deadly."

Before Crawford could respond, a commotion in the hallway drew their attention. Through the conference room window, Emma saw two state troopers escorting Walter Kendrick toward an interview room. His hands were cuffed, but his posture remained upright, almost defiant.

"He's requested to speak with the lead investigators," Crawford announced as he ended a brief phone call. "Specifically asked for Detective Stone and Agent Steele."

Emma exchanged a glance with Steele. "He wants to confess?"

"More likely wants to justify," Steele replied. "Based on his psychological profile, he probably believes we'll understand his motivations once he explains them properly."

Twenty minutes later, Emma and Steele sat across from Walter Kendrick in the spartan interview room. A recording device captured every word, and a one-way mirror allowed Crawford and other investigators to observe. Kendrick had waived his right to an attorney, insisting he wanted to tell his story without legal interference.

Up close, the toll of the past few days was evident on Kendrick's weathered face. His gray hair was disheveled, his outdoor clothing torn and stained from his flight through the wilderness. But his pale blue eyes remained sharp, alert, calculating.

"You read my journals," he said without preamble, addressing Emma directly. "Tell me what you saw."

Emma kept her voice neutral, professional. "Thirty years of documented environmental crimes. Detailed records of regulatory failures and corporate malfeasance. The work of someone deeply committed to conservation."

Kendrick nodded approvingly. "Someone who understands. Good." He leaned forward slightly. "Do you know what it's like to spend your entire career watching them destroy everything you've sworn to protect?"

"Explain it to us," Steele said, his tone carefully noncommittal.

Kendrick's gaze shifted between them, assessing their level of interest. "I joined the Forest Service in 1992, fresh out of college, full of idealism about protecting America's natural heritage. I believed the system worked, that environmental laws meant something, that regulatory agencies served the public interest."

His voice took on the bitter edge Emma had heard in the forest. "It took me exactly eighteen months to realize I was naive. My first major case involved a copper mining operation in the Wrangell Mountains. Beautiful country, pristine watershed, home to one of Alaska's last intact salmon runs."

Kendrick paused, his expression distant with memory. "The company's environmental impact study was a joke, obvious fabrications, manipulated data, bribed consultants. I documented everything, filed a report recommending denial of their permits."

"What happened?" Emma asked, though she suspected she knew.

"Political pressure. My supervisor informed me that the mining operation would create jobs, generate tax revenue, and demonstrate

Alaska's commitment to resource development. My recommendation was overruled, the permits were approved, and within two years, that salmon run was extinct."

Steele studied Kendrick's body language, noting the genuine pain beneath his controlled delivery. "That was your first exposure to regulatory capture?"

"The first of many," Kendrick confirmed. "Over the next three decades, I watched the same pattern repeat dozens of times. Timber harvests in old-growth forest, oil drilling in sensitive habitats, mining operations in protected watersheds. Every time, my scientific recommendations were overruled by political considerations."

Emma could see how years of such experiences might drive someone to extremes, but murder remained unjustifiable. "So you decided to take matters into your own hands?"

"I decided to stop pretending the system would ever work," Kendrick corrected. "When I discovered the gold in that stream three years ago, I saw an opportunity to do something meaningful—to preserve one small piece of wilderness by controlling access to its resources."

"By killing people who discovered it," Steele stated flatly.

For the first time, Kendrick's composure cracked slightly. "By preventing the destruction that would inevitably follow academic documentation. You didn't know Marcus Chen, but I researched his background after he started showing interest in the area. His graduate advisor had consulting contracts with three major mining corporations. His research wasn't purely academic—it was resource reconnaissance."

Emma leaned forward. "That's a serious accusation. Do you have evidence?"

Kendrick smiled coldly. "Dr. Elaine Winters received consulting fees totaling $47,000 last year from Yukon Mining Consortium, Northern Resources Inc., and Alaska Mineral Development Corporation. Chen's research into alluvial gold deposits was funded by a grant that traced back to industry sources."

The specificity of his information was unsettling. Emma made a mental note to verify these claims, though she suspected Kendrick's research would prove accurate.

"Even if that's true," she said, "Chen was a graduate student. He wasn't making policy decisions about mining permits."

"He was the advance scout," Kendrick replied with conviction. "Academic studies that identify valuable resources invariably lead to corporate exploitation. I've seen it happen countless times. Chen's research would have put the stream location on the public record, making it available to any mining company with the resources to file claims."

Steele interjected, "So you decided to eliminate him rather than trust the legal system to protect the area."

"I decided to prevent irreversible damage to a pristine ecosystem," Kendrick corrected. "That stream supports wildlife corridors that have existed for millennia. The gold deposits create unique mineral conditions that support rare plant species found nowhere else in Alaska. Commercial mining would destroy all of that for short-term profit."

Emma studied his face, seeing genuine passion beneath the rationalization. "What about Dr. Peterson? He was a local geologist, not a corporate agent."

Kendrick's expression darkened. "Peterson was already making contact with commercial mining consultants. I intercepted communications between him and Northern Resources Inc. He was providing detailed analysis of Chen's samples, preparing the groundwork for a formal mining claim."

"Intercepted how?" Steele asked.

"Peterson used the same internet café in Talkeetna where I monitored local communications. Simple keystroke logging software revealed his correspondence." Kendrick spoke as if discussing routine surveillance rather than invasion of privacy.

The methodical nature of his approach was chilling. This wasn't impulsive violence but calculated elimination based on systematic intelligence gathering.

"You established yourself as the sole judge of who posed a threat to the area," Emma observed.

"I accepted the responsibility that the government had abdicated," Kendrick replied without shame. "Someone had to protect that watershed from exploitation. The Forest Service wouldn't do it. The EPA couldn't do it. Congress certainly wouldn't do it. So I did."

Steele exchanged a glance with Emma, both recognizing the complete moral framework Kendrick had constructed to justify murder. In his mind, he wasn't a killer, he was a guardian of the wilderness, protecting nature from human greed.

"Tell us about the Alliance," Emma said, shifting focus. "How did Barrett become involved?"

Kendrick's demeanor changed slightly, a hint of disdain entering his voice. "James approached me two years ago, claimed he wanted to establish a sustainable community in the area. I thought he might be a genuine ally in conservation efforts."

"But that changed?"

"Barrett's vision of sustainability included controlled resource extraction for community benefit," Kendrick explained. "He saw the gold as funding for his social experiment. I saw it as a resource that needed protection from any human exploitation."

Emma realized the philosophical split that had driven the recent tensions. "You wanted to preserve the stream completely. Barrett wanted to exploit it carefully."

"Barrett wanted to become another type of colonizer," Kendrick said bitterly. "More sophisticated than corporate mining companies, but ultimately serving the same destructive impulse to extract wealth from the natural world."

Steele leaned back in his chair, processing the complex dynamics. "So you maintained your association with the Alliance while planning to eliminate anyone who threatened the stream's secrecy?"

"I used their security infrastructure while pursuing my own conservation objectives," Kendrick confirmed. "Most Alliance members genuinely believe in sustainable living. Barrett's corruption hadn't infected the entire community."

Emma felt a chill at his casual reference to corruption and infection, the language of someone who saw human contact with nature as inherently destructive.

"What was your long-term plan?" she asked. "You couldn't kill everyone who might discover the gold."

Kendrick's eyes took on a distant quality. "I was developing a permanent solution. Legal mechanisms to have the area designated as protected habitat, using my documentation of its unique ecological features. The murders were... temporary measures while I established proper protections."

The clinical way he discussed the killings was perhaps most disturbing of all. Chen and Peterson had been obstacles to be removed, not human beings with lives and families.

"You documented their deaths in your journal like scientific observations," Emma noted.

"I documented the successful protection of a critical ecosystem," Kendrick corrected. "The deaths were regrettable but necessary consequences of my conservation mission."

Steele had heard enough. "Walter Kendrick, you're being charged with two counts of first-degree murder, conspiracy to commit fraud, illegal mining on federal land, and multiple environmental crimes. Do you understand these charges?"

Kendrick nodded calmly. "I understand that you're prosecuting me for protecting one of Alaska's last pristine watersheds from industrial destruction. History will judge whether my actions served a higher purpose than your laws."

As the interview concluded and Kendrick was led back to his cell, Emma and Steele sat in the now-empty room, processing what they'd heard.

"He genuinely believes he's a hero," Emma said finally. "In his mind, murder was environmental activism."

"Thirty years of regulatory failures created a zealot," Steele agreed. "Someone who lost faith in legal protections and appointed himself guardian of the wilderness."

Emma gathered her notes, troubled by the interview's implications. "The worst part is, some of his concerns about the stream's ecological value might be legitimate. If the area really does support unique species..."

"Then it should be protected through proper legal channels," Steele finished. "Not by murdering people who discover it."

As they prepared to leave, Emma found herself thinking about the complexity of environmental protection in a state where economic interests often trumped conservation concerns. Kendrick's methods were monstrous, but his passion for preserving Alaska's wilderness came from a place of genuine love for the land.

"Crawford wants a full debrief in an hour," Steele said, checking his watch. "Then we can finally head back to Anchorage."

Emma nodded, surprised by how much she was looking forward to returning to the city. The case had been exhausting, not just physically but emotionally. The revelation of Kendrick's environmental zealotry had added layers of moral complexity she hadn't expected.

As they walked toward the conference room, Emma felt Steele's hand briefly brush against hers, a subtle gesture of connection after the intensity of their confrontation with Kendrick.

"Good work in there," he said quietly. "Your questions revealed the depth of his rationalization system."

"Your analysis of his psychological profile was accurate," she replied. "He did want us to understand his motivations."

They paused outside the conference room, neither quite ready to return to the bureaucratic aftermath of the investigation.

"Emma," Steele said, his formal tone softening slightly. "When this case officially closes, I'd like to discuss... our partnership."

Emma felt her heart rate increase despite her attempt to maintain professional composure. "Professional partnership?"

"Among other possibilities," Steele replied, his eyes holding hers with an intensity that had nothing to do with the case.

Before Emma could respond, Crawford emerged from the conference room, ready to begin the debrief. But as they settled into their seats to document the successful conclusion of their investigation, both knew that something significant had changed between them, something that extended far beyond professional collaboration.

The truth had emerged from the wilderness of Talkeetna, bringing justice for two murdered men and exposing the complex motivations of their killer. But for Emma Stone and Jeremiah Steele, another truth was just beginning to surface, the recognition that their partnership had evolved into something neither had sought but both now found invaluable.

Walter Kendrick would face trial for his crimes, his environmental passion no defense against the charges of murder. James Barrett and the Alliance leadership would answer for their conspiracy. The golden stream would be properly protected through legal means rather than violence.

And two federal agents who had started as reluctant partners had discovered that some connections transcend professional necessity, creating bonds strong enough to survive even the darkest secrets hidden in Alaska's vast wilderness.

❋ ❋ ❋

While Emma and Steele pursued their investigation in Talkeetna, Randall Bauer's vision for The Blue Note manifested with remarkable speed, and with the kind of financial backing that raised questions among those who knew how to ask them.

Detective Ray Mitchell stood in the shadows across from the old Mariner Building at Ship Creek, watching construction crews work through the night under portable floodlights. The building that had been an abandoned warehouse just six weeks ago was now Anchorage's most sophisticated jazz venue, complete with upscale office spaces on the upper floors that would serve as fronts for Randall's various shell companies.

Mitchell's encrypted phone buzzed with a text from Agent Kahn. *Document everything. Night construction suggests they're rushing to launder funds before federal scrutiny increases.*

The speed of the transformation was indeed suspicious. Floor-to-ceiling windows had been installed to showcase the waterfront view, with the mountains rising beyond like a picture postcard designed to impress investors and auditors alike. The expansive space featured tiered seating centered around a proper stage illuminated by professional lighting that cost more than most people's annual salaries. The bar, triple the size of the original, curved elegantly along one wall with top-shelf spirits displayed against backlit glass, each bottle carefully selected and priced to justify the large cash transactions that would soon flow through the register.

Most importantly, the gleaming Steinway grand piano commanded center stage, positioned to make its player the focal point of the entire room. Mitchell knew that particular piano had cost $180,000, a sum that appeared on Randall's books as "acoustic consultation fees" but served a darker purpose as a way to move money through the renovation budget.

Bernie Holloway stood at the entrance, surveying the space that bore only the name of his original club. Everything else had been reimagined on a scale he had never dared to envision, and Mitchell could see the older man's discomfort even from across the street. Bernie had no idea he was now the unwitting front man for a sophisticated money laundering operation.

"The acoustics are perfect," Randall said, appearing beside Bernie with architectural plans tucked under his arm. "We used the same consultant who designed the Seattle Symphony Hall."

Mitchell adjusted his surveillance equipment, making sure to capture both men's voices clearly. The FBI needed documentation of every conversation, every decision that showed Randall's control over the operation.

"It's not even the same place," Bernie murmured, both awestruck and unsettled. "No one will recognize it."

"That's the point. Evolution, Bernie." Randall gestured toward the stage where three musicians were setting up equipment, the house band he'd hand-selected from the Pacific Northwest jazz scene at salaries that seemed generous until you realized they were being paid with laundered funds. "The best talent deserves the best showcase. Speaking of which, any word from Detective Stone?"

Mitchell's blood chilled at the mention of Emma's name. Through his earpiece, he could hear the possessive undertone in Randall's voice, the way he said "Detective Stone" like he owned her.

Bernie shook his head. "Still out of town on that case. She doesn't even know we've moved, let alone..." he waved his hand to encompass the dramatic transformation.

"She'll appreciate quality," Randall said with absolute confidence. "I've arranged press coverage for the grand opening next week. The feature will run in Alaska Beyond magazine as well, reaching potential customers throughout the state."

Mitchell made a mental note to alert Agent Kahn about the press coverage. Media attention would provide perfect cover for the large crowds and cash transactions that would help legitimize Randall's money laundering operation.

What had started as a renovation had morphed into a complete reinvention, and Mitchell had watched every stage of it unfold. The modest loan Bernie had initially discussed had expanded into a complex web of financial instruments that made Randall a "silent partner" with controlling interest in the business. The details were buried in paperwork that Bernie had signed without scrutinizing closely enough, documents that Mitchell had photographed and forwarded to the FBI's financial crimes unit.

The construction costs alone told the story of the scheme's scope. Official invoices showed $2.3 million in renovations, but Mitchell's investigation had revealed the real number was closer to $800,000. The extra $1.5 million existed only on paper, creating a clean pathway for dirty money to enter the legitimate financial system.

"We should consider renaming it," Randall suggested, studying the elegant blue neon sign that preserved the original name. "Something that reflects its elevation. 'Blue Note Waterfront,' perhaps. Or 'Bauer & Holloway's.'"

Mitchell tensed. Putting Randall's name on the business would make the money laundering connection even more obvious, but it would also feed his ego and desire for control.

"The name stays," Bernie said firmly, one of the few stands he still felt empowered to take. "Emma knows The Blue Note. That doesn't change."

Randall smiled indulgently, and Mitchell could see the calculation behind his eyes. "Of course. Maintaining certain... touchpoints will ease the transition." He checked his watch, a Patek Philippe that cost more than Bernie's original annual lease, and which Mitchell knew had been purchased with funds from a shell company tied to this very project. "The sound engineers need another hour. Shall we discuss the hiring of additional staff? I've selected several candidates with experience in upscale establishments."

As they walked toward what was now Bernie's "office", a space that Bernie increasingly felt was merely on loan to him, Mitchell continued his surveillance. The office would serve multiple purposes: a legitimate workspace for Bernie, a meeting place for Randall's various business associates, and a convenient location for the kind of cash transactions that the FBI was working so hard to document.

From his position across the street, Mitchell could see Bernie's growing unease. The old man couldn't shake the feeling that he'd made a deal with a force he didn't fully understand. The Blue Note had been his life's work, modest but authentic. This gleaming showcase at Ship Creek, while undeniably impressive, felt more like Randall Bauer's elaborate lure than Bernie's dream realized.

But the contracts were signed, the renovations complete, and the grand opening just days away. Mitchell knew that Bernie had no idea how those contracts implicated him in a federal money laundering investigation, or how his signature made him legally responsible for funds that originated from sources that would horrify him.

Mitchell's phone buzzed with another encrypted message from Agent Kahn.

Opening night is when they'll move the most money. We need you in position to document everything.

As Mitchell prepared to respond, he thought about Emma Stone, somewhere in Talkeetna pursuing a murder investigation while completely unaware that her musical sanctuary had been transformed into the centerpiece of a federal financial crimes case. When she returned, she would find her refuge rebuilt with dirty money, operated by a man who'd unknowingly become a criminal accomplice, all orchestrated by someone whose obsession with her had driven him to increasingly reckless behavior.

The irony wasn't lost on Mitchell. In trying to impress Emma, Randall was creating exactly the kind of evidence trail that would ultimately destroy him. His obsession was making him sloppy, and the FBI was ready to capitalize on every mistake.

Whatever Emma Stone would think when she returned to find her sanctuary transformed and relocated, that was a reckoning yet to come. But Mitchell knew that reckoning would involve much more than hurt feelings about a relocated jazz club. It would involve federal agents, handcuffs, and the kind of betrayal that would shatter Emma's faith in the people around her.

The only question was whether Mitchell could help the FBI build their case fast enough to protect Emma from the fallout when Randall's world inevitably collapsed around him

CHAPTER 25:
Escape

The transport van's interior reeked of industrial disinfectant and stale coffee, a familiar cocktail of law enforcement efficiency that Walter Kendrick had grown to despise over the past week. Shackled in the rear compartment, he studied his captors with the same methodical attention he'd once applied to forest surveys and mining assessments.

Deputy Marshal Tom Reeves sat in the passenger seat, occasionally glancing back through the steel mesh partition with the bored vigilance of someone who'd transported hundreds of prisoners without incident. Behind the wheel, Transport Officer Janet Mills maintained steady focus on the rain-slicked highway, her hands positioned precisely at ten and two despite the deteriorating weather conditions.

Predictable, Walter thought, testing the range of motion his restraints allowed. Complacent.

Both officers wore standard-issue tactical vests over their uniforms, service weapons secured in retention holsters, radios clipped to their shoulders. Protocol dictated they check in with dispatch every thirty minutes during prisoner transport, maintain visual contact with their charge, and follow predetermined routes that avoided remote areas where assistance might be delayed.

Walter had spent forty years learning to read human patterns, first as a mining engineer calculating crew efficiency, then as a Forest Service ranger observing tourist behavior in wilderness settings.

These officers operated within systems designed by people who'd never faced a desperate man with specialized knowledge and nothing left to lose.

The modified paper clip he'd concealed in the seam of his boot had taken three days to perfect. Straightened, sharpened against his cell's concrete floor, then carefully bent into a tension wrench and pick combination that would defeat standard restraint locks. The technique was crude but effective, a skill learned during his early mining days when broken equipment locks couldn't stop necessary work.

Timing is everything, he reminded himself, watching the landscape roll past through rain-streaked windows. They were approaching the most isolated section of the route, a twenty-mile stretch between Talkeetna and Anchorage where cell coverage was spotty and backup response times measured in tens of minutes rather than seconds.

The storm that had been brewing for days was finally arriving with the violence Alaskan weather systems were famous for. Wind gusts rocked the van periodically, and Mills had to fight the steering wheel to maintain their lane position. Perfect conditions for confusion and delay, assuming Walter could create the opportunity he needed.

He'd been practicing the lock manipulation during their journey, using micro-movements that appeared to be normal shifting in his seat. The modified paper clip was positioned correctly, the restraint mechanism partially disengaged. One quick twist and his hands would be free.

Not yet, he cautioned himself. Wait for the moment when their attention is completely focused elsewhere.

As if summoned by his patience, that moment arrived in the form of a massive pine tree that chose that instant to surrender to the storm's assault. The sixty-foot giant crashed across the highway directly ahead of them, its massive trunk completely blocking both lanes while its crown disappeared into the forest on the opposite side.

Mills hit the brakes instinctively, the van's anti-lock system engaging with a rapid chattering sound as they skidded to a stop thirty feet from the barrier. Both officers stared at the obstruction in stunned silence for several seconds.

"Just our luck," Reeves muttered, reaching for his radio. "Dispatch, this is Transport Unit Seven. We've got a complete highway blockage at mile marker forty-two. Gonna need DOT and probably a crane to clear this mess."

While Reeves coordinated with dispatch and Mills assessed potential alternate routes on her GPS unit, Walter executed the lock release with practiced precision. The restraints opened with barely audible clicks, though he kept his hands positioned as if still secured.

"How long for alternate routing?" Reeves was asking Mills.

"Minimum two hours to backtrack and take the mountain route," she replied, studying the small screen. "More if this storm keeps getting worse."

"Negative on extended delay," came the response from dispatch. "Prisoner needs to be processed by 1800 hours for federal transfer. Maintain schedule using best available route."

Walter listened to their discussion while calculating his own options. The storm was intensifying, visibility dropping as sheets of rain swept across the windshield. Both officers were focused on navigation problems, their situational awareness degraded by weather stress and route planning.

Now.

Walter's hands slipped free of the restraints completely, though he maintained the appearance of being secured. The van's interior configuration gave him limited options, the partition between prisoner compartment and driver area was solid steel mesh with no gaps large enough for physical access. But the vehicle's electrical systems ran along the walls within reach of someone who knew what to look for.

His years maintaining Forest Service equipment had included extensive electrical troubleshooting. Every government vehicle was built to similar specifications, with predictable wire routing and standard component placement. The dome light fixture above his head contained not just illumination but junction points for multiple circuits.

Working with the careful precision of someone whose life depended on stealth, Walter began disconnecting specific wires inside the light housing. Not a crude sabotage that would trigger immediate alarms, but a selective disruption that would create exactly the confusion he needed.

"Dispatch is getting antsy about our schedule," Reeves was saying. "We need to make a decision here."

"There's a logging road about half a mile back," Mills replied. "Might connect to the old mining access routes. Could save us an hour if it's still passable."

As they debated alternatives, Walter completed his electrical modifications. A few precisely severed connections would disable the van's communication systems, interior lighting, and door locks while leaving the engine and basic driving systems functional. The officers would be able to drive but unable to call for help or prevent his escape.

Almost ready.

The final component was the timing device, a simple chemical reaction using cleaning supplies from the van's emergency kit mixed with aluminum fragments scraped from the light fixture. The combination would produce a dense, foul-smelling smoke after a predictable delay, creating panic and forcing the officers to evacuate the vehicle.

Walter had approximately ten minutes before the reaction triggered.

"Let's try the old road," Mills decided. "Worst case, we turn around and go back to the main highway."

As the van reversed toward the old road, Walter positioned himself for action. The moment the smoke began, both officers would exit the vehicle to investigate what they'd assume was an electrical fire. Standard protocol would keep them together initially, two officers never separated when dealing with vehicle emergencies while transporting prisoners.

That protocol would give him the window he needed.

The old road was rougher than Mills had anticipated, forcing her to reduce speed as the van bounced over permafrost bumps. The storm's intensity seemed to increase as they moved deeper into the forest, away from the main highway and any possibility of assistance.

Walter watched the seconds tick by on his mental countdown. Five minutes. Four. Three.

Any moment now.

The smoke began as a thin wisp near the dashboard, barely visible in the dim interior lighting. Within seconds, it had thickened into a choking cloud that filled the van's cabin with acrid chemical fumes.

"What the...?" Mills coughed, immediately pulling to the side of the narrow road.

"Electrical fire," Reeves confirmed, already unbuckling his seatbelt. "Get us stopped. Now."

Both officers exited the van simultaneously, leaving doors open as they moved to the front of the vehicle. Mills popped the hood while Reeves tried his radio, discovering that communications had mysteriously failed.

Walter heard their muffled conversation through the open doors—confusion about the electrical failure, debate about whether to abandon the vehicle, concerns about prisoner security during an emergency evacuation.

They would spend precious minutes trying to assess the situation, locate the source of the smoke, and establish communication with dispatch. By the time they realized their prisoner was missing, he would be deep in the forest where their urban training and equipment gave them no advantages.

Moving silently despite his urgency, Walter slipped from the van's rear compartment and melted into the forest. The storm that had created this opportunity now became his ally, the driving rain washing away tracks and the howling wind masking any sounds of movement.

Behind him, he heard Reeves shouting, "Check the prisoner!"

But Walter Kendrick was already gone, swallowed by Alaska's vast wilderness where he'd spent four decades learning every trick of survival. The storm that threatened everyone else was simply weather to him, dangerous but manageable for someone who understood the land's moods and possibilities.

The hunt would continue, but now the predator had become prey. And in this environment, Walter held every advantage except time.

The conference room at Alaska State Troopers headquarters buzzed with urgent energy as officers and federal agents filed in, shaking rain from their uniforms. The wall-mounted weather display painted a grim picture: a massive low-pressure system churning across the Gulf of Alaska, its spiral arms reaching inland like skeletal fingers. What forecasters had dismissed as a minor April shower had morphed into something far more sinister.

"Alright, people, listen up." Trooper Holden's voice cut through the chatter. "We've got a Category 3 situation on our hands, and on top of that, Walter Kendrick is once again a fugitive. He somehow managed to escape during his transport to Anchorage."

A collective murmur rippled through the room. Agent Steele leaned forward, his coffee mug forgotten on the table. Emma Stone stood against the back wall, her arms crossed, eyes narrowing as she processed the information.

"Details on the escape?" Steele asked, his voice steady despite the growing dread in his gut.

"Transport van was found abandoned fifty-two miles outside Anchorage. Driver and guard both down, tranquilized, but alive. Blood smears on the interior door panel suggest Walter broke out using some kind of hidden tool. We're analyzing the van now." Holden clicked through crime scene photos on the overhead screen. "He's been gone approximately two hours."

"Two hours in this storm?" Emma's voice carried a note of disbelief. "That's a death sentence."

"Maybe for someone else," Steele countered, studying the weather radar. "But Walter's resourceful. He's survived worse conditions during his Forest Service career. The question is, what's his play without his usual support network?"

The room fell silent as the reality sank in. Walter's entire operational methodology relied on preparation and deep understanding of the land. Stripped of his backup hideouts and equipment caches, he was now fighting for survival against Alaska's merciless wilderness.

"Current conditions," Holden continued, "show sixty-mile-per-hour sustained winds, gusts up to eighty. Visibility down to a quarter-mile. Temperature dropping to thirty-two degrees with wind chill factor. This isn't your typical April weather system, NOAA's calling it unprecedented."

Steele stood and approached the topographical map spread across the conference table. His finger traced possible routes Walter might take from the escape point. "He'll need shelter. Fast. The nearest populated areas are too far given these conditions."

"There are abandoned mining settlements throughout this region," offered Trooper Holden. "Most are forgotten, unmapped. Perfect hiding spots."

"Walter would know about them," Emma interjected. "He researched everything about this state during his planning phase. That knowledge could save his life now."

Steele's mind worked rapidly, calculating distances, factoring weather patterns against human endurance. "He's got a maximum two-hour window before hypothermia becomes a real threat. If he's smart, and we know he is, he's already found or is heading toward a specific shelter."

"Agent Steele," Crawford interrupted, "what's your recommendation?"

The room waited. Outside, rain lashed the windows with increasing violence, the building groaning under nature's assault. Steele felt Emma's gaze boring into him from across the room.

"We mount an immediate search and pursuit operation," Steele declared. "Every minute we delay gives Walter more advantage. In this storm, he's operating on desperation and survival instinct, that makes him more dangerous than any of his previous schemes."

"Steele," Holden spoke up hesitantly, "regulations state we ground all aircraft in these conditions. Road visibility is next to zero. It's suicide to..."

"The regulations were written for normal circumstances," Steele cut in sharply. "This situation is anything but normal. Walter is desperate and dangerous. It could be fatal if he reaches innocent people seeking shelter in the wilderness. We cannot let him slip away."

Emma pushed off the wall, her boots clicking against the linoleum as she approached the map. "I'm coming with you."

"No." Steele's response was immediate and nonnegotiable.

"Excuse me?" Her eyes flashed with an unfamiliar fire he hadn't seen during their partnership.

"Detective Stone has proven invaluable in this investigation," Steele addressed the room while holding Emma's challenging stare. "Which is precisely why I need her here, coordinating search efforts from headquarters. If my theory about where Walter might be headed proves wrong, we'll need a comprehensive grid search. No one knows this case file better than Stone."

"That's nonsense, and you know it," Emma shot back. "You're going out there alone into that hurricane because you think you have some personal score to settle with Walter."

"This isn't personal," Steele lied smoothly. "It's tactical. Walter's alone and without his usual resources. I'll be alone. Equal footing. No distractions, no backup to worry about getting caught in crossfire."

"Agent Steele raises a valid point," Crawford interjected carefully. "Detective Stone's coordination skills would be invaluable for the broader search operation."

Emma's jaw tightened, but before she could argue further, the lights flickered ominously. A crack of thunder rattled through the building's foundation.

"The storm's intensifying," noted one of the local guides who had stepped in to help. "Latest readings show pressure dropping faster than predicted. We could be looking at a historic weather event."

Steele gathered gear methodically: tactical vest, encrypted radio, specialized GPS unit, emergency supplies. "I need topographical surveys of all mining sites within a hundred-mile radius of the escape point. Focus on locations with creek access, Walter has an obsession with water sources."

"Agent Steele," Emma's voice carried a warning note as she followed him to the equipment room. "If you're wrong about this lone wolf strategy, if Walter manages to…"

"He won't." Steele checked his sidearm, secured extra ammunition. "I've profiled killers for fifteen years, Emma. Walter's brilliant, but he's also predictable in crisis situations. He'll seek familiar patterns: secure shelter, water access, high ground for observation. The mines tick all those boxes."

"And if you get caught in the storm? If you can't find him before hypothermia sets in?"

He paused at the door, meeting her eyes directly. In them, he saw concern warring with frustration, professional respect battling personal connection. "Then you'll have a comprehensive search plan ready to deploy at first light. That's why I'm counting on you here."

"Jeremiah," she whispered fiercely. "Don't you dare die on me trying to prove something."

"I'm not trying to prove anything," he replied softly. Then, louder for the others: "Maintain radio contact on channel five. If I haven't checked in within six hours, initiate full recovery protocols."

The conference room had transformed into a command center, with officers spreading maps, establishing communication lines, preparing emergency response teams. Steele felt the weight of their collective gaze as he headed for the exit.

"Agent Steele." Crawford's voice stopped him. "Whether regulations approve or not, you're our best shot at recovering Walter before he disappears completely. Bring him back."

"Preferably alive," Emma added pointedly.

Outside, the storm raged with primordial fury. Rain sheeted across the parking lot like horizontal curtains. Wind howled between buildings, carrying debris that clattered against walls and vehicles. The FBI SUV sat isolated in the maelstrom, a small island of metal and glass against nature's assault.

Steele climbed in, instantly soaked despite the brief exposure. The engine roared to life, headlights cutting weak swaths through the downpour. As he pulled onto the road, his radio crackled.

"Steele?" Emma's voice, distorted by static and rain.

"I'm here."

"I've plotted seventeen possible mine locations based on Walter's research patterns. Sending coordinates to your GPS now. The closest cluster is the Caribou Creek complex, thirty-eight miles northeast."

"Copy that." He accelerated carefully, feeling the tires fight for grip on the flooded asphalt.

"Steele?" A pause. "Be careful out there."

"Always am, Detective."

The lie tasted bitter. There was nothing careful about driving into a hurricane to hunt a desperate fugitive. But as Steele pushed into the storm's heart, he felt oddly calm. This was what he'd trained for: pursuit under impossible conditions, decisions made at the knife's edge of life and death.

Twenty minutes into the drive, visibility dropped to mere feet. The wipers struggled futilely against the deluge. Lightning illuminated snapshots of chaos: trees bending at impossible angles, power lines whipping like snakes, debris transformed into deadly projectiles.

At a mile marker just outside of Talkeetna, a birch blocked the highway, possibly the same tree that had enabled Walter's escape. Steele braked hard, hydroplaning slightly before the tires gripped. He sat for a moment, watching rain batter his windshield, feeling the SUV rock with each gust.

This was Walter's reality now: no GPS, no weather apps, no satellite communications. Just human instinct against Alaska's raw power. The irony wasn't lost on Steele. For all Walter's technological sophistication during his crimes, their final confrontation would be decided by primitive elements: shelter, survival, and the will to endure.

He reversed, seeking an alternate route. The storm seemed to intensify with each passing minute, as if nature itself had chosen sides in this lethal game of cat and mouse. Lightning struck close, the flash burning afterimages into Steele's vision. Thunder followed immediately, a sound like artillery fire echoing through the air.

Two miles past the downed tree, his phone lost signal completely. The GPS flickered, struggled, then died. Even technology designed for harsh conditions couldn't cope with this anomalous weather system.

Perfect. Now he truly was alone, stripped of modern advantages just like Walter. The playing field had been leveled by forces neither man could control.

Steele continued deeper into the storm, navigating by dead reckoning and occasional lightning flashes. The Caribou Creek mines lay somewhere ahead, promising shelter to whoever reached them first. In his rearview mirror, the lights of Talkeetna disappeared into the churning darkness.

Behind him, in the State Troopers headquarters, he imagined Emma coordinating the massive search grid, her keen mind working through contingencies, preparing for outcomes both hopeful and dire. She would be furious at his unilateral decision, but she would execute the plan flawlessly. That's who she was, professional to her core, even when personal feelings complicated matters.

A pine branch exploded across the hood, leaving deep scratches in the paint. Steele swerved automatically, nearly sliding off the road. His heart hammered with sudden adrenaline. One mistake out here could be fatal.

The mountains loomed ahead, barely visible through sheets of rain. Somewhere in those ancient peaks, Walter Kendrick fought for survival. For all his crimes, for all the lives disrupted by his schemes, he now faced the ultimate equalizer: nature's indiscriminate fury.

Steele pressed onward, hunter and hunted locked in a deadly dance with the storm. Whatever happened next, whatever price either man would pay for this night's decisions, it would be decided without the civilized safety nets of backup, medical support, or easy extraction.

Just two men, Alaska's wilderness, and a raging tempest that recognized no human authority.

The ghost mines of Caribou Creek waited patiently in the darkness, aged witnesses to this modern drama of pursuit and escape. Somewhere in that desolate landscape, Walter Kendrick was making his final stand against both the elements and the justice that had finally caught up with him.

The storm would determine which force proved stronger.

CHAPTER 26:
Irony

The rain pounded relentlessly as Steele navigated the muddy trail toward Caribou Creek. His boots struggled for purchase on the slope slick with runoff and decomposing pine needles. The storm had stripped away the forest's natural stability, transforming familiar hiking paths into treacherous slides of mud and loose rock. No more thunder shook the sky, no lightning illuminated his path, just the steady, monotonous deluge that had turned the landscape into a death trap.

Fresh boot prints led down the steep embankment, already half-dissolved by the relentless precipitation but still visible to Steele's trained eye. Walter Kendrick had passed this way recently, perhaps within the last thirty minutes. The prints were deep, suggesting haste rather than the careful placement someone would use if they were thinking clearly. The direction was unmistakable: toward the cluster of abandoned mining structures that dotted this remote valley.

Steele descended carefully, each step threatening to send him sliding into the churning creek below. The rain had swollen the normally placid stream into an angry torrent of brown water carrying debris from miles upstream, fallen branches, chunks of eroded bank, and the detritus of a forest under assault. Through the gray veil of precipitation, he spotted movement ahead near the largest of the old cabins.

But Walter Kendrick hadn't stopped at the shelter. Through his binoculars, Steele watched the figure continuing up the mountainside, ignoring the only viable refuge for miles. The fugitive was climbing toward even more exposed terrain, away from any possibility of warmth or protection.

He's panicking, Steele realized with a mixture of professional satisfaction and human concern. All his careful planning has been reduced to animal flight instinct.

"Kendrick!" Steele called out, his voice barely carrying over the sound of wind and rain. "It's over! This is suicide! The cabin's your only chance!"

The figure ahead paused for a moment, then continued climbing with what appeared to be desperate energy. Clearly, rational thought had been overridden by pure survival panic. The man who had orchestrated sophisticated murders through careful manipulation was now running scared, his intellectual superiority no match for the primal terror of pursuit.

Steele pushed himself harder, closing the distance meter by muddy meter. Each breath came harder at the increasing altitude, his lungs working against the thin air and physical exhaustion accumulated over hours of pursuit. But his federal training sustained him, cardiovascular conditioning, mental discipline, and the knowledge that stopping meant losing his quarry forever.

The trail wound through stands of spruce and birch, their branches heavy with accumulated moisture that showered Steele with additional water each time the wind gusted. His tactical gear, designed for durability rather than comfort, had reached its limits hours ago. Water had found every seam, every gap, turning his clothing into a cold, clinging second skin that sapped body heat with each step.

At the riverbank, where the trail crossed a narrow ford that had probably been manageable before the storm, Steele finally caught up. Walter stood knee-deep in the rushing water, clearly weighing whether to risk the crossing. The normally shallow creek had become a torrent at least four feet deep in the center, moving with enough force to sweep a man downstream in seconds.

At the sound of Steele's approach, boots squelching in mud, equipment rattling, Walter spun around with wild eyes.

"Stay back!" Walter's voice cracked with exhaustion and something approaching hysteria. Water dripped from his gray hair, his expensive outdoor gear now plastered with mud and rendered useless by the conditions. No trace remained of the confident forest ranger who had orchestrated murders with cold precision just days earlier. This was a man stripped of all advantages, reduced to his most basic survival instincts.

"You can't cross that, Walter. Look at the current, it's suicide. Come back to the cabin. We can work this out."

"Work this out?" Walter let out a bitter laugh that bordered on hysteria. "You want to put me in a cage for the rest of my life. After everything I've built, everything I've accomplished for the preservation of this wilderness. You want to reduce me to a prisoner number."

Steele took a careful step closer, testing the water's edge while keeping his hands visible and non-threatening. "What you've built is a foundation of corpses, Walter. You've killed two innocent people…"

"Innocent?" Walter's interruption was sharp, his voice rising despite the danger of their position. "I eliminated obstacles to environmental protection. I moved pieces on the chessboard to preserve something far more valuable than individual human lives. You do the same thing, Agent Steele, you just do it with government approval and legal justification."

"I don't murder civilians, Walter. I don't crack people's skulls with rocks and leave them to die in the wilderness."

"Civilians?" Walter scoffed, taking another step deeper into the torrent. The water now reached his waist, the current pulling at him with visible force. "No one is innocent in the struggle to preserve our planet's last wild places. There are only those who understand the stakes and those who serve corporate interests. You just haven't accepted that truth yet."

Steele could see Walter's legs trembling with the effort of maintaining balance against the rushing water. Hypothermia was clearly setting in, his speech was becoming slurred, his movements less coordinated. If he went much deeper, the current would claim him whether he chose it or not.

"The truth is that you're done, Walter. Your operation is finished. Barrett's talking, your records have been seized, and the entire Alliance leadership is in custody. Turn yourself in now, and you might live to see trial."

"Never." Walter pushed deeper into the river with desperate determination. The water rose above his belt, and Steele could see him fighting to maintain footing on the submerged rocks. "I'll take my chances with nature's justice over your corrupted legal system any day."

"Don't be stupid!" Steele moved forward to the very edge of the bank, close enough now that he could see the exhaustion and desperation in Walter's pale blue eyes. "Your paranoia and environmental fanaticism got you here. Don't let them kill you too."

"Fanaticism?" Walter's eyes blazed with the fervor that had driven his crimes. "Vision, Agent Steele. I had vision while you just followed bureaucratic orders. I created new realities to protect irreplaceable wilderness while you clung to laws written by politicians who serve mining corporations."

"Your realities killed innocent people, a graduate student and a local geologist who were just doing their jobs!"

"Their jobs threatened the last pristine watershed in this region!" Walter pushed even deeper into the torrent, his voice rising to match the river's roar. "Chen's research would have brought commercial mining operations. Peterson was already making contact with extraction companies. I saved thousands of acres of wilderness from destruction caused by industries!"

The water reached Walter's chest now, and Steele could see him struggling against the current with increasingly desperate movements. His face showed the grayish pallor of advancing hypothermia, and his words were beginning to slur.

"The world I'm protecting has no room for those who would destroy it for profit," Walter continued, his voice taking on the rambling quality of someone whose cognitive function was being impaired by cold and exhaustion. "I won't let them turn this place into another poisoned wasteland…"

His foot slipped on the submerged rocks.

Steele watched in horrified fascination as Walter's arms windmilled frantically, fighting to regain footing, but the current seized him with implacable force. In what seemed like slow motion, Walter went under, his head disappearing beneath the brown water. He resurfaced twenty feet downstream, gasping and flailing, then disappeared again as the river swept him toward a jumble of boulders and fallen trees.

Without conscious thought, Steele raced along the riverbank, his boots slipping on the muddy rocks, each step a battle against the steep terrain beside the torrent. Fifty yards ahead, Walter's body tumbled between boulders like a broken doll, arms and legs striking the rocks with sickening impacts.

There, Steele spotted a potential stopping point, a massive fallen tree trunk that had wedged between two boulders, creating a temporary dam across a narrow section of the creek. If Walter hit it, he might have a chance. If he missed it or went under it, the next obstacle was a quarter-mile downstream over increasingly violent rapids.

Walter slammed into the tree trunk with devastating force, his body making a sound like a sack of grain being dropped. But worse was the wet crack that followed as his head struck a protruding branch with the kind of impact that Steele had seen too many times in his career, the sound of bone giving way under blunt force trauma.

Steele reached the unconscious form within seconds, sliding down the muddy bank and into the icy water without regard for his own safety. Blood mixed with river water around Walter's head, painting crimson swirls that dissipated instantly in the current. The protruding branch had opened a gash across Walter's temple and above his left ear, a wound that looked disturbingly familiar.

The same injury pattern he inflicted on Chen and Peterson, Steele realized with grim irony. Blunt force trauma to the head, bleeding into the wilderness.

Poetic justice had a cruel sense of symmetry.

Checking for a pulse revealed shallow, erratic breathing. Walter was dying, but not dead yet. Blood continued to seep from multiple head wounds where his skull had struck the branch, and his skin had taken on the waxy pallor that indicated severe blood loss and shock.

Steele faced a choice that seemed to freeze time itself. Save the man who had orchestrated the murders of two innocent people? Or let the river finish what Walter's own desperation had started?

Every instinct cultivated through fifteen years of law enforcement screamed for justice. Walter Kendrick was a killer who had shown no mercy to his victims, who had left Chen and Peterson to die slowly in the wilderness after inflicting similar head trauma. He had demonstrated no remorse, no recognition that his crimes were anything other than necessary conservation measures.

But Steele's training won out over his desire for vengeance. Despite everything, despite the images of Chen's shattered skull and Peterson's broken body, he couldn't execute a man, even this one. Whatever Walter's crimes, whatever justice he deserved, it wouldn't come from Steele's decision to let him die.

With tremendous effort, Steele hauled Walter's deadweight to the bank, his muscles screaming with the strain. The fugitive's body was awkward and heavy with waterlogged clothing, dead weight that threatened to pull Steele back into the current. Each step up the muddy slope was a battle against exhaustion, hypothermia, and the knowledge that he might be saving a monster.

Getting Walter back to the cabin required every ounce of Steele's remaining strength. The return journey tested his limits as he half-carried, half-dragged the unconscious man over terrain that had become even more treacherous. Rain continued its assault, turning the trail into a soup of mud and pine needles that provided no stable footing.

By the time Steele dragged Walter through the cabin door, his lungs burned with each breath, and his limbs trembled with exhaustion that went beyond the physical. He had pursued a killer through hell itself, and now found himself trying to preserve the life of someone who had shown no such mercy to others.

The cabin offered basic shelter but no medical supplies beyond a rusty first aid kit that contained little more than bandages and antiseptic from decades past. Steele did what he could, applying pressure to the head wounds, checking vital signs, trying to stabilize Walter's position to prevent further injury.

His radio produced only static when he tried to call for medical evacuation. His phone displayed the dreaded "No Service" message that was all too familiar in Alaska's remote regions. He was truly isolated with a dying fugitive, hours from help even if the storm cleared enough for helicopter rescue.

Time became meaningless as Steele maintained pressure on Walter's wounds, monitoring his increasingly labored breathing, rationing his own remaining energy against the possibility that he might need to hike out for help. Walter never regained consciousness, his body occasionally convulsing as his brain struggled with the trauma it had sustained.

The irony was not lost on Steele as he watched Walter's life ebbing away. The man who had killed Chen and Peterson with calculated blows to the head, who had left them to die slowly in the wilderness, was now experiencing the same fate. The same trauma, the same gradual bleeding out, the same isolation from medical care that might have saved him.

Walter's breathing gradually weakened to rattling gasps that echoed in the small cabin, then stopped entirely at 4:47 AM according to Steele's watch.

Steele remained with the body as rain continued to drum against the cabin roof in endless rhythm. He had pursued Walter Kendrick through a hellish storm, and nature had delivered its own verdict. The man who had manipulated deaths from a position of calculated safety had died in precisely the same manner as his victims, skull broken by blunt trauma, bleeding out in Alaskan wilderness, alone except for someone who could only watch helplessly.

The symmetry was almost supernatural in its completeness.

Dawn crept through gray clouds, and with the weak morning light came renewed hope for communication. Steele stepped outside, scanning the sky for any break in the weather pattern. The storm had finally exhausted itself overnight, rain now reduced to a light drizzle that felt almost gentle after the night's assault.

His radio crackled to life with blessed static-filled voices.

"Agent Steele, this is base. Do you copy? Over."

"Steele here," he responded hoarsely, his voice rough from hours of cold and strain. "Target is down. Repeat, Walter Kendrick is dead. Need extraction at Caribou Creek mine cabin."

"Copy that. Team leader, we have contact!" Another voice broke through the static, Emma's, laden with emotion and relief. "Jeremiah. We thought… how are you? Are you injured?"

"Cold, tired, alive. Kendrick is deceased. Drowning followed by head trauma from impact with submerged obstacles. Same mechanism of injury as his victims."

A long pause filled with static and the sound of people conferring in the background. Then Emma's voice again: "Crawford's sending a helicopter. Storm's finally broken enough for aerial support. ETA forty minutes. Hold tight."

"Copy. Standing by."

Steele returned to the cabin where Walter's body appeared smaller in death, his grandiose plans and murderous environmental crusade reduced to cooling flesh on a rough wooden floor. The man who had appointed himself guardian of Alaska's wilderness had been claimed by the very forces he'd claimed to protect.

Outside, the sun made its first appearance in eighteen hours, turning raindrops into diamonds on pine needles and casting long shadows through the clearing around the cabin. The forest was beginning to reclaim its normal rhythms after the storm's chaos, birds calling tentatively from hidden perches, small animals emerging to assess the damage.

Exactly thirty-seven minutes later, the helicopter appeared like a mechanical angel threading between mountain peaks. Steele waved from the clearing, relief flooding his exhausted system as the aircraft descended in a whirlwind of rotor wash and flying debris.

Emma stood at the open door as the helicopter touched down, her dark hair whipping in the downdraft. Professional composure warred with visible relief on her face as she spotted Steele walking toward them under his own power. Behind her, Crawford maintained his usual stern expression, but Steele could see approval in the senior agent's eyes.

"Good work, Agent," Crawford said as Steele climbed aboard, accepting the thermal blanket and hot coffee that Emma pressed into his hands. "Though your methods remain questionable from a procedural standpoint."

"I understand, sir." Steele wrapped the blanket around his shoulders, feeling human warmth for the first time in hours. "But Kendrick won't kill again. The case is closed."

"No, he won't," Crawford agreed, studying the cabin below as the helicopter lifted off. "The cleanup crew will handle body recovery and scene documentation. You need medical attention and debriefing. But first, you need rest."

As the helicopter gained altitude, Emma sat beside Steele, close enough that their shoulders touched through the thermal blanket. She didn't speak while he drank coffee and processed the night's events, respecting his need for silence after the nightmare pursuit. But her presence anchored him to reality, a reminder that not everyone in his world dealt in death and violence.

Below them, Alaska's wilderness spread out in magnificent indifference, already beginning to reclaim its secrets. The mining cabin grew smaller until it disappeared entirely among the trees, hiding its newest ghost. Walter Kendrick's environmental empire had crumbled completely, his life ended by the same violence he'd wielded so carelessly against others.

"You scared me," Emma finally said softly, hours of fear and worry breaking through her professional facade. "When we lost radio contact, when the storm got worse... I thought we might lose you too."

"I scared myself more than once," Steele admitted, his voice still rough with exhaustion. "But it's over now. Walter Kendrick is dead, and he died exactly the way he killed Chen and Peterson. There's a certain justice in that."

Emma studied his face, reading the complex emotions there, relief, exhaustion, and something that might have been satisfaction at the cosmic justice of Walter's end. "How do you feel about that? About watching him die?"

Steele considered the question carefully, testing his own emotional response to the night's events. "I tried to save him," he said finally. "Despite everything he'd done, despite the fact that he showed no mercy to his victims, I couldn't let him die if I had the power to prevent it. But when he did die..." He paused, searching for the right words. "I felt like the universe had balanced its own scales."

The helicopter banked toward Anchorage, leaving the mountains' shadows behind. Steele closed his eyes, letting exhaustion claim him as they flew toward warmth, safety, and the complex process of justice that would follow. Walter Kendrick was dead, his victims could rest, and the survivors could begin to rebuild.

Some cases ended with arrests and trials, careful documentation and legal proceedings that stretched on for months. Others ended with rivers and rocks delivering a verdict beyond appeal, nature serving as both judge and executioner. Steele had witnessed both kinds of justice in his career, and had learned to accept that sometimes the universe delivered its own form of cosmic irony.

Walter Kendrick had died by the same mechanism he'd used to murder Chen and Peterson, blunt force trauma to the head, followed by slow bleeding in the wilderness. The symmetry was so complete it seemed almost supernatural, as if Alaska itself had demanded retribution for the blood spilled on its soil.

As the helicopter carried them home, Steele reflected on the strange justice of Walter's end. The man who had appointed himself guardian of the wilderness had been claimed by the very forces he'd claimed to protect. The killer who had shown no mercy had received none in return.

Sometimes, Steele thought as sleep finally claimed him, the universe had a better sense of justice than any human court could provide.

CHAPTER 27:

Wrap It in Jazz

The Alaska State Troopers' office in Talkeetna buzzed with the controlled chaos of case closure. Reports needed filing, witness statements required signatures, and evidence demanded proper chain-of-custody documentation. Emma Stone worked methodically through the paperwork, her pen scratching across forms while dawn light filtered through the blinds.

"You sure this mining claim's legitimate?" she asked Diana Hickok, who was personally overseeing the final details.

"Clean as they come," she replied, spreading geological survey maps across the conference table. "Michael Dawson filed proper permits six months ago. The mining operation is real enough. Gold deposits stretch deep into that mountain."

Steele entered the room, freshly showered and wearing clean clothes for the first time in three days. Dark circles under his eyes betrayed his exhaustion, but his posture remained military straight.

"The compound's secured," he reported. "Most of the group wants to continue as legitimate survivalists. They're signing cooperation agreements as we speak."

Emma looked up from her paperwork. "What about the few who were involved?"

"Handful heading to federal holding. Aiding and abetting charges mainly. Nothing that'll stick long without Kendrick's leadership."

"One week ago, I was wrestling with theft cases and DUIs," Emma mused, stacking completed forms. "Now international espionage and murder conspiracies feel almost normal."

"Welcome to the federal world," Steele smiled wryly. "Where normal means everything's suspicious."

Holden gathered the maps, his movements precise as always. "You two did exceptional work. The State Department will want full debriefs, but that can wait until you're back in Anchorage."

"Actually," Steele interjected, "I was thinking of extending my stay in Alaska. Consider this an unofficial vacation request."

Emma's pen paused mid-signature. She didn't look up, but Steele noticed the slight tension in her shoulders.

"The Blue Note still does live music on Friday nights, right?" he asked casually.

"Every week," she confirmed, her voice carefully neutral. "Though I don't play public gigs anymore."

"Maybe you should start again. I'd pay good money to hear you play."

Emma finally met his gaze. Something unreadable flickered in her dark eyes, surprise, pleasure, wariness perhaps. "I'll think about it."

The drive back to Anchorage stretched long and quiet. Steele focused on navigating the Glenn Highway while Emma gazed out the passenger window at the recovering landscape. The storm's fury had passed, leaving clear skies and mountains painted in fresh snow.

"You know," Emma finally broke the silence around mile marker 152, "most federal agents disappear after cases wrap. No goodbye, no forwarding address."

"I'm not most agents."

"No, you're not." She turned toward him. "Question is, what are you?"

"Someone who's tired of chasing ghosts. Maybe it's time to try something different."

"Like what? Playing tourist in Alaska?"

"Like figuring out who I am when I'm not hunting killers." Steele glanced at her briefly. "Maybe hearing some live jazz while I do it."

Emma's lips curved into a hint of smile, the first genuine expression he'd seen from her in days. "The Blue Note has terrible acoustics. Old building, low ceilings."

"I don't think I'd notice."

The conversation lapsed again, but comfortable this time. As Anchorage's skyline appeared on the horizon, neither spoke of what came next. Some possibilities required silence, space to breathe before taking shape.

At the State Troopers headquarters, Steele parked but left the engine running. Emma gathered her files, hesitating with her hand on the door.

"Friday nights," she said finally. "Set usually starts at eight."

"I'll be there at eight-thirty. Get a good seat."

She nodded, stepped out, then paused. "Jeremiah?"

"Yeah?"

"Don't expect anything fancy. I'm out of practice."

"Emma?"

She looked back.

"I think you're perfect exactly as you are."

For a moment, they held each other's gaze across the console. Then Emma closed the door and walked into the building, her silhouette disappearing through glass doors.

Steele sat watching until she vanished completely. Friday was three days away. Three days to decide if pursuing this connection was wisdom or foolishness. Three days for Emma to decide the same.

He shifted into drive and headed toward his hotel. Anchorage felt different now, less like a temporary assignment, more like a place that might become home. The Blue Note awaited, with its terrible acoustics and one remarkable musician.

Some cases closed with bullets and body bags. Others with handshakes and flight tickets home. This one might close with jazz and whiskey, and the tentative hope that two damaged people could create something whole.

The radio played softly as Steele navigated city streets. Outside, Alaska continued its eternal dance of light and shadow, mountain and sea. Inside his rented SUV, possibility hung in the air like a half-finished melody.

Friday couldn't come soon enough.

CHAPTER 28:
Bureau Proposal

The FBI regional office in Anchorage gleamed with polished wood and government efficiency. FBI Director Caldwell stood behind his massive desk, official commendation certificates laid out with military precision. Morning light carved sharp shadows across his weathered face as he regarded Emma Stone and Jeremiah Steele with rare approval.

"In my thirty-two years with the Bureau," Caldwell began, his gravelly voice filling the office, "I've rarely seen such effective coordination between local and federal law enforcement. Your work on the Kendrick case prevented what could have been catastrophic."

He lifted the first certificate, reading the formal language that transformed danger into bureaucratic accolade. Emma accepted hers with a slight nod, her professional mask firmly in place. Steele's hand was steady as he took his, though his mind lingered on the bodies they'd found, the lives damaged in Walter Kendrick's web.

"Which brings me to an unconventional proposal." Caldwell settled back in his leather chair. "Detective Stone, the Bureau rarely extends consulting offers to local law enforcement. However, your insight into this case, particularly your psychological profile of Kendrick, proves invaluable. We'd like to offer you a position as special consultant on complex investigations."

Emma's eyebrows lifted fractionally, the only outward sign of her surprise. "I have obligations to the State Troopers."

"Already cleared with Chief Rogers. Part-time arrangement, full discretion on case selection. Specifically partnered with Agent Steele for investigations requiring…" Caldwell paused, choosing words carefully, "…your combined expertise."

Steele caught Emma's sideways glance. Their partnership had worked, despite initial friction. The unspoken elements, their growing attraction, the tension that sometimes helped, sometimes hindered, remained deliberately unaddressed in the professional setting.

"I accept," Emma said simply. "Pending review of specific terms."

"Excellent. Agent Steele, you'll remain lead on collaborative cases. Administration will handle details." Caldwell tapped a thick file on his desk. "Actually, something's already emerged that requires immediate attention. Unusual embezzlement pattern. We brief Monday."

The meeting concluded with handshakes and the quiet satisfaction of bureaucracy satisfied. Outside, Anchorage's April weather had achieved that rare balance, crisp without cutting, bright without blazing. Spring in Alaska arrived cautiously, testing the ground before committing to the bloom.

"Coffee?" Steele suggested as they reached the parking level.

"I've got paperwork at the office." Emma's response was automatic, protective. Their partnership carried electricity that needed careful handling until she fully understood what it meant.

"Emma." He stopped her with a gentle touch on her elbow. "About us working together…"

"I know." She turned, eyes meeting his. "We need boundaries. Professional distance. The partnership works because we respect each other's skills, not because…" She let the sentence drift.

"Not because I think about you constantly?" he finished softly. "Because that kiss changed things for me."

"Jeremiah." His name sounded different when she said it, intimate, cautious. "What we went through intensifies everything. We need time to sort what's real from what's adrenaline."

"Fair enough." He stepped back, giving her space while his heart protested. "But Friday night at the Blue Note, that was my idea before… before everything. Pure interest in you."

She smiled then, transforming her serious features. "Eight o'clock. Don't be late."

✳ ✳ ✳

The debriefing with Crawford had gone longer than expected, the paperwork on Walter Kendrick's case required meticulous documentation. It was nearly evening by the time Emma returned to her apartment, muscles aching from weeks of tension. The familiar space felt strangely foreign after her time in Talkeetna, as if she had changed in ways her unchanged surroundings couldn't accommodate.

Her fingers itched for piano keys. After setting down her bags, she reached for her phone and dialed Bernie's number.

"Blue Note," came the familiar gruff voice, though there was something different in his tone, a new energy that hadn't been there before.

"Bernie, it's Emma. I'm back in town."

"Detective Stone!" Bernie's voice brightened considerably. "Perfect timing. How'd the case go?"

"Successfully concluded," she replied, not elaborating on the danger and drama of the past weeks. "I was hoping to stop by tonight, if you're open. I could use some piano time."

There was a slight pause on the line. "About that... we're not at the old location anymore."

"Are you kidding?" Emma frowned. "I thought you were just fixing the plumbing."

"Well, that was the original plan," Bernie said, an undercurrent of excitement in his voice. "But I've been keeping a secret. We didn't just renovate, we moved. To Ship Creek. Got a waterfront location in the old Mariner Building."

Emma sank onto her couch, surprised. "Ship Creek? Bernie, how did you manage that? Those properties are...."

"It all came together unexpectedly," he interrupted. "Got some investment help. You wouldn't believe the place, Emma. Real stage, proper lighting, and the piano..." He trailed off, then added with reverence, "It's a Steinway concert grand. Black. Beautiful."

Emma's pulse quickened with a complex mix of emotions, surprise, excitement, and an inexplicable unease. "A Steinway? That's… quite an upgrade from the old upright."

"That's not all," Bernie continued enthusiastically. "We've got a house band now too. Top-notch musicians from the Pacific Northwest scene. Bass, drums, sax. They can back you up if you want, or you can still play solo. Your choice, always your choice."

Emma's unease deepened. This wasn't just a renovation or relocation, it was a complete transformation. The Blue Note had been her sanctuary precisely because of its modest, unpretentious nature. A spotlight stage with professional backing seemed the opposite of the private musical refuge she'd valued.

"This sounds like a major change, Bernie."

"It is, but in the best way possible," he assured her. "The essence is the same, I promise. Just… elevated. You should see it. Tonight. The house band's there rehearsing, but the place is officially closed until the grand opening next week. You could have a private preview."

Emma glanced at her watch, conflicted. Part of her wanted to retreat, to process this unexpected change before experiencing it. But her need for musical release after the Talkeetna case outweighed her hesitation.

"Text me the address," she said finally. "I'll be there in an hour."

After hanging up, Emma sat still for several moments, trying to make sense of her unease. The Blue Note had been one of the few constants in her life, reliable, unchanged, hers in a way few things were. This sudden transformation felt like yet another shift in a world that had already tilted on its axis during her partnership with Steele.

As she showered and changed, Emma tried to focus on the positives, a better piano, potential for musical collaboration, a waterfront view. Yet she couldn't shake the feeling that something important had changed without her consent, that a piece of her carefully controlled life had been rearranged while she was away.

Meanwhile, across town, Detective Mitchell sat in his car outside FBI headquarters, his hands shaking as he reviewed the encrypted messages from Agent Kahn. Tonight was supposed to be the night they took down Randall Bauer's money laundering operation. The grand opening would provide the perfect opportunity to document large cash transactions and arrest the key players with evidence in hand.

But everything had gone sideways in the past 24 hours.

"The warrant was quashed," Agent Kahn had told him during their emergency meeting that afternoon. "Federal judge in Seattle ruled that our surveillance was obtained through questionable means. Something about jurisdictional issues and improper coordination with local law enforcement."

Mitchell knew exactly what had happened. Randall had discovered the FBI investigation, probably through connections Mitchell hadn't even known about, and had triggered a legal challenge that brought everything to a screeching halt.

"How?" Mitchell had asked, though he dreaded the answer.

"Someone tipped him off. Someone with access to federal case files and knowledge of our surveillance protocols." Kahn's eyes had been cold as ice. "Someone who knew exactly which legal pressure points to hit to kill our investigation."

The implications were staggering. Randall didn't just have Detective Mitchell on his payroll, he had someone inside the federal system itself. Someone with enough access and influence to derail an FBI financial crimes investigation through bureaucratic maneuvering.

"So what happens now?" Mitchell had asked.

"Now we start over. New warrants, new surveillance protocols, new evidence gathering. But it'll take months, maybe years. And Bauer will be ready for us next time."

Mitchell's phone buzzed with a text from Randall.

Opening night proceeds as planned. Your services will no longer be required. Consider our arrangement concluded with mutual satisfaction.

The message was clear: Randall was cutting ties, probably already moving his operations to new fronts and shell companies that the FBI would have to spend months tracking down. By the time they rebuilt their case, Randall would be three steps ahead with entirely different schemes.

An hour later, as Emma parked outside the impressively renovated Mariner Building with its elegant new "The Blue Note" sign illuminated in sophisticated blue neon, she felt a strange nervousness she hadn't experienced since her first public performance as a child.

The new Blue Note took Emma's breath away. But it was the gleaming Steinway grand, positioned to catch both natural and stage lighting, that made her heart race.

"What do you think?" Bernie asked, hovering nervously as Emma circled the piano, running her fingers lightly over its polished surface.

"It's magnificent," she admitted, still processing the dramatic transformation from the humble club she'd known. "But it's so... much. How did you manage all this, Bernie?"

Before he could answer, the house band approached, a bassist, drummer, and saxophonist who introduced themselves with the easy confidence of seasoned professionals.

"We've heard great things about you," the saxophonist, Manny, said with genuine respect. "Bernie shared some recordings from your solo nights at the old place. Your interpretation of Evans is something special."

Emma raised an eyebrow at Bernie, who shrugged apologetically. "Just on my phone. For reference."

They suggested a casual rehearsal, just to feel each other out before opening night. Emma hesitated, protective of her solitary musical space, but the Steinway's allure was irresistible. She settled onto the bench, took a deep breath, and began with a simple melody line.

What happened next surprised her completely. Rather than overwhelming her playing, the trio fell in behind her with remarkable sensitivity, finding the spaces between her notes, enhancing rather than competing. The bassist caught her rhythmic intention almost before she knew it herself; the drummer added texture so subtle it felt like an extension of her own expression; and the saxophonist wove melodic responses that complemented her improvisation perfectly.

After the first piece ended, Emma found herself smiling with genuine pleasure. "That was…"

"Magic," Manny finished, the others nodding in agreement. "Doesn't always happen that way, even with players who've worked together for years."

They continued for another hour, the music flowing effortlessly between them. Emma found herself taking new risks, exploring harmonic territories she'd never ventured into alone, buoyed by the supportive foundation the trio provided. For the first time in years, playing felt not just therapeutic but joyful.

Friday, opening night, Emma texted Steele.

At the new Blue Note on Ship Creek. Different location, same sanctuary. Come if you're free.

She wondered if he'd accept. Maybe he'd changed his mind. But forty minutes later, he appeared at the entrance, scanning the room with his characteristic thoroughness before spotting her close to the piano.

"You look absolutely stunning!" he said.

"Thanks"

"This is… not what I anticipated," he said as he joined her, taking in the transformed space.

"Me neither," Emma admitted. "But the piano is exceptional, and the musicians…" She gestured toward the trio setting up for another set. "They somehow know exactly what I'm going to play before I play it."

Steele settled at a table near the piano with perfect sightlines to both Emma and the room's entrances, ever the agent, even in relaxation. As the music resumed, Emma found herself occasionally glancing his way, surprised by his evident appreciation. His usual analytical expression had softened into something more receptive, his focus absolute.

Emma Stone remained oblivious to the admiring crowd as she took her place at the Steinway, a vision of understated elegance in a fitted midnight blue dress that fell just below her knees, the most feminine thing she'd worn since Harrison's retirement party. Her chestnut hair, normally pulled back in a practical style for detective work, cascaded in soft waves around her shoulders, catching blue highlights from the stage lighting that seemed designed specifically to illuminate her.

As she began to play, a transformation overtook her, the reserved, guarded detective melted away as her fingers danced across the keys with both precision and passion. Her face, usually composed into professional neutrality, became extraordinarily expressive, eyes sometimes closing in complete absorption, sometimes opening to reveal a depth of emotion she never permitted in her daily life.

The crowd was silent, captivated not just by her remarkable skill but by the rare glimpse of Emma's true self, vulnerable, passionate, and possessed of a profound musical intelligence that spoke directly to something primal in her listeners. Even those who knew her from her detective work barely recognized this version of Emma, a woman completely surrendered to her art, radiating the kind of authentic beauty that comes only from being utterly, unselfconsciously immersed in something one loves. The house trio behind her exchanged knowing glances as they followed her lead, aware they were witnessing something extraordinary in this detective whose soul emerged only through music.

While Emma played, Steele's attention was momentarily drawn to movement near the bar. A man sat in the shadows, partially concealed by a structural column but with a clear view of the stage. Even in the dim lighting, Steele recognized Randall Bauer from Emma's brief description after the unwelcome phone call in Talkeetna. The real estate developer's intense focus on Emma carried an unsettling possessiveness that immediately triggered Steele's investigative instincts.

The pieces connected rapidly in his mind, Bauer's real estate background, the sudden relocation to prime waterfront property, the high-end renovations far beyond what a small jazz club owner could typically afford. This transformation wasn't just Bernie's unexpected good fortune; it was calculated acquisition.

Steele considered informing Emma but hesitated as he watched her play. For the first time since he'd known her, she appeared completely unguarded, lost in the music and the rare perfect chemistry with fellow musicians. Her usual vigilance had temporarily dissolved into pure artistic expression.

He made his decision. Tonight would remain hers, untainted by the revelation of Bauer's manipulation. Tomorrow would be soon enough to discuss the concerning implications of the developer's involvement. For now, he would simply ensure that Bauer kept his distance.

When Emma concluded a particularly moving piece, Steele joined the audience's appreciative applause. The connection between them when their eyes met carried newfound understanding, something deeper than professional respect or emerging friendship.

In that moment, amid the music and subtle blue lighting, Steele acknowledged to himself what his analytical mind had been cataloging for weeks. Patterns of increased heart rate in her presence, involuntary prioritization of her wellbeing, unprecedented willingness to adapt his established protocols. The data was conclusive.

He was in love with Emma Stone.

From his shadowed corner, Randall Bauer observed the exchange between them with narrowing eyes, his fingers tightening around his glass as he noted the unmistakable connection. This unforeseen complication would require adjustment to his plans, but Randall had built his empire by anticipating and neutralizing obstacles. The federal investigation that had threatened to destroy him was now nothing more than a temporary inconvenience, dispatched through careful legal maneuvering and well-placed connections. His resources ran deeper than the FBI had imagined, and tonight's successful opening proved he remained untouchable.

Sometime before closing, Randall slipped out, already planning his next moves. The FBI would regroup eventually, but by then he'd have restructured everything through new shell companies and offshore accounts. More importantly, he'd have found a way to eliminate the growing obstacle that Agent Steele represented.

For tonight, Emma remained blissfully unaware of both men's realizations, losing herself once more in the perfect harmony of piano and accompaniment, finally at home in the music that had always been her truest voice.

"Drink's getting warm," Jeremiah observed as she reclaimed her seat next to him.

"Some things are worth the wait."

They talked then, carefully at first, testing boundaries. The embezzlement case provided safe ground, professional fascination with how criminals evolved paralleling technological advancement. But conversation drifted to personal territory: Emma's father, Steele's childhood, the moments that shaped their very different paths to law enforcement.

"You know what's interesting?" Emma mused around midnight, her third gin lending slight softness to her usually precise diction. "Six months ago, I would have arrested you for suspicious behavior. All that brooding federal agent energy."

"Six months ago, I would have considered you too rigid for field work. All that by-the-book detective protocol."

"And now?"

"Now I think we balance each other. Your structure, my instinct. Your local knowledge, my resources. Your music, my appreciation for it."

She smiled, a real one, rare and valuable. "The jazz helps, doesn't it? Shows I'm not completely made of reports and regulations."

"Shows you're human underneath all that intimidating competence."

"Intimidating?" She arched an eyebrow. "Is that your professional assessment, Agent?"

"Professional and personal." He leaned forward slightly. "Most intimidating, most fascinating, most complicated person I've met. And I work with international spies."

The compliment hung between them, too honest to dismiss, too charged to pursue. Emma's expression shifted, vulnerability flickering beneath her controlled exterior.

"We're playing with fire, Jeremiah."

"I know."

"Office romances complicate cases. Clouds judgment. Creates liability."

"I know that too."

"And yet..."

"And yet here we are. Friday night, jazz playing, two people who nearly died together trying to figure out what's real."

Emma drained her gin, decision crystallizing behind her eyes. "Slow, then. We agreed on slow."

"Glacially slow. Professional by day, occasional jazz and whiskey by night."

"With clear boundaries."

"Completely clear."

They shook on it, formal, almost comical given the intimate nature of their agreement. But the gesture established parameters, created structure within their growing attraction.

The Blue Note began closing around them, staff clearing tables as the last musicians departed. They walked out together, stepping into Anchorage's spring night. The city hummed with weekend energy, cars passing, distant laughter, the ever-present sound of water meeting land.

At her car, Emma paused, keys dangling from long fingers. "Monday. Briefing at eight."

"I'll bring coffee."

"Make it strong. Embezzlement cases are tedious."

"Not with the right partner."

She looked at him then, a lingering study that made his pulse quicken. In heels, she nearly matched his height. The professional armor had temporary cracks, revealing glimpses of the woman beneath.

"Goodnight, Jeremiah."

"Night, Emma."

Their eyes met under the amber streetlight. She rose on her toes, hesitating for half a heartbeat. When her lips brushed his, it was slow and deliberate, a test and promise combined. Her hand found his chest as his fingers touched her jaw, the kiss deepening to something between professional goodbye and personal beginning. When they parted, rain had started falling, though neither noticed.

She drove away, and Steele remained on the sidewalk, watching taillights dissolve into Anchorage's darkness. Their partnership carried new weight now, professional respect seasoned with personal connection. Dangerous territory, yes, but worth navigating carefully.

Back at his hotel, Steele reviewed case files for Monday's briefing. Embezzlement schemes demanded different skills than murder investigations, but patterns emerged in human behavior regardless of crime. He considered how Emma's analytical mind would approach financial fraud, already anticipating her questions, her insights.

His phone buzzed, a text from her number.

Thanks for tonight. Forgot how much I missed performing. See you Monday.

He typed back.

You didn't forget. You just needed the right audience.

The response came immediately.

Careful with compliments, Agent.

He smiled alone in his room. They'd established boundaries while acknowledging attraction. Professional collaboration with personal potential, a delicate balance requiring patience and wisdom.

Outside, Anchorage settled into its brief spring night. Somewhere across the city, Emma Stone probably reviewed the same files, her brilliant mind working through fraud patterns while Ellington played softly in her apartment. They'd built something rare, a partnership that survived extreme duress while maintaining professional integrity.

Monday would bring new challenges, the embezzlement case testing their coordination in calmer circumstances. But Friday had proven something important: their connection transcended crisis-bonded attraction. Emma's music revealed depths that matched his own complexities. They were equals in ways that mattered, intelligence, courage, damaged edges carefully managed.

Steele closed the files, satisfied with slow beginnings. Some investigations required patience, allowing evidence to accumulate naturally. Their relationship followed similar logic, building trust through shared purpose while exploring cautious intimacy.

The Blue Note would see them again. Jazz and whiskey offered safe spaces for boundaries to breathe, for connection to grow without pressure. They'd found rhythm in their partnership. Now came the delicate work of harmonizing professional excellence with personal possibilities.

Alaska's endless light waited beyond the horizon. In 2 weeks, they'd face midnight sun instead of starlit darkness. By then, their collaboration would be tested by complex cases, the embezzlement investigation stretching across corporations and cultural boundaries.

But that was future uncertainty. Tonight held simpler truths. Emma Stone played piano like she solved crimes, with precision and passion.

Sleep finally claimed him, promising dreams of jazz and mysterious eyes, of cases solved by their combined strengths. Tomorrow began another chapter in their story, professional partners testing whether a slow burn might eventually ignite something worth the risk.

The Blue Note's music lingered in memory, a promise of Friday nights yet to come.

Meanwhile, Detective Mitchell sat alone in his apartment, staring at the severance check Randall had deposited into his account, enough money to pay off his debts and start fresh, but also a clear message that their arrangement was permanently closed. The FBI's investigation had been neutralized through legal channels Mitchell didn't even understand, leaving him as the only remaining loose end.

His phone showed seventeen missed calls from Agent Kahn, but Mitchell had already made his decision. Tomorrow he would submit his resignation from the police force and disappear into the lower 48, where Randall's influence couldn't reach him. The alternative, staying to face questions he couldn't answer without destroying innocent people like Bernie, wasn't an option he could live with.

Randall Bauer had won this round completely. The money was clean, the FBI was stalled, and Emma Stone remained unaware that her musical sanctuary had been purchased with dirty money by a man who believed he owned her. The only question was how long Randall's victory would last, and what he might do next time someone tried to come between him and what he wanted.

The game was far from over.

CHAPTER 29:
Home

Three weeks after returning from Talkeetna, Emma Stone drove the familiar route to Spruce Haven Assisted Living. The Alaska landscape looked different now, not just because autumn was painting the birch trees gold, but because she saw it through eyes that had witnessed its capacity for both beauty and danger. The mountains that had once seemed like distant guardians now held memories of pursuit through wilderness, of gold hidden in streams, of a killer who had used the land's remoteness to hide his crimes.

She parked in her usual spot but sat for a moment longer than normal, gathering not just her resolve but her thoughts. The past weeks had changed her in ways she was still discovering. Working with Steele, surviving Walter Kendrick's attempts on their lives, finding connection with another person despite her carefully maintained walls, all of it had shifted something fundamental inside her.

Inside, Nurse Marlene greeted her with a knowing smile. "He's having one of his clearer days," she said. "Been asking about you since yesterday."

Emma nodded, grateful for the warning. Clear days with her father could be harder than the confused ones. When his mind was sharp, their conversations carried the weight of years of unresolved tension.

She found him in his chair by the window, dressed neatly in a cardigan she'd bought him for his birthday. His silver hair was combed carefully, and his pale blue eyes tracked to her immediately as she entered.

"Emma," he said, and she was relieved to hear recognition and warmth in his voice. "You look different."

"Different how?" she asked, settling into the chair across from him.

"Less angry," he said simply, studying her with the perception that sometimes surfaced through his declining cognition. "Something's changed."

Emma considered deflecting, making small talk about the weather or his meals. But something about his directness, and perhaps something about her own recent experiences with letting walls down, made her choose honesty instead.

"I've been working a difficult case," she said. "In Talkeetna. With a federal agent."

"The partner you mentioned before?"

She was surprised he remembered. "Yes. Agent Steele."

"You said his name differently just now," her father observed. "Like it means something."

Heat rose in Emma's cheeks. Even with dementia, Thomas Stone remained perceptive about human nature. "We've... developed a good working relationship."

"More than that, I think." He leaned forward slightly. "Emma, I know I wasn't the father you needed. Too rigid, too controlling. I tried to protect you from the world by building walls around you, but I just made you build walls around yourself instead."

The unexpected apology caught Emma off guard. In all their conversations since his decline began, he'd never acknowledged the damage his rigid parenting had caused.

"Dad...."

"Let me finish," he said with a flash of his old authority. "I've been thinking about it a lot lately. About the mistakes I made. You were so bright, so capable, but I was afraid. Afraid of losing you the way I lost your mother to her independence, her talents, her dreams that took her away from me."

Emma stared at him. This was a version of their family history she'd never heard.

"Mom didn't leave you for her dreams," she said carefully. "She died of pneumonia."

"Before that," he said, his voice growing softer. "She was always creating something amazing, always the person other people needed. I thought if I could keep you close, keep you safe, I wouldn't lose you too. But I did anyway. Just in a different way."

The room fell quiet except for the distant sounds of the facility's daily life. Emma processed this revelation, understanding for the first time that her father's controlling nature hadn't just been about religious conviction, but about fear of abandonment.

"I chose my isolation, Dad," she said finally. "Even as an adult. It wasn't just your rules, I kept building walls because they felt safer."

"And now?" he asked.

Emma thought about Steele, about the way he'd positioned himself between her and danger, about the kiss that had acknowledged something neither of them had been looking for but both had found. About how terrifying and exhilarating it was to let someone matter.

"Now I'm learning that some walls can come down," she admitted. "Slowly. Carefully. But they can come down."

Her father smiled, the expression transforming his weathered features. "This Agent Steele, does he make you happy?"

"He makes me... better," Emma said, surprising herself with the honesty. "He sees things I miss and I see things he misses. We balance each other."

"That's what your mother and I had, before I got so afraid of losing it that I destroyed it," her father said. "Don't make my mistakes, Emma. Don't let fear rob you of connection."

They sat together in comfortable silence for a while, watching the afternoon light shift across the mountains visible through his window. Something warm spread through her chest. Something loosening in her chest, a knot of resentment and hurt that had been there so long she'd forgotten it was separate from her core self.

"I brought something," she said, pulling out her phone. "A recording of me playing piano. At a jazz club in Anchorage."

His eyes lit up with genuine pleasure. "You're performing again?"

"Just occasionally. But yes." She queued up the recording Bernie had made the night Steele first heard her play. "I thought you might like to hear it."

As the music filled the small room, Emma watched her father's face. His eyes closed, and she saw tears tracking down his cheeks. When the piece ended, he reached over and took her hand.

"She would have been so proud," he whispered. "Your mother. She always said you had the gift and your own voice."

"I wish I remembered her better," Emma said.

"She used to play you to sleep," her father said, his voice distant with memory. "Said music was the language you understood before you had words. When you were fussy, nothing else would calm you down, but the moment she started playing piano, you'd stop crying and just listen."

Emma felt tears threatening her own composure. "Why didn't you tell me these things before?"

"Because I was a fool," he said simply. "Afraid that if I talked about her gifts, you'd follow her path away from me. Instead, I pushed you away myself."

As the afternoon wore on, they talked more openly than they had in years. He shared memories of her mother that painted a picture of a woman Emma barely remembered but could now begin to understand. She told him about the case in Talkeetna, carefully edited to avoid the more dangerous details, focusing instead on how working with Steele had taught her the value of partnership.

When it was time to leave, her father held her hand as she stood to go.

"Emma," he said. "Don't wait too long to tell him how you feel. Life is shorter than we think it is, and regret is heavier than risk."

She leaned down and kissed his forehead. "I love you, Dad."

"I love you too, sweetheart. I always have, even when I showed it poorly."

Driving back to Anchorage, Emma felt lighter than she had in years. The conversation hadn't erased decades of tension or healed all wounds, but it had opened a door to understanding that she hadn't known existed. Her father's fear of loss had created the very abandonment he'd tried to prevent, but recognizing that pattern meant she didn't have to repeat it.

Her phone buzzed with a text from Steele.

Dinner tomorrow? I found a place that serves decent Thai food and has terrible acoustics for eavesdropping on federal agents.

She smiled, typing back.

It's a date. Literally this time, not just work.

The response came quickly. *I was hoping you'd say that.*

As she drove through the outskirts of Anchorage, Emma made a mental note to visit her father more often. Not out of duty, but out of genuine desire to rebuild what they'd both thought was irreparably broken. The case in Talkeetna had taught her that even the most carefully hidden secrets could be brought to light, that truth had its own power to heal as well as to wound.

And perhaps most importantly, she'd learned that the walls she'd built to protect herself had also isolated her from the very connections that made life worth living. With Steele, she was discovering the courage to let someone in, not completely, not recklessly, but genuinely.

That night, she played piano in her apartment for the first time in weeks, choosing a piece her father had mentioned her mother used to play, Amazing Grace. As her fingers found the melody, Emma felt a connection not just to her musical heritage, but to the possibility of a future where her past informed but didn't imprison her.

The music flowed through her apartment and out into the Anchorage night, a bridge between who she had been and who she was becoming.

Later that evening, Emma sat in her apartment, still processing the afternoon's revelations. Her phone rang, Steele's name appearing on the screen.

"Stone," she answered, falling back into professional habit.

"Emma," Steele's voice came through, and she could hear something different in his tone, less measured, more immediate. "Are you all right? You mentioned visiting your father today, and I've been…"

He paused, and Emma could practically hear him calculating whether to continue.

"You've been what?" she prompted gently.

"I've been worried about you," he admitted, the words coming out in a rush. "All afternoon. Which is… inefficient. Counterproductive. I had reports to review, but instead I kept thinking about you sitting in that assisted living facility, dealing with painful family history alone."

Something warm spread through her chest. "Jeremiah…."

"No, let me finish. I know this isn't how I usually operate. I don't typically call colleagues to check on their emotional well-being. My training suggests maintaining professional boundaries, avoiding personal entanglements that could compromise operational effectiveness." His voice grew quieter. "But my training didn't account for someone like you."

Emma closed her eyes, hearing the cost of this admission in his carefully controlled tone.

"I care about you, Emma," he continued, abandoning his usual formal precision. "Not just as a partner, not just professionally. I care about whether you're hurting, whether you're processing difficult emotions alone, whether you need someone to listen or just… be present."

The vulnerability in his voice was almost painful to hear, this man who had been trained from childhood to view emotional expression as weakness, deliberately choosing connection over control.

"I realized today that my father spent his whole life afraid of losing people, so he never really had them," Emma said softly. "I don't want to make that mistake."

"Neither do I," Steele replied. "Which is why I'm calling instead of analyzing my concern from a distance. Which is why I'm telling you that when you disappeared at the Alliance compound, something in me broke that can't be repaired with logic or procedure."

Emma felt tears threatening her composure. "Where are you right now?"

"In my car. Outside your building. I've been sitting here for twenty minutes, debating whether to call or just drive away."

She moved to her window and looked down to see his rental car parked under the streetlight. "Come up," she said. "Please."

When she opened her apartment door five minutes later, Steele stood in the hallway looking uncharacteristically uncertain. His usually perfect composure showed cracks, hair slightly disheveled as if he'd been running his hands through it, tie loosened, expression vulnerable in a way she'd never seen.

"This is uncharted territory for me," he said without preamble. "Caring about someone enough to worry when I have no logical reason for concern. Wanting to comfort someone when I was trained to maintain emotional distance."

Emma stepped closer, close enough to see the flecks of amber in his brown eyes. "How does it feel? This uncharted territory?"

"Terrifying," he admitted. "And essential. Like breathing."

She reached up and loosened his tie completely, then let her hands rest against his chest. "My father gave me some advice today. He said not to let fear rob me of connection."

"Statistically sound advice," Steele said, his analytical nature asserting itself even in this moment of vulnerability.

Emma laughed softly. "You can't help yourself, can you?"

"Apparently not. Though I'm discovering that some things can't be quantified or categorized." His hands came up to frame her face. "Like this. Like you."

When he kissed her this time, it was different from their first tentative contact. This was deliberate, unguarded, a choice made not from proximity or adrenaline but from genuine emotional need. Emma felt his usual control dissolve as he pulled her closer, his carefully maintained barriers finally, fully dropping.

When they broke apart, both breathing unsteadily, Steele rested his forehead against hers.

"I don't know how to do this," he confessed. "Long-term relationships, emotional intimacy. My marriage failed because I couldn't access these feelings. I don't want to fail with you."

"Then we'll figure it out together," Emma said, surprised by her own certainty. "One imperfect day at a time."

As they sat together on her couch, Steele's arm around her as she told him about her conversation with her father, Emma realized they were both learning the same lesson, that true strength sometimes meant choosing vulnerability, that the greatest risk was also the greatest possibility.

"Thank you," she said as the evening wound down, "for calling instead of analyzing from a distance."

"Thank you for answering," he replied, "for letting me try to be someone different than I was trained to be."

Outside, Anchorage settled into its autumn night, while inside Emma's apartment, two people who had spent their lives maintaining careful control discovered the profound relief of letting someone else matter enough to worry about, to comfort, to love.

Epilogue

As Emma explored the transformed venue, she experienced a complex mix of wonder and displacement. The Blue Note she'd known, modest, familiar, unambiguously hers, had been replaced by something that demanded a different relationship. Here, she would be a featured performer rather than a private seeker of solace.

"It's magnificent," Emma admitted to Bernie, running her fingers over the piano's polished surface. Yet beneath her appreciation lay an unspoken question: what would this transformation cost her in return?

Bernie watched her reaction with nervous pride, though he couldn't entirely shake his growing discomfort with arrangements he didn't fully comprehend. Partnership documents had multiplied beyond his understanding, filled with terminology about "equity structures" and "performance metrics" that made his role feel less like ownership and more like stewardship of someone else's vision.

From his carefully chosen vantage point, Randall observed Emma's every gesture with the satisfaction of an architect watching blueprints come to life. Her obvious connection to the Steinway, the way she unconsciously positioned herself within the space's carefully designed acoustics, confirmed his calculations about her psychological needs.

"She belongs here," he murmured to himself, noting how the lighting he'd specified highlighted her profile perfectly when she played. Every design element had been chosen to showcase Emma's talent while creating an environment that would feel irreplaceable to her.

What pleased Randall most was Emma's visible struggle between gratitude and unease. She recognized quality but sensed strings attached, creating exactly the emotional tension he'd intended. The venue would become necessary to her musical expression, while remaining perpetually dependent on resources only he could provide.

The detective observed this dynamic with growing alarm, recognizing the psychological manipulation even as he remained powerless to expose it. Randall had crafted a trap so elegant that warning Emma would require explaining his own compromised position, knowledge that would destroy several lives in the process.

Emma's adaptation to the space would happen gradually, each performance binding her more deeply to its particular acoustics, its professional atmosphere, its elevated expectations. By the time she realized how thoroughly she'd been captured, extraction would require sacrificing the very musical growth Randall had made possible.

The strategy revealed Randall's understanding of Emma's character with disturbing precision. He hadn't bought her affection directly, he'd purchased her artistic dependencies, creating a situation where rejecting him meant rejecting her own creative fulfillment.

The last notes of The Dave Matthew's Band faded from the Bluetooth player in Detective Emma Stone's apartment. She sat on her couch, the stress of the past week's case slowly melting away. The familiar burn in her right shoulder, a reminder of the tension, now a dull manageable ache.

Her phone buzzed against the wooden surface of her desk. Steele flashed across the screen.

"Stone," she answered, already reaching for her jacket.

"Get ready to pack," came Jeremiah Steele's gravelly voice. "Director wants us in briefing room in 30 minutes."

"The embezzlement case?"

"Yes. Five million from a Dallas business called Richardson Energy Partners." He paused. "Word is they're connected to the Cardenas cartel."

Stone felt her chest tighten. Cartel cases were messy, dangerous. But she'd worked three months alongside Steele now, and despite their differences, her intuitive approach versus his methodical logic, they'd developed an effective rhythm.

"Details?" she asked, already pulling clothes from her closet.

"Forty-year-old CPA named Marcus Wheeler. Worked their books, then vanished for nine years. Got a tip he was seen in Alaska recently. Job is two-fold. Bring down the embezzler and the cartel operation."

Stone grabbed her jacket. "Meet you at the office?"

"Already here. I've got coffee and preliminary files."

She ended the call and stood before her mirror, running a hand through her dark hair. At thirty-six, she still looked younger than her years, though the past few months had added new lines around her green eyes. The badge on her hip felt heavier each day, the weight of responsibility, and secrets, growing with each case.

Captain Harrison's voice echoed in her mind: "Samantha, rebellion without purpose is just noise. Find your purpose."

Maybe she had. Even if that purpose meant partnering with a man who questioned her every instinct while somehow always having her back.

Forty minutes later, Stone pushed through the glass doors of the federal building. Steele waited by the elevator, two coffee cups in hand, his tall frame impeccably dressed in a charcoal suit. Good looking at forty-one, he carried himself with the confidence of someone who'd spent fifteen years proving he belonged in rooms where others doubted him.

"Black, two sugars," he said, handing her a cup.

"You remembered."

"I'm trained to remember details, Detective."

She smirked. "Is that what we're calling it?"

As they rode the elevator up, Steele pulled out his phone. "I've already contacted the Anchorage field office. If Wheeler's here, he's been smart about staying off the grid."

"Or he's not here at all," Stone countered. "The Alaska story could be misdirection."

"Possible. But we start with the most credible lead."

The elevator dinged open. As they walked to the conference room, Stone asked, "Did they tell you why they want us on this? We literally just closed the Hammond murder case."

Steele's expression darkened. "The cartel connection. After what happened in El Paso last year…" He didn't finish, but Stone knew the story. Steele had lost his partner to cartel violence, another reason they'd been paired together. She understood loss.

Inside the conference room, files and photographs covered the table. Marcus Wheeler's face stared up from a DMV photo, average features, receding hairline, glasses. The kind of man who blended into crowds.

"Five million," Stone murmured, studying financial documents. "That's not impulse. That's planned."

"Methodically planned," Steele agreed. "He's been funneling money into offshore accounts for eight months. The question is whether he acted alone."

As they headed for the door, Steele paused. "Stone?"

"Yeah?"

"Watch yourself on this one. If this is connected to cartel… they don't play by our rules."

She met his gaze, seeing genuine concern beneath his professional mask. "When have they ever?"

Neither knew it yet, but the five million dollars was just the beginning. The investigation into Marcus Wheeler's disappearance would become their longest case, weeks of dead ends, dangerous encounters, and unlikely revelations. By the time they finally cornered Wheeler, Stone and Steele would understand that the five million was never the real prize.

The truth was worth far more, and far deadlier.

Learn More

www.AuthorMelissaSaulnier.com
https://www.facebook.com/MelissaEadesSaulnier

www.ingramcontent.com/pod-product-compliance
Lightning Source LLC
Chambersburg PA
CBHW071831020726
47502CB00004B/1315